Treasure Hunt

Paul deMena

IRISH CROWN JEWELS?

The true mystery that inspired my book

"The theft of the Irish Crown Jewels by a person or persons unknown in 1907 is one of the most famous and puzzling mysteries of Irish history and has been the subject of numerous books and articles."[1] So writes Sean J. Murphy in the introduction of his 2008 report to the Centre for Irish Genealogical and Historical Studies.

Well, Mr. Murphy, I think the world needs one more book on the topic! I'm sure the reader is aware that Ireland did not truly lose their crown jewels, at least not such as the Crown Jewels lost by Mr. Bean from the Tower of London. The so-called Irish Crown Jewels were the insignia of the Order of Saint Patrick, which was formed in 1783 as a source of honor and patronage for nobility on the Emerald Isle. Five decades later, King William IV of England presented a set of jewels, consisting of a star and a badge composed of rubies, emeralds and Brazilian diamonds, to the Lord Lieutenant of Ireland. These jewels mysteriously disappeared from Dublin Castle in 1907 and have never been found.

There have been many theories about who stole the jewels. The names you will read in this book, Francis Shackleton (brother of the famous Antarctic explorer) and Francis Bennett-Goldney, are the men who top of the list of suspects, but no one knows who removed the jewels from the Bedford Tower in Dublin Castle, or where they are today.

For the most part, I have tried to keep the description of the jewels and other historical information accurate, up until the death of Francis Bennett-Goldney in Brest, France in July of 1918. Everything in this story that took place after his death is a figment of my imagination—well, almost everything.

---

[1] Murphy, Sean J. "A Centenary Report on the Theft of the Irish Crown Jewels in 1907." Centre for Irish Genealogical and Historical Studies, Windgates, County Wicklow, 2008.

DELIGHTFUL

Falling in love was the last thing on my mind that day. I had promised myself to never again put my heart in harm's way, but harm seems to go out of its way to find my heart.

When she first walked into my life, I was instantly attracted to her good looks, and over time, I grew to appreciate her talent. But the quality that overwhelmed my defenses was her ability to read my soul. For the first time in my life, I was with a woman who truly saw me, who liked what she saw, and wanted to see more. The evening we met, I was entirely unaware that I would soon fall in love with her, and then face the possibility of losing her forever.

My longtime friend, Philip Pennfield, had invited a large gathering to a housewarming party at his Fifth Avenue apartment. I was alone on the patio as usual, because I was repulsed by the ritual of engaging in mindless chatter with people I didn't know.

"Look at all those poor sods, Philip," I said when he came outside to check on me. I was leaning over the railing, looking down at the bumper-to-bumper, Friday night traffic below. "They're all chasing the same thing, all wishing they could get rich."

"Maybe they're just wishing they could get home," Philip replied.

"They're wishing they could live in a place like this, because if they did, they'd be home already. They think that would make them happy."

"How do you know they aren't happy?" he asked, peering over the railing.

"They're not happy. They're miserable, but they think having more money would make them happy."

"Maybe so," he said, turning toward me. "What's it to you, anyway? Why do you care?"

"It irritates me—the way they think about us. They think all rich people should be happy, but we're not."

1

"We're not?" he asked.

"No, we're not. I have everything they're yearning for. I have more money than I could spend in two lifetimes, but I'm just as stinking miserable as they are."

"You weren't so gloomy before you broke up with Vanessa," Philip replied. "What did that woman do to you?"

"I've always been this way. Although, I used to hide it better. Why do you always act so happy?"

"I'm not acting. I am happy. I enjoy the things I do. I enjoy being with Stephanie. I enjoy riding horses. And I really enjoy beating you at racquetball," he said.

"That's my point. What good is it beating me at racquetball? You know in a couple of days we're going to play again and get the same result. How can you find meaning in that?"

"My parents find meaning in helping people," he replied after a moment's reflection. "That's why they are involved in so many charities."

"I respect that," I said, treading carefully because I held his parents in such high regard, "I'm sure they mean well, but think about it." I pointed to the street below. "Your parents support programs that help kids down there get a good education, right?"

"Right."

"What will they do with their education?" I continued.

"Better themselves, learn skills that would enable them to enter the workforce as productive citizens, I suppose," he said.

"Exactly. They want an education so they can get a job, and they want a job so they can make more money. And they think if they make more money, then they will finally be happy."

"OK, maybe you're right. What's wrong with that?"

"What's wrong with it? Everything is wrong with it! It's patently false, but they'll have no way of knowing until it's too late and the damage has been done. Damage to themselves and their families," I shouted.

My passionate response seemed to take Philip by surprise at first. Then he looked at me and with a knowing nod of his head, he said, "Ah, I think I understand."

"There you are, Philip," said his girlfriend, Stephanie, poking her head through the sliding glass door. "Brian says they need more ice."

"Did he look in the freezer?" Philip replied without turning toward her.

"I don't think he knows how to operate a freezer. If a device doesn't have a keyboard, he's lost."

"I need a butler," Philip said. "Not for myself, mind you, but to help me take care of all my friends."

Philip was born into one of the wealthiest families in Philadelphia. His parents' estate in St. David's was teeming with servants who took care of all the mundane tasks busy socialites didn't care to perform themselves. Needless to say, Philip never served ice in his father's home.

As he was going back inside, I said, "While you're in the kitchen, would you mind getting me another drink? My glass is nearly empty."

"Therein lies your problem, Clay," he said to me as he followed Stephanie toward the door, "you need to see that your glass is half-full."

"Either way," I replied, "it will soon be dry."

"Oh, by the way," he said, before stepping inside, "you're going antiquing with us this weekend, right?"

"Two days rummaging through dusty shops, searching through piles of old junk nobody has wanted to own for hundreds of years? How could I refuse such an incredible offer?"

"Good. So, it's settled. We'll fly from Teterboro in the morning. Don't be late," he said, closing the door behind him.

As I turned back to reflect on the people below, I heard the door open behind me. "I promise I won't be late," I said.

"Late for what?" came an unfamiliar voice.

As I turned, I saw a stunningly beautiful woman standing directly in front of me. She was wearing a fiery red sequin mini dress with a heavy silver choker chain necklace. I was so struck by her beauty and poise, it took me a moment to realize she had asked me a question.

"I can't remember," I said.

"So much for your promise," she replied.

"I saw you inside earlier, didn't I? You were surrounded by a pack of hungry wolves in the living room."

"Those guys weren't that bad. I've seen worse," she said as she took a place at the railing beside me. "That's a lot of traffic down there."

"I hadn't noticed," I replied, catching the scent of her perfume.

"Are you a friend of Philip's or Stephanie's?" she asked.

"Philip and I went to secondary school together. We've been great friends ever since."

"So, you're one of the Gang of Four that I've heard about?"

"I'm Clayton. First of the Four," I said, extending my hand toward her.

She shook my hand and said, "Olivia, of course. Pleased to meet you." The way she said her name made me think we must have been introduced already. "So, you went to high school in London?"

"Tonbridge School, in Kent. Yes, that's where we all met. Philip and I were roommates. Brian and Robert were in our house, but in different rooms."

"Did Brian and Robert go to university with you, too?" she asked.

"Brian? No, we all came back to the States, but Philip and I went to Harvard. Brian started in Princeton, but never finished. Don't get me wrong. He has a brilliant mind, but he gets distracted easily. School never was his thing."

"And Robert?"

"Robert went to Yale. We never understood why. We still talk to him, but it's not the same," I said with a wink.

"I went to Yale," she said.

"Of course, I was joking," I shot back. "A fine institution, even if it is located in Connecticut."

"Why are rich people such snobs?"

"I don't know," I said. "When I meet one, I will ask, first chance I get."

"You don't consider yourself rich?"

"I'm not as wealthy as Philip," I replied. "And, by the way, Philip is no snob. Nor are his parents."

"Fair enough. I'll give you that. But what about you? Were you born into snobbery, or are you a self-made snob?"

"You don't want to know about my family," I replied, "and I don't want to talk about them. Suffice it to say my father would be considered nouveau riche. We weren't born into money, but money killed us."

"I can tell you suffered a lot," she countered, snickering.

"And what about you?" I asked, "What have you done with your degree from Yale?"

She studied my face for a moment, then asked, "Are you joking again?"

"No. I mean where do you live? What do you do for a living? The usual questions."

Once more, she studied my face and furrowed her brow. "You really don't know who I am?"

My first reaction to this question was to wonder if I had ever dated this woman before. In my early twenties, I was the stereotypical wealthy playboy, spending my nights in the clubs and my days wondering where I had been the night before.

"Have we met before?" I asked. "I apologize, I—"

"You really don't recognize me? No, we haven't met before."

"Then, I take it you must be someone famous. A model, perhaps? You assumed your celebrity status would create instant recognition."

She rolled her eyes at my reply and shook her head.

I continued, "Hey, you expected me to wag my tail and drool in your presence, just like the pack of wolves in the living room. Now who's acting the snob?"

"At least those wolves, as you call them, were polite."

"How did you become famous?" I asked. "Or were you born into it?"

"I'm an actor," she replied. "I worked incredibly hard to get where I am."

"On Broadway?" I asked doubtfully. I had been to every show on Broadway, and I had never seen her before.

"I act on television."

I laughed. "Oh, television. Where all the highest quality productions can be found. How, ever, did you manage to descend from the Ivy League into that quagmire?"

"I guess it's just what happens to people who go to university in Connecticut," she replied as she turned to go back inside.

Before she could open the door, however, Stephanie and Philip came out to the patio.

"Oh, wonderful," Stephanie began. "I had been planning to introduce you two."

"We've just been getting to know each other," I said.

"Excellent!" Philip said as he turned to the actress. "Olivia, you'll be happy to know that Clay, here, is coming with us on our trip to Vermont. Isn't that great?"

"Delightful," she said, pulling back her shoulders and brushing past me into the apartment.

THE WINGED CHAIR

The flight from Teterboro, New Jersey, to Burlington, Vermont, took just under an hour in Philip's father's Gulfstream 650. Philip and Stephanie slept arm-in-arm in the first row of luxury recliners. Behind them, Brian amused himself with a handheld video game and placed his oversized backpack on the seat beside him.

I sat behind Brian and next to me was Olivia, leaning as far away as possible and looking as if she would rather be sharing the seat with Brian's backpack. The red sparkling dress had been replaced by an oversized plaid blazer, white scalloped blouse, skinny jeans, and knee-high leather boots below. A pair of sunglasses hung from the blazer's breast pocket.

"Are those so no one will recognize you?" I asked her, pointing to the sunglasses.

"I prefer to go unnoticed," she said, "but things don't always go the way I prefer."

"You'd rather be sitting next to Brian, wouldn't you?" I asked.

"Not that it is any of your business, but he's the one who invited me to Philip's party. So, yes." she replied.

"You aren't the first of Brian's dates to be cast aside for his computer game. I told you he gets distracted easily."

"You also said he was brilliant," she said watching him grunt, grimace, and gesticulate wildly as he played his game. "He doesn't look very intelligent to me."

"That game he's playing is one he designed himself. He plays it over and over, then he disappears into his man cave to rewrite the code. Looks can be deceiving."

She looked out the window, then said, "Philip tells me you have never been antiquing before. Why did you come?"

"It's not often I get to hang out with a television star," I quipped.

6

"Look," she said, "I'm stuck with you for this trip, OK? Philip and Stephanie are going to be together, and Brian is in his own world. That leaves you and me. Do you think you can handle being courteous for two days?"

"Forty-eight hours is an awfully long time for a guy like me to quit making wise cracks. But if you promise you won't force me to spend those hours digging through junk yards, I'll do my best to keep a civil tongue."

"It's a deal," she said. "In truth, I'm not a huge fan of antiques, either. My mother, on the other hand, is an avid collector of jewelry boxes."

"Jewelry boxes?" I asked. "With or without the jewels inside?"

"Just the boxes. She's got dozens of them, all shapes and sizes, from all over the world. It's a very interesting collection. I told her I would keep an eye out for something special."

"Well, that settles it. The game's afoot," I replied, happy to have any sort of purpose for the trip. "We must find your mother a special jewelry box without the jewels."

A light rain was falling as we landed, which is typical for Vermont in September. Robert was waiting for us outside the charter arrivals area, and he drove us to the bed-and-breakfast he and his wife purchased after they graduated from Yale. It was a Victorian-style home, built in the 1850s, with nine well-appointed rooms, including a few that overlooked Lake Champlain. Robert's wife, Roberta, welcomed us at the front door and showed each of us to our rooms. Mine was not one of the rooms with a view of the lake, but there was an inviting fireplace and a wingback chair that spoke to me, urging that I should tarry long within its embrace.

"I could spend the whole weekend with you," I assured the chair. "We will be good friends." I placed my copy of Sophocles' Theban plays on the table by the fireplace and settled into the chair.

"That will have to wait, Clay," said Philip, entering through the open door of my room. "It's time to hit the antique trail. Ancient treasures await us."

"Most of the furniture in my room is antique, including my friend, the chair. Perhaps I should soak in the atmosphere longer, so I can appreciate those treasures more fully."

"Tonight, you can soak all you want," he said. "Now, you need to accompany Olivia. I don't want her out there on her own. Once people begin to recognize her, she'll need someone to run interference."

"What about Brian?" I asked. "She's his date, isn't she?"

"That was yesterday. Steph invited her to come with us today. That means she's currently unattached."

"I don't think she likes me very much," I said. "In fact, I'm pretty sure she'd rather be with Brian."

"Brian's not going to be able to help her, you know that," Philip said. "C'mon, expand your horizon's a bit. Antiques are a window into a world we rarely see any more. They speak of the life and times of the people who walked these lands before we were born. There's intrigue and mystery in those humble shops, if one has the eyes to see and the mind to investigate."

"All right, all right, don't oversell it."

"Besides," he continued, "you have to admit that Olivia is gorgeous."

"Stunningly beautiful."

"It wouldn't hurt you to find some companionship again. How long has it been since Vanessa?"

"Not long enough," I sighed.

"What's not long enough?" Olivia said, smiling and peeking her head through the door. I hadn't heard her approach.

"We were having a private conversation."

Stephanie was with Olivia in the hall and said, "Clayton, what's gotten into you? Where are your manners?"

"My apologies, Stephanie. I'm just not accustomed to eavesdroppers," I replied with a sharp glance at Olivia as she and Stephanie began walking down the stairs, laughing.

"You're not accustomed to people, Clay," Philip said. "You've been living alone too long. It's time to go."

I took another hungering look at the chair and fireplace in my room. "Good night, good night, parting is such sweet sorrow," I said as I closed the door behind me.

"That I shall say good night till it be morrow," said Olivia from the stairs below.

NAME YOUR PRICE

Philip drove us in Robert's car to Church Street, a brick road in the middle of Burlington brimming with cafés, restaurants, gift shops, and antique stores. Scattered throughout the center of the pedestrian street were small wrought-iron tables with glass tops and sturdy chairs, mostly empty. The rain had stopped, but there were puddles everywhere. We hadn't walked one block before something inside a jewelry store caught Stephanie's eye. A little further on, Brian, game console in hand, stumbled into an empty table and knocked over a paper cup that had been left behind. Then he sat down on the available chair, all without looking up or missing a beat in his game. Olivia and I walked on together, each of us wishing to be somewhere else, with someone else.

"I can't think of a more likely street on which to find music boxes. I like our chances of success," I said, trying to break the tension.

She was wearing her sunglasses, even though the sky was overcast, so I couldn't read the expression in her eyes. She said coldly, "Jewelry boxes. Not music boxes. My mother collects jewelry boxes."

I started to point out that some jewelry boxes make music when one opens them, but I quickly realized that wasn't going to help.

"This place looks promising," I said, pointing to the first antique shop we saw. "Let's see what intriguing and mysterious treasures await us inside."

I held the door open for her, and she walked through without acknowledging me. Inside the shop, she took off her sunglasses and once again, I was astounded by her beauty. The shopkeeper did a doubletake when she approached. I didn't know whether he recognized her, or if he was just unaccustomed to seeing a face as beautiful as hers.

The shop was packed with the very types of items I expected to see. Old chairs and old tables. Old lamps and old plates. Old clocks and old jewelry. Every inch of every surface was packed with a seemingly random collection of items with only one attribute in common: they were timeworn.

"Whoever do you hire to dust this place?" I asked the proprietor. "They must be a magician."

Without taking his eyes off Olivia, he ignored me and asked, "How can I help you, ma'am?"

"Do you have any jewelry boxes?" I replied, waving to get his attention.

Olivia immediately turned to me, cocked her head, pursed her lips, and widened her eyes.

The shopkeeper sized me up with a quick glance at my well-worn shoes and my comfy jeans. His dour expression told me he wasn't pleased with what he saw. "Against the wall," he said, pointing to the other side of the store and clearly disappointed Olivia had brought me along.

"You aren't supposed to tell them what you're looking for," she whispered in my ear. The warmth of her body and the sensation of her breath on the side of my face made me shiver.

"Why not?" I whispered into her ear, lingering long enough to savor the fragrance of her conditioner.

"Because they raise the price when they know you are interested."

I looked around the shop again and said, "I could buy and sell this dump. No matter. Your mother must have her jewelry box. Price is no object."

"Well, don't say that either," she said, and she smiled at me for the first time.

As we walked through the shop, she carefully examined the selection of antique clocks and handled a blue and white vase on a tabletop before casually making her way to the jewelry boxes. There was a wide selection: big ones and small ones, some that looked old and others that looked even older. I had a feeling we were going to be there for a while. She found one that caught her eye, and when she opened the lid, it began to play music.

I put my hand to my mouth and pretended to cough, saying "Told you so."

She looked at me and then rolled her eyes and shut the lid. "None of these are any good," she declared as she moved toward the door.

"What makes one good?" I asked, surprised, but happy to be leaving that place.

"It's hard to explain, but I'll know it when I see it. For one thing, a collector is always looking for something unique, something they don't have already."

"And your mother already has those?"

"No," she replied, adding to my confusion.

We popped into several other stores and were met with similar reactions whenever Olivia showed her face. In one of the more crowded stores, some customers recognized her and asked to take selfies with her. In each of these shops, Olivia pronounced the jewelry boxes not good enough for her mother.

As we came to the end of the street, we reached a shop that specialized in antique furniture. "Last chance," I said, hoping beyond hope there wasn't another row of shops behind that one.

"No use going in there," she said. "Furniture stores don't sell jewelry boxes."

"Ah," I said. "For that very reason, we must check this place out. For if they do have a jewelry box, then it must needs be unique."

"You are the strangest man I've ever met," she said. Then waving her hand toward the shop, she said, "Lead the way."

As we entered the store, we were met by an older gentleman wearing thick, black glasses with thick, smudged lenses. His hair was black and curly, and his face was thick with stubble. He wore a heavy brown sweater that covered his plump frame. He did not seem to notice Olivia, who was standing beside me.

"We're looking for a jewelry box," I said. "But not just any jewelry box, a special box."

"Yes, I have it," he replied as if he had been expecting us and indicated we should follow him to the back of the store. Olivia and I exchanged puzzled looks, but we followed without asking any questions.

He led us to a small nook with a boarded-up fireplace beneath a sturdy wooden mantel and said, "Here are the items I acquired from Mr. Salus. Each item was arranged just so when the discovery was made."

On the mantel before us was a small wooden box, a bundle of letters tied together with a string, and a leather pouch with a rusted metal key on top.

"What do you mean, *discovered?*" I asked.

He gave me a quizzical look; his thick lenses magnified the confusion in his dark eyes. "Didn't you say you were looking for this special collection?" he asked.

Intrigued, I decided to play along. "Why, of course," I said. "What I meant to ask was, 'Who made the discovery?'"

"Mr. Salus hired a local contractor to renovate his home and expand the master bedroom."

"Here in Burlington?" Olivia asked.

"Yes, ma'am," he said. "When they took down the bedroom wall, they found a hidden compartment. Inside that space, they discovered these items."

"Is that the jewelry box?" I asked, pointing to what looked like a cigar humidor.

"It certainly is," he asserted, picking it up gingerly from the shelf. "It's solid oak, richly stained, with a cobalt blue velvet interior." He pulled the lid from the base, pointing to the two broken hinges in the back. "Whoever had it last, it looks like they lost the key and had to open it from the back."

"Looks like it would be difficult to repair," said Olivia as she took a closer look.

"Any idea who owned it?" I asked. "And why they hid it inside a wall?"

"Jake Salus bought the home at auction and never spoke to the previous owner."

"Did he do any research at all before bringing these things to you?"

"Jake fixes up houses for sale or rent. He's not interested in the past."

"The dult," I said.

The shopkeeper glowered at me. The magnification of his glasses made his eyes more menacing. "Jake knows his limitations. Unlike you and I, he's not an expert in antiques."

Olivia feigned a cough saying, "Expert," then poked me hard in the ribs with her finger.

"Ah!" I cried, lurching forward, as if to get a better look at the other items on the shelf.

"Furthermore," the shopkeeper continued, "this box is clearly even older than the house. There's no way of being sure if it was the former owner who put it there."

Olivia spoke up again, "This is all very interesting, but it's not the kind of jewelry box I'm interested in."

"What's the story of these other items?" I asked. "Have you looked through the letters? Do you have any idea what the key is for? And how about the pouch, what's in there?"

Olivia was enjoying the fact that I was beginning to take an interest. "Clayton, I'm shocked. An expert like you doesn't know what kind of key that is? You must have seen hundreds like it before," she teased.

"I did not untie the bundle of letters," said the antiques dealer, "and as for the key, your guess is as good as mine."

"What about the pouch?" I asked.

"It's a book."

"A book?" I replied, my curiosity heightening.

"A diary, I think. Handwritten in French. Beautiful handwriting, but terrible grammar," he replied. Then he paused and said, "How did you hear about this special collection? I haven't advertised it yet and you obviously don't know Jake. Who told you about it?"

"I'd rather not say," I shot back, wanting to sound elusive. "But I am sufficiently intrigued. We'll take the lot, my man. Name your price."

THE BOOK

"I can't believe you bought that stuff," Olivia said, tilting her head toward the cardboard box on the floor.

After leaving the furniture store, we turned back on Church Street and found a pleasant café just as it was starting to drizzle. It was a cozy affair with rustic oak tables, mismatched colonial chairs, and roaring fire in a grand fireplace. We were seated at a table near a wall with Olivia facing away from others who might recognize her when a waitress came to our table and took our orders.

"Looks like you had a successful morning," she said pointing to the box. "Find lots of good treasures?"

"It's his first time to shop for antiques," Olivia mocked. "Like most first-timers, he overpaid for stuff he knows nothing about."

"You gotta bargain with these people," the waitress said. "My boyfriend used to work at one of these shops and they always quote a price much higher than what they expect to get."

"I bargained," I said with a wry smile.

"Yeah, you gave the guy more than he asked for," Olivia said.

"This stuff is clearly worth more than a few hundred dollars," I said.

"Six hundred dollars. He asked for six hundred dollars, and you gave him a thousand."

"And I will sleep just fine tonight, thank you."

"Nothing wrong with being generous," the waitress said, smiling at me and clearly hoping my generosity extended to tipping servers of food and beverages. "My name is Gracy, with a y. Why? I don't know why."

"I don't know why, either" I told her, "but I will never forget it as long as I live."

We ordered our lunches, and while we were waiting, I pulled the leather pouch out of the box.

"You're going to open it here?" Olivia said.

"My inquisitiveness has taken over. I can stand it no longer."

"Antiques need to be handled with care. You can't just open an antique book on a table in a restaurant."

"Sure, I can. Remember, I paid a thousand dollars for this stuff. I can do whatever I please with it."

"Who's the dult now?"

"Fabulous!" I exclaimed, opening the pouch and eyeing the prize it contained.

The book inside was bound with thick, dark leather, weathered and worn, and the edges of its leaves were ragged. There was no title on the cover and no title page inside, nothing to indicate what it contained nor to whom it belonged, except the initials, *LPM* on the inside of the front cover. I turned the pages carefully, glancing at Olivia to gauge her reaction. She looked as curious as I.

"Well?" she said after a moment.

"It looks to be an autobiography of a French-speaking woman, handwritten in beautiful script, as the shopkeeper pointed out. Nothing wrong with her grammar, however. She was Belgian, and she mixes in Flemish words from time to time."

"You speak Flemish, too?"

"I grew up in Europe," I replied as I continued examining the text.

"I didn't know that. I thought you just went to high school in England."

"It would seem there are many things you don't know about me," I said, not looking up from the book.

"You're mad because I called you a dult?"

"It did seem a bit harsh." I kept my nose in the book and tried to seem more annoyed than I was. "You can't fault a man for being curious."

"Not true. I know lots of people who are curious to a fault," she replied, lifting my chin so I could see a smiling Gracy standing beside the table. "Our drinks are here."

She placed two glasses of Diet Coke in front of Olivia, being careful to keep mine far away from my book. "I wasn't sure if you wanted lemon or lime—or neither—in your drinks, so I brought you a plate of both," she explained, with a smile in my direction.

"Service with a smile, Gracy with a y" I said, smiling back.

"And special consideration for the generous man who overpays for things," Olivia muttered as Gracy walked away. "Lemon or lime?" she asked, holding one of each above my glass.

"Surprise me," I replied and returned to my book. I was fascinated and began to recount some of what I was reading. "The author was born in Sint-Niklaas, a town in Belgium, not far from Antwerp. She writes that her father was working against the Germans, trying to keep them from obtaining something valuable. The Germans hired him to go to France to get the object, but he had cooked up a plan to double-cross them."

"The Nazis?" Olivia asked.

"No," I replied, "The date is August 1918. It's World War One." I closed the book and looked at her. "In the Great War," I said with air quotes, "the Germans occupied Belgium, even though it was supposed to be neutral."

"What was the plan?"

"I don't know yet, but her father wants her help."

"What's the woman's name?" Olivia asked.

"I can't find her name anywhere. It's not a daily diary, per se. It's more like an autobiographical account written some time afterward. It's like she's telling her story to people who know who she is but don't know where she came from."

"Maybe to her children?"

"Something like that, yes," I answered, looking at her. "Do you think you'll ever write your own story?

"I keep a diary, but I shudder to think that someone else might read it," she said.

I raised one eyebrow and asked, "Will you be writing something about me in there?"

"Believe me, I already did."

"Exceptional things, I presume."

She laughed. "Lots of superlatives, yes. He's a great big this and a great big that," she said with air quotes each time she used the word, great.

I laughed with her. "You're clever," I said. "I'm sure I deserve all the remarks you made about me, and more."

Our lunches arrived, and once again we were showered with all manner of attention. "Are your sandwiches alright? Is the soup hot enough? Would you like a different dressing on your salad? How about some grated Parmesan cheese?"

After we assured Gracy that we were wonderfully satisfied in every way possible, she reluctantly left our side, allowing us to eat in peace.

"The soup needs salt," I said to Olivia.

She quipped, "Would you like me to get Gracy over here? She could grind up some Himalayan rock salt for you."

"Just pass the salt, please."

After a few minutes, Olivia asked, "Are you coming back out with me after lunch to look for a jewelry box?"

I froze with my spoon mid-way to my mouth. "Why would we do that?" I whined. "We searched all the stores already. And besides, we have a jewelry box."

"That little cigar box thing?" she asked. "I don't think that's the kind of item my mother would want in her collection."

"Why not? You said she doesn't have one like it. It's clearly something special. If it's the broken hinge that bothers you, I'm sure we can get that fixed."

"You don't understand," she protested. The intensity of her reaction puzzled me. She acted as if I had stood her up at the prom.

"You say I don't understand? Well, on that we are in complete agreement. I don't understand a lot of things when it comes to you."

She let out a barely audible, "Hmph!"

"Furthermore, I can't understand why anyone would want to collect old junk in general, let alone the subtleties of why one piece of old junk is valuable while another is worthless."

"And I can't understand why a man with so much time on his hands can't spare enough to spend it on someone other than himself, doing something that someone else wants to do."

"That's not fair. I came on this trip, didn't I? And I spent the whole morning out there with you, didn't I?"

"You did. And you complained the whole time. That is, until you found something that interested you. Now, you can't even be bothered to look at me—I mean look with me out there for a gift for my mother."

Gracy approached the table cautiously. "Is everything all right here?"

"I'm leaving," Olivia said, pushing her chair back from the table. Gracy surveyed the table and saw that Olivia had hardly touched her food. Her face drooped as her hopes of a cheerful tipper vanished.

"Didn't you like your sandwich? Would you like me to box up the leftovers?" she asked her.

Olivia assured her, "The food was great, Gracy, but the company was a little too sour."

"Don't forget your sunglasses," I replied, trying to appear indifferent.

She picked up her glasses from the table and marched out the door without any more words.

"Aren't you going to follow her?" Gracy asked when she saw I wasn't moving. "I can watch your things for you."

I thought for a moment. I wanted to follow her, and it bugged me. *Why should I care?* I thought. On the other hand, I wondered if she wasn't right. Perhaps I was being selfish, which is what happens when one is alone all one's life. For sure, it hurt to see her walk away, which is what happens when one gets too close to someone else.

"It's all right. I'm OK," I said. "Go ahead and clear away her plate so I have more space to read my book. Oh, and bring me a cup of that coffee they're brewing. It smells delicious."

said. "They can find their own way home."

"How did I end up in trouble?" Philip asked the back of the door when the women left the café.

"It was your idea to bring me along, wasn't it?" I asked.

"Yes, come to think of it, it was my idea. Stephanie predicted you'd be trouble, but I persuaded her you could behave when you needed to."

"It would seem that my presence has caused you distress," I replied.

"It is partly my fault, at least. I should have given you some of Olivia's backstory," Philip said. "She comes across as strong and independent, but she's easily upset when she faces a crowd alone."

"She's a television star who's afraid of her fans?" I asked. "That's inconvenient."

"When Olivia was a junior at Yale, her sorority sisters staged her kidnapping during rush week to scare the new pledges. They arranged for a bunch of guys from a fraternity to pretend to abduct her and hide her somewhere."

"Brilliant idea. What could possibly have gone wrong with that plan?" I mocked.

"Right. Unfortunately, some of the guys didn't realize it was supposed to be a fake abduction. They got rough with her, tied her up, and locked Olivia in a closet."

"Yale men."

"It was awful. She nearly had to drop out of school because of the trauma. I think she took some time off, but with counseling she was able to make it back and finish her degree."

I was moved inside, but tried to stay intellectual on the surface. "And she still suffers post-traumatic stress?"

"Whenever a person or a group of people gets too close, yes. So, when those fans back there were up in her face asking for selfies, she started to panic."

"How was I supposed to know? She hides it well."

"She is an actor, after all," Philip said.

"She's on television," I replied. "That doesn't say much."

"Have you ever seen Olivia act on television? I've seen her show. She's quite proficient."

"Anyone can act on television, Philip. You read your lines off a cue card, and if they don't come out the way the network wants it, you just read them again." I looked around and lowered my voice, "The audience won't notice anyway, because their collective brain has been numbed by the commercials."

Philip replied, "It's not as bad as you make it out to be. Moreover, Olivia's show is especially well done."

"What redeeming qualities have you discovered?" I asked.

"The concept is good. It's a show about faculty politics within a prestigious university."

"OK, the premise sounds interesting," I admitted.

"Olivia has one of the lead roles. She plays a university vice-president who is trying to push the boundaries against sexism, cronyism, and corruption."

"Worthwhile themes to explore."

"My point is this: you should not make uninformed judgments. You haven't seen her work, so you have no right to assert that it's trash."

"Fair point," I conceded. "OK, from now on I will broaden my horizons."

"How broad? Broad enough to watch her show?"

"Are you serious? I don't even own a TV."

"No problem," Philip said. "We can stream it at Robert and Roberta's."

"Tonight?" I gasped, thinking of my fascinating book and the winged back chair near the fireplace in my room.

"Tonight. You can read that thing any time," Philip said, reading my mind and pointing to the book on the table between us. "Let's go. Brian's waiting outside. Grab your book and your box. The girls took the car, so we're Ubering back to Robert's place."

BAD ACTING

We sat in the living room of Robert and Roberta's bed and breakfast watching an episode of Olivia's program on their giant television. The fireplace was roaring, and Robert passed out soft fleece blankets for each of us. Brian sat cross-legged on the floor near the fireplace. The two couples sat together, each on one end of the large sectional sofa. Olivia sat in a rocking chair near the sofa, under her blanket with her hand on her forehead and trying to avoid looking at the screen. She was as uncomfortable as a teenager whose mother broke out baby pictures for a gathering of her friends. I sat in a large comfortable chair in the back corner of the room. I had no interest in watching her performance, but if it meant she would be squirming in real life for an hour, then I was all for it.

The episode was about a scandal involving the respected dean of the university's science department. He was a Nobel laureate who singlehandedly brought in more grant money each year than several other departments combined. His world was rocked one day, however, when the FBI came to his office with a search warrant requesting a sample of his DNA. They were alleging that the dean sexually molested a woman while an undergraduate student at California Institute of Technology, forty years earlier. Of course, he refused to comply with the search warrant, calling the allegations a frivolous smear campaign.

To keep the story out of the hands of the hungry media, the university immediately challenged the warrant in court for lack of probable cause. After all these years, they argued in a closed hearing, how could there suddenly be reason to suspect the professor's DNA would match samples taken at the scene? In the hearing, the FBI admitted that DNA collected forty years earlier had never led to matches in the Combined DNA Index System, or CODIS, but they went on to say there was recent evidence from genetic genealogy that implicated the dean. The dean's grandson, they claimed, had sent a DNA sample to an ancestry website, and investigative geneticists were able to triangulate his genetic profile into a vector headed straight toward the celebrated dean.

"That's crazy," Stephanie said. "They can't do that, can they?"

"It's true, Stephanie," Olivia said. "It's how they caught the Golden State Killer."

"Seems pretty far-fetched to me," said Philip.

Brian, who was still playing his game console while watching the show, said, "It's simple bioinformatics. You don't need an exact match; you just need to find someone within a few hundred centimorgans of the DNA found at the scene of the crime. Once you have that, you can work backwards to find a common ancestor and then work forward to the guilty party."

"What's a centimorgan?" Stephanie asked. "I sent a sample to twenty-three dot com. Are you saying the police could use that to accuse my brother of a crime?"

Philip replied, "Is there something about your family you're not telling me, Steph?"

"It just feels like an invasion of privacy," Stephanie said, hitching up her blanket.

Olivia's character appeared on-screen again, so I said, "Some of us are trying to watch the show," which caused just about everyone to roll their eyes at me.

The college president was arguing with her that they should play down the story in the press and continue fighting the allegations in court. Olivia's character, the vice president, on the other hand, was trying to convince the president and the board that the best way forward was to fully cooperate with investigators. Only a transparent investigation, she argued, would settle the issue in the minds of donors and prospective students.

What she didn't realize, however, was that her political enemies in the administration were plotting to make her the scapegoat. They were planting evidence to make it look as if she knew about the dean's history and fought to keep him at his post, even though the president wanted to remove him years earlier. By pushing for an investigation, she was unsuspectingly plotting her own destruction.

The story was much more engaging than I had anticipated, and I was surprised by how quick-witted and insightful the dialog was. I also had to admit to myself that Olivia was a good actor. Her argument with the president in front of the board was extremely believable. And later in the episode, when the bursar publicly accused her of covering up the dean's actions against the wishes of the college president, she communicated her character's disbelief and indignation with a nuance that felt authentic.

When the scene had reached its peak of tension, I could feel Olivia's eyes watching me, assessing my level of interest in the story. I don't know how long she had been observing me, but I hoped it wasn't long because I did not want to let on that I was enjoying the show. I pulled out my phone to pretend checking my text messages, and I heard her exhale loudly.

"Tsk," she said, as she turned away. "I know you were watching, and I could tell you were hooked."

"I'm sorry," I said, turning to her. "Were you talking to me? I had made some inquiries this afternoon about the house where the book was found, but I struck out. I was thinking of how I could find more information."

"You were watching the show—the *television* show—and you were enjoying it. Admit it."

"Of course I was watching. There's a huge TV on the wall in front of us. It would have been physically impossible not to watch it," I shot back.

The credits started to roll, and Stephanie and Philip shouted, "Huzzah!" when Olivia's name appeared on screen.

"What did you think of it, Clayton?" Stephanie asked me, her face toward the screen, still watching the credits.

"Of all the television shows I have watched, that was one of them," I said, continuing the pretense.

"You're a lousy actor," Olivia said. "Your disdain is so far from believable as to be ridiculous."

"He loved it," Philip countered. "I know Clay. If he didn't like it, he would have thought of some small thing to praise. The only reason he would say he didn't like it is because he loved it and he's too ashamed to admit it."

Philip knew me too well. "As a matter of fact, I was going to say that I thought the set decorations were very authentic. I felt like I was back in school again."

"Too late," Philip replied, seeing right through me. "You already gave away your true feelings. You watched a television show, and you liked it. But don't worry, your secret is safe with us."

"How about another episode?" Stephanie asked.

Both Olivia and I groaned at the same time.

"I don't know," she said. "I think people have had enough for one night."

"People? What people?" Stephanie asked, pointing at me. "You mean him? Ignore him, that's what he prefers, anyway."

"Don't let me stop you from continuing to watch this quality programming. As for me, I can only take so much entertainment in one night. I need to pace myself."

"Same goes for me," Brian said, jumping to his feet while both hands continued to work the controls on his game.

"I promised that exceptional chair by the fireplace in my bedroom that I would spend some quality time in its warm embrace," I said.

As I left the room, I heard Olivia ask, "What is he so afraid of?"

AMERICA

The fireplace was of the fake gas-powered variety, which disappointed me at first, but within seconds, it was burning brightly, and I was sitting comfortably in my chair. The book was open on my lap, my feet were propped up on the ottoman, and I let out a comfortable sigh.

"Finally," I said to no one at all as I opened the leather-bound manuscript for the first time since Philip scolded me at the café. I turned the pages in wonder at the beautiful script, carefully written in neat rows across the unruled pages. Each leaf turned crisply and cleanly with a satisfying sound that told me few, if any, had ever read this volume before me.

I skimmed its contents and noticed immediately that the book was divided into three chapters followed by what appeared to be an epilogue. The first chapter was about her life in Belgium and her father's scheme to fool the Germans. The next chapter told the story of her own journey from Europe to the New World in North America. The longest chapter was the third, and that described her life in Burlington. The fourth section was the shortest and the most captivating.

You may never understand why I left you, she began. *But if I hadn't left, bad people would have come and hurt us all. I couldn't take both you and your sister with me, so I had to choose. I took her because I knew she would not be strong enough to live in the house with your father. Furthermore, he always loved you more than her, and I knew he could never live without you. I hope you can forgive me. I hope you can understand that I had to leave you because it was the only way to protect you.*

Several water spots on the bottom of the page marked the places where that mother's tears fell. My heart went out to her, but I ached even more for the boy whose mother left him alone with his father. The story hit too close to home.

The page that followed was written by the same hand, but it was written in haste. The luxuriously flowing script of the preceding pages was gone, replaced with sharply angled letters that leaned forward as if they were already racing off on a speeding train. The book ended with this:

30 March 1924. I have no time to say more, dear Edward. I will write you whenever I can. When you are old enough to understand, I will send you the key to find this book, so you will know the mother who loves you more than life itself. Now, I must go. They are coming.

I closed the book and stared into the burning fire. My thoughts rushed to my own mother, and I wondered if she ever wanted to write a book like this. I longed to know more about her and to understand what forces drove her from her home and from her sanity.

These thoughts were interrupted by the sound of a text message. It was from Olivia. She wrote to tell me she regretted the fact that we got off on the wrong foot. She knew about my bad breakup with Vanessa and wondered if I wasn't projecting some of my feelings toward Vanessa onto her. She wanted to let me know she'd be willing to start over in the morning if I was willing to do the same.

"Maybe it's Vanessa, or maybe it's just me," I said to my empty room. I tapped out and deleted several responses before turning off my phone and throwing it on the floor.

Opening the book at the beginning, I said, "Now, LPM, tell me your story. Who are you? Where did you come from, and who has frightened you enough to tear apart your family?"

I picked up the story from where I had left off in the café. LPM and her father traveled to Brest to purchase the stolen item. However, in Brest, everything fell apart. While driving to a remote place to make the exchange, Goldney realized they weren't who they said they were. He figured out that they were going to return the stolen item to Britain and that his crime would be discovered. With one hand on the wheel, he pointed a gun at her father, who was sitting in the passenger seat. LPM grabbed the gun from the back seat, but the car swerved and hit an army truck head on. Being in the back, she wasn't injured badly, but those up front did not fare as well.

"Get the bag from the trunk," her father instructed her with his dying words. *"Bring it to England and stay there until the war is over. I'm going to your mother. It won't be long now."*

She opened the trunk and found only a leather briefcase inside. Soldiers from the truck and a nearby tavern were running to the car, so she hurriedly grabbed the case, which was lighter than she expected, and ran in the opposite direction. She never saw her father again, and she never discovered what happened to Goldney.

Making her way to the banks of the Iroise Sea, she found the boat that would have taken her and her father to England, and to safety. Her father had given her their tickets and traveling money before getting in Goldney's car. She wondered if he had foreseen trouble that would befall them, and she was determined to complete the work that he had begun. Once across the Channel, she would turn over the briefcase to the British government.

It wasn't until she disembarked in Portsmouth, England, that she became aware of a glaring oversight in her plan. She had no idea what she was carrying or how to turn it over to the British government. She began to grow fearful of what would happen if anyone questioned her about the briefcase.

Would anyone believe me if I told them I recovered this briefcase from a British officer who had stolen it? Rather, wouldn't they accuse me of being a thief and a smuggler? she wrote.

She talked her way past customs, holding the briefcase, and walked towards a small grove of trees along the road that hugged the edge of the harbor. She had been burning with curiosity to know what she had removed from the trunk of Goldney's car, but the crowded ferry had offered no place of privacy suitable for opening the satchel and examining its contents. She hurried toward the grove, and looking from side to side to make sure no one was watching, she hid herself amongst the trees.

She opened the bag and found a small wooden box swaddled inside a bundle of fine linen handkerchiefs all bearing the monogram, *FBG*. The box was locked, but there was a small key sewn into the hem of one of the handkerchiefs.

"Incroyable!" I shouted in French, jumping to my feet and clapping. "I knew that jewelry box was special. Just wait 'till I tell Olivia!" A few moments later, a sleepy guest from the room below me came and knocked on my door. He asked very politely if I wouldn't mind keeping the noise down. He was craning his neck to look around the room, trying to see who I had been talking to. "No more jumping," I promised and closed the door.

I picked my phone up off the floor, turned it on, and tapped out a text to Olivia. I answered her message by affirming that tomorrow would be a new day and I'd be happy for a new start. Also, I went on to write that she would not believe what I learned about her mother's newest jewelry box. Then, I sat down by the fire and continued reading LPM's fascinating tale.

As I was about to use the key to open the box, I suddenly noticed two men, one old and one young, on the street near my hiding place. They were looking up and down the street as if they were lost. I was concerned because the older man looked familiar; I remembered seeing him on the ferry crossing from Brest to Portsmouth. Curiosity to know what was inside the box overwhelmed my sense of caution, however. I opened the box, and to my amazement, I saw two breathtaking pieces of jewelry. The larger one was a dazzling, eight-pointed silver star encrusted with hundreds of tiny diamonds, so brilliant were they that even in the shade of those trees they were too bright for my eyes to behold. In the center of the star there was a cross of rubies, encircled by a crown of emeralds. Next to the star was a smaller item, a pendant suspended from a magnificent silver harp and similarly decorated in glittering diamonds, rubies, and emeralds.

I gasped at the sight of these objects, which were far more beautiful than anything I had ever beheld in my life. And when I did, the men on the street in front of me immediately turned their heads, peering between the branches that hid me. I quickly closed the box and the briefcase, bolted out of the trees, and began to run down the street away from the men. When they saw me, the older one shouted, 'Schnell, verfolge,' and I could hear the footsteps of the young man chasing me—and getting closer.

I made a quick turn onto a road marked King Street because I saw the backs of a line of soldiers two blocks away, marching toward the entrance of a large grassy area. I ran toward the soldiers praying to Saint Patrick that they would turn around and help me.

The younger man's footsteps were getting closer by the second, and I knew I would never make it to the soldiers in time. I tried to run faster, but my legs were burning and felt like they were made of rubber. The faster I tried to run, the closer my pursuer's footsteps approached and the louder the sound of his breathing came into my ears.

When I could feel his breath on the back of my neck, he stretched out his hand to grab the briefcase, which was hanging from the strap over my shoulder. When he did so, I quickly thrust my shoulder forward, and I could feel his fingers slide from the shoulder strap to the back collar of my dress. With all the breath I could muster, I shouted toward the column of soldiers in English, 'Help me! Help me! Help!' Two soldiers in the rear of the column turned in time to see the young man tearing the back of my dress and pulling me to the ground.

'You there!' they shouted and moved toward us with bayonets lowered.

My attacker froze, then he tried one more time to wrench the briefcase from my grasp.

'He's German!' I shouted to the soldiers. They quickened their pace and were abruptly joined by a dozen more soldiers from the column.

The young man swore in German, then ran down King Street in the opposite direction, empty handed. I crossed the street to get out of the way of the soldiers, who were closing in on the man, and slipped into a darkened alley unnoticed. In the stillness of that alley, I made a decision that changed the course of my life. There was only one thing for me to do. I would go to America.

ADMIRATION

I don't know what time it was when I finally stopped reading her book, but when I awoke Sunday morning, it was after eight. The house was quiet, and I feared I had missed out on the greater 'B' of the B&B: breakfast. I jogged downstairs to the dining room through the eerie silence and was delighted to see someone still sitting there.

"Oh, it's you," I said when Olivia turned to look at me.

"Good morning, to you, too," she said and turned back to her coffee cup.

"Sorry," I said. "I meant no offense. I was only hoping you were Roberta waiting with some more of her fabulous blueberry pancakes."

"None taken. And you're in luck," Olivia said. "Roberta is still in the kitchen. I asked her to wait for you a little while longer."

"I could kiss you," I said, before immediately wishing I hadn't spoken. I could feel the warmth of circulation rushing to my face as I continued, "Just an expression. What I meant to say is, simply, thank you."

"You're simply welcome," Olivia said, smiling. "I received your texts," she continued. "An hour or so after midnight, I might add."

"Sorry to text you so late. I had no idea what time it was. I was so captivated by what I was reading."

"So, I figured."

"Where are the others?" I asked and plopped myself down in chair near her table.

"Stephanie and Philip went for a hike up the mountain to see the leaves, and Brian went back to his room. He mumbled something about a critical juncture and detailed documentation, or something like that. I didn't hear it clearly, but I got the message."

"You should have gone on that hike," I said. "The mountains are beautiful this time of year."

"I didn't want to be a third wheel, and also..." she began.

Roberta came out of the kitchen with a large plate bearing a beautiful stack of pancakes, two eggs, bacon, and toast. "We don't usually serve breakfast after eight a.m.," she said. "But Robert said we have to expect people from Harvard to be a little slow."

"Say what you want about me or my alma mater; it's not going to ruin my enjoyment of your outstanding breakfast," I replied, licking my lips.

"Coffee is self-serve," Roberta said, pointing to the mugs on a table near the wall. "Enjoy your breakfast."

"You know I will, Roberta," I said to her as she went back into the kitchen. And then to Olivia, I said, "And also... what?"

"And also, I was waiting for you."

"Waiting for me? Why?" I replied, maybe too vigorously. It was the last answer I expected to hear.

"Don't sound so surprised," she said. "Just because you were a jerk to me yesterday, doesn't mean I'm going to treat you the same way. Remember? A fresh start?"

"A jerk? I don't think that's fair. After all, I went shopping with you, didn't I? And I watched your show, hmm?"

"Of course you watched it, and you liked it. Only, you didn't have the decency to admit you were enjoying it. And a man without decency is a jerk, is he not?"

I thought for a moment, searching for the right comeback, but I drew a blank. Maybe it was the fact that she had waited for me, maybe it was her breathtaking good looks, or maybe it was the blueberry pancakes. Whatever the reason, my hostility melted, and I apologized. "A man without decency is, indeed, a jerk, and I am that man. Forgive me. The show was quite good. The dialogue was crisp and witty, and your performance was spot-on."

"That's big of you to admit. Apology accepted," she said and joined me at my table.

"There's one thing I would have changed in the story, though," I continued.

"Oh, what?" she asked, leaning back in her chair and glancing at me sideways.

"I only wish your character had punched that bursar right in the mouth. How dare he talk to her that way!"

Olivia laughed out loud. Her laugh was warm-hearted and melodious. "I know, right? He deserved to be punched. Wait till you see what happens in the next episode."

"Looking forward to it," I said, and I meant it.

"I believe you. You see? You're not such a jerk after all. I always suspected you were a good man hiding behind a façade."

"Really? What made you think so?"

"You remind me of my father," she said, turning her face away. "He kept us all at arms' length because he was afraid to let us get too close, but once in a while I would see glimpses of kindness on the inside."

"Your father? I never heard you mention him before. You've only talked about your mother and her insatiable desire for old jewelry boxes."

"He left us when I was a senior in high school. For years, he had been fighting his demons, and the demons finally won. He packed up and moved to Arizona."

"I'm sorry to hear that," I said. "Fathers can be quintessential jerks."

"He's not evil, he's just lost. I hear from him from time to time. How about you? What is your father like?" she asked.

"Let's not talk about him. You were about to elaborate on why you think I am a good man."

"I said I suspected you were good. I'm still looking for evidence."

"I hope your research is successful," I replied. "Truth be told, I have my doubts."

Olivia smiled at me with a sweet, yet sorrowful smile. "Finish your pancakes," she said. "I want you to take me out on the town."

"Perfect," I replied. "That will give me a chance to tell you what I read in my book last night. I've gained some dazzling insights regarding my purchase at the furniture store yesterday."

"Dazzling? Seriously?"

"I'll explain later."

I finished my breakfast and washed it down with more of Roberta's coffee. When I picked up my plate and cup to bring it into the kitchen, Roberta came out and relieved me of the burden. "I'll take those," she said. "Sounds like you two are finally starting to get along."

"I didn't realize the walls here are so thin," I said, only half-joking.

"We've been doing this long enough now that I can tell when couples are hitting it off and when they are counting the minutes until check-out time."

"What can you recommend we do this morning, Roberta?" Olivia asked. "We are flying back to New Jersey around four o'clock. What's there to do in Burlington on a Sunday morning?"

"And please don't say 'shopping for antiques,'" I quipped.

"Have you ever heard of *The Spirit of Ethan Allen?*" Roberta asked.

"I didn't know his ghost haunted these parts," I said.

"Not funny. Don't quit your day job," she shot back. "Oh, that's right. You don't have a job. *The Spirit of Ethan Allen* is a tour boat. It's for scenic cruises on Lake Champlain."

I turned to Olivia and said, "I'm not opposed to working. It's just that I'm not qualified to do anything."

"What did you study at Harvard?" she asked.

"Classics, with a concentration in Greek Drama."

"So, you were a drama major?" she laughed.

"Something like that. I don't know how to act, but I can read a play in multiple dead languages. What did you study at Yale?"

"I was an English major, and my concentration was on the plays of Shakespeare," she said with a convincing British accent.

"Seriously? So, please tell me—and I'm not trying to be rude anymore—why television?"

Roberta laughed and said, "Clayton's so talented, he can be rude without even trying."

"Clayton's so privileged, he is mindless of the fact that some people need to earn a living," Olivia said to her. "With my father out of the picture, my mother depends on me for support. When I was offered the part on a TV series, I jumped at the chance."

"Admirable," I responded. "I am duly chastised for my ignorance. In fact, I am beginning to believe that I can learn a lot from you."

"My work here is done," said Roberta. "Now get out of here before this gets awkward for me. *The Spirit of Ethan Allen* is docked on College Street. Go out the front door and turn left, then walk until you reach the lake. You can't miss it."

A FALLACY OF FAULTY COMPARISON

As we walked to the waterfront, I told Olivia all I had read the night before. I decided to start from the beginning and build up to the big reveal when I would tell her about the jewels. I told her all about their scheme to double-cross the Germans and turn over the stolen object to the authorities in England. She was shocked to hear that LPM's father died in a car accident because she grabbed the gun while Goldney was driving.

"What happened to Goldney?" she asked.

"I've no idea. She didn't stick around to find out. She grabbed the bag out of the trunk and started making tracks for the boat to England."

"What was in the bag?" Olivia asked. "I can't remember what you told me. Was it the little box?" As we approached the boat dock and bought our tickets, she began to seem distracted, even distant.

"Hey now, don't get ahead of me," I joked as we joined the long line of tourists waiting to navigate the islands of Lake Champlain. "I'm building up to an exciting climax."

"Sorry, I thought you said something about the box."

"No. I didn't say that. Now, where was I?"

"The exciting climax," she said without looking at me.

For a moment, I thought she was being intentionally obtuse, and I was about to respond with one of my trademarked zingers. But something inside me told me to stop and look for another explanation for her sudden change in attitude. It was at that point that I noticed Olivia was beginning to act agitated. Even though her baseball cap hung low across her forehead and her large, black sunglasses covered much of her face, I could tell she wasn't herself. The beautiful serenity that normally adorned her face was replaced with worry—almost panic.

"Are you OK?" I asked her.

"These people," she whispered in my ear.

I looked around us from left to right. "No one recognizes you here. I doubt anyone will recognize you wearing those welding goggles."

"It's a boat," she said.

I opened brochure they handed me when I purchased our tickets, and said, "*The Spirit of Ethan Allen* is one hundred forty feet long and has been in service for decades. We'll go north, towards Lone Rock Point, then loop around Juniper Island into Shelburne Bay. All protected waters. Furthermore, the lake monster hasn't sunk it yet, so I think we'll be OK."

"No back door," came another whispered response, with more urgency.

"It's a boat," I said.

"Clay," she whispered. She was barely audible this time. She was breathing rapidly, and beads of sweat were forming on her cheeks. "I'm afraid. I mean it. I'm really afraid. If people recognize me on that boat, I will have no place to go. I'll be trapped."

My heart went out to her, and I marveled at how deep the scars of her trauma from the college prank years earlier still cut. "Well then, let's get out of here," I replied. "The only way off that boat would be by jumping into the lake, and I have no intention of swimming back to shore from Shelburne Bay."

"I'm sorry, Clay. I should've said something before you bought the tickets, but I was hoping I could do it."

"Forget about the tickets," I said, tearing them into several pieces and throwing them in a nearby trashcan. "Let's get some air."

The moment I tore the tickets, a visible change came over her face, and in fact, her whole body seemed to relax. Her shoulders straightened, and her breathing slowed. She took off the sunglasses and baseball cap that had been hiding her gorgeous face and flung loose her matted hair.

After walking a long time in silence, I picked up my story where I had left off. When I finally got to the part where she opened the box, Olivia was duly impressed. She reacted with as much shock and excitement as I had been hoping for. I went on to tell her briefly about the Germans, but I left out the part where the younger guy chased her and grabbed her by the back of the collar in her dress. I just told her the Germans had been chased away by some soldiers who happened to be nearby.

"What an incredible story, Clay. Dazzling, indeed. So, you found what we had set out to find, a jewelry box without the jewels."

"Haha, I guess you're right."

"So, what happened next?" she asked. "Or is this one of those 'To be continued' episodes?"

"That's as far as I got translating the book. The language is a little dated, so it's slow-going."

She looked at me and said, "I want the whole story, episode by episode. And I don't care if you take your time."

Olivia took my hand as we continued walking in silence along the waterfront. Then, it became my turn to panic. The day Vanessa told me she wanted to date someone else, I promised myself I was done with relationships. Starting with my parents, everyone close to me left me. 'To know me is to reject me' became my tagline. Now this beautiful woman—talented, intelligent, and kind—was holding my hand, and it scared me.

We stopped to watch the skaters at the skateboard park and stepped into the Gallery at Main Street Landing and enjoyed some creations of local artists. Olivia had completely recovered her composure, but she noticed that I had become stiff along the walk.

"Your palm is sweaty," she said, tilting her head and raising one eyebrow. "Something wrong?"

I stopped walking and looked out over the lake. "You know how you fear being mobbed by a crowd?"

"Yes?"

"I fear being abandoned by an individual."

"Me?"

"Whoever I care about. And, yes, that includes you. I was attracted to you from the moment I met you. Your captivating looks and your intelligent banter ensorcelled me. When you went toe-to-toe with me in a battle of snide remarks, I was intrigued. Then, back at the house yesterday, you completed a line from Romeo and Juliet, and I was hooked. This morning, I learned you're not only good company, but you're also a good daughter. I said I admired that, and I meant it."

"You've been pushing me away all this time so that I wouldn't reject you, huh?"

"You can't reject me if you never accept me."

"It's too late. I'm already intrigued and slightly attracted," she said, presenting her thumb and forefinger spread a half-inch apart. "But look at the bright side."

"Never tell a pessimist there's a bright side."

"All your other relationships began with the girl liking you, but over time, she became disillusioned, am I right?"

"Lather, rinse, repeat."

"Right. But don't forget, I couldn't stand you at first."

"Is that so?"

"Absolutely. I wasn't feigning aversion. I honestly didn't like you."

"I'm not sure where this is going."

"So, it stands to reason," she continued, "that we will get along better and better over time."

The thought of our relationship growing deeper and closer over time scared the daylights out me, but I was too ashamed to show it. "Sounds like a faulty comparison fallacy," was the only response I could utter.

"Let's ride bikes!" she exclaimed, pointing to a small shop with a dozen or more mountain bikes lined up like dominoes waiting to be knocked over or rented.

I was so willing to change the subject I would have agreed to dental work if she had suggested it. "That's a splendid idea," I said. "I'll rent them all to make sure no one follows us."

"Two's enough," she said. "We can ride faster than the viewing audience."

Olivia was right. We rode our rented bikes along a trail that followed the lake shore, and although several people recognized her along the way, she took it in stride. Each time it happened, she would say something short and sweet, then peddle faster until we were safely away. A few miles up the coast, we came to a wooded area on a peninsula that jutted far into the lake. There was a small stone patio there, with a single stone bench and a Celtic cross carved from the same stone as the bench.

"Rock Point Open Air Chapel," I read aloud the metal plaque affixed to the floor at the entrance.

"You're bringing me to a chapel, Clay?" Olivia joked, as she took a long drink from her water bottle.

"By no means!" I protested.

"Drink your water," Olivia said, and gestured for us to sit down. The coolness of the stone bench was refreshing, and we enjoyed the view of the lake, seen through the thin, young trees that hid us from tourists. "Can I ask you a personal question?"

"You can ask," I replied. "Of course, I won't answer."

"Tell me about your family."

"That's not a question."

"Would you please tell me about your family?"

"No."

"Why not? I told you about mine," she said.

"Very little. You shared about your mother's penchant for special antique jewelry boxes, and you said your father moved to Arizona because the devil made him do it."

"And you shared that your father is rich. That's all."

"I also implied he was a jerk, like your father. Except in my father's case, he didn't leave us; he kicked us out."

"He kicked you out? That's terrible."

I turned to her and said, "My father made a fortune banking in Europe. He owned a bank that specialized in currency exchanges before the inception of the European Union. When the EU was formed and the currencies were all folded into the Euro at the turn of the century, my father found himself in possession of the goose that lays golden eggs. To be more precise, he had multiple golden geese in several European capitals that laid dozens of eggs faster than anyone could count. He became a gazillionaire several times over."

"So, he was in the right place at the right time, huh?"

"I'm not sure it was the right place. As far as I can tell, the money ruined everything. I was just a kid, and most of those years I was away at boarding school, but everything at home went to hell in a handbasket. The richer he got, the worse things got. By the time I was in Tonbridge, my mother was hospitalized with some kind of mental illness. He said it was drugs, but I think that's a lie."

"Tonbridge was your high school in England?"

"Secondary school, they call it, but yes. It's in Kent, on the southeast coast of England."

"Is she OK now? Your mom?" Olivia asked. The look of concern on her face moved me.

"She's dead. I never saw her again after she went into the hospital."

"I'm so sorry," she said, placing her hand on mine.

"Then, while I was in university, my jerk of a father decided to replace my mother with a woman younger than my older brother."

"No way!" Olivia exclaimed, placing her other hand over her mouth.

"She's a couple years older than me, and a couple years younger than him. But she didn't want stepchildren her age around to make things awkward, so she persuaded my father to send us packing."

"So, he kicked you and your brother out?"

"He gave us a reverse-prodigal-son deal. He offered us our huge inheritance on the spot if we signed an agreement that we would leave and never try to contact him again."

"Sounds like he divorced you," she said.

"Kind of. More like he disowned us, and he bribed us to go along with it."

"I'm sorry I asked. I mean, thank you for your honesty, but I'm sorry to make you say all that. I can understand why you didn't want to talk about it."

"You are the only woman with whom I've shared that story," I said, sliding my hand out from under hers and placing it on top.

"Not even Vanessa?" she asked.

I pulled my hand away abruptly, and said, "Seriously?"

"I'm sorry. That just came out. It was rude of me."

"I'm used to it," I lied. "Let's get going. We don't want Philip to fly back to New Jersey without us."

We returned the rented bikes, then walked quickly to Robert and Roberta's bed and breakfast with only a few words of superficial conversation. I don't even remember what we were talking about when I opened the front door to see Robert's frowning face glaring at me.

"What do you expect me to do with *this*?" He growled and pointed behind him with his thumb.

I looked past him to see standing in the middle of his living room, an ornate walnut and glass case that contained the circa 1890 musical carousel I bought for Olivia's mother. It was the size of a refrigerator.

"We're going to need a bigger plane," said Brian, laughing and walking past me wearing his backpack for the return trip to Teterboro.

THE GAME'S AFOOT

"It makes quite a nice addition to my home," I said while looking at the oversized music box in my living room. I was in New York, speaking with Olivia on the phone. A few weeks earlier, she had gone back to California to film more episodes of her television show. Since our weekend in Burlington, we had been calling each other almost every day.

"I'm surprised Robert didn't want to keep it for the bed and breakfast. I think his guests would love it."

"You don't think it a bit much?" she asked.

"I find it soothing to watch the carousel as it spins, while the horses and boats frolic up and down tirelessly. Furthermore, the music sounds fabulous. The oak cabinet provides wonderful resonance."

"You sound like someone trying to sell something that no one wants to buy," Olivia said.

"I'm sure your mother would have loved it, but I've decided to keep it. Don't even bother asking me to change my mind."

"Deal."

"I mean it. You can ask all you want, but it's not leaving my home," I declared.

"In case you hadn't noticed, I already agreed to never ask you for it."

"You don't know what you're missing."

"I'm pretty sure I do," she replied. "But listen, I need to get back to the set in a few minutes. You promised you'd bring me up to date on your translation of the book."

"I'm almost done with the second section," I said. "It's all about her journey from England to Burlington, Vermont. Long story short, she boarded a vessel for Canada that stopped in Ireland. At the port in Galway, a fellow joined the passengers who turned out to be quite an important figure in her life."

"Really? Sounds intriguing. Why Canada, though. I thought she wanted to go to America."

"It was August 1918. Because of the war, there weren't any passenger ships available for ports in the United States; they were all being used to carry soldiers. Quebec City was her closest option. And it's a good thing, too, because if she hadn't gone to Quebec City, she never would have met Michael."

"A tall, dark, and handsome stranger from Galway?"

"She describes him as being kind of short, compared to the men in Belgium, and not very handsome, but he was kind. They met on deck when he saw her shivering and he offered her his wool overcoat. She was cold, and he was chivalrous."

"That'll do it. If a man gave me his warm coat on a cold night, I'd be his."

"I'll bear that in mind," I said. "So, most of the second section concerns the journey to Canada and her budding romance with Michael. She also seems worried that the Irish passengers will learn that she is carrying The Order of Saint Patrick. That's what her father named it."

"Does she say what she plans to do with the jewels?"

"Not yet, but I learned a critical piece of information."

"What's that?" Olivia asked.

"Her name is Louisa Peeters. Two e's," I said.

"Louisa Peeters is LPM? What does the M stand for?"

"I'm guessing it's Michael's last name. He is in the story for a reason."

"She's explaining to her son how she met his father? That's sweet," she said.

"Very sweet. Of course, by the end of the book, she is going to leave him behind."

"That must have been gut-wrenching for her. As it was for your mother, Clay."

I held the phone to my ear but didn't speak.

"You OK?" Olivia asked.

"When are you coming back?" I asked her.

"As soon as I can," she said. "I want to see my mother. Furthermore, I have a friend with a place in New York City."

"Does this friend have an antique music box the size of a refrigerator that plays six tunes and sports a carousel with horses and boats?"

"He does, indeed, and I can't wait to see it."

"And him?" I asked.

"And I can't wait to see him," she said. "But now I really need to go. I'm already late for makeup."

"How soon is soon?" I asked.

"I'm not sure. The showrunner doesn't like the pacing of the season finale. She wants to re-shoot a bunch of scenes. I expect to be home for Thanksgiving."

"Thanksgiving is over a month away," I whined.

"It'll be here before you know it. The time will fly by."

"That's easy for you to say because you have a job. What do I have? I sit at home watching toy horses inside a music box."

"I thought you said it was therapeutic."

"I lied. It's awful. The horses are laughing at me."

"We need to get you a job," Olivia said.

"Funny you should say that. I have an idea about a job," I replied.

"That's great, Clay. What's your idea?"

"I want to find the missing jewels."

She laughed. "That's not a job."

"No, I mean it. The jewels are still missing. I think that's because Louisa hid them somewhere. With a little detective work, I bet I can find them."

"They've been missing for over a hundred years. What makes you think you can find them when no one else could?"

"Because we know things no one else knows. Louisa Peeters M-something took the jewels to Burlington, Vermont. We are the only living people in the world who know that."

"What do you mean, 'we'?" she laughed. "How did this go from 'I' to 'we'? I already have a job, remember?"

"Naturally, I expected you would be excited to join the hunt."

"Naturally," she said sarcastically. "But even if I were interested in this quest, and I'm not saying I am, what's the point? We wouldn't be able to sell them, and you don't need any more money."

"That Goldney character stole them from someone. If I can find them, I can return them to their rightful owner. I can be a hero."

"Then your music box will stop laughing at you?"

"That, too."

After a brief pause, Olivia said, "Well, Superman, I just looked up something on Google while you were having delusions of grandeur."

"Go on."

"I searched for 'Goldney-jewel-heist,' and you'll never guess what I found online."

"What?" I asked and wondered why I hadn't thought to do the same.

"'One Francis Bennett-Goldney,' it reads, 'died at an American hospital in Brest, France on July 26, 1918, from injuries sustained in a car accident.'"

"That's our man. Does it say anything about stolen jewels?"

"He has a very impressive résumé," Olivia said while skimming the article.

"He was appointed Athlone Pursuivant at the Dublin Castle in February 1907. He was mayor of Canterbury and a member of Parliament, too. In October 1917, he joined the British Embassy in Paris as an honorary military attaché and was promoted to Major General in May 1918."

"Not your typical jewel thief," I said.

"There's more," Olivia continued slowly, "'It should be noted that Francis Bennett-Goldney was discovered to have been something of a thieving magpie. After his death in 1918, among his possessions were found ancient charters and documents belonging to the City of Canterbury, as well as a painting by Romanelli which was the property of the Duke of Bedford.'" She paused to keep reading, then with more enthusiasm, said, "'He has also come under suspicion in relation to the 1907 theft of the Irish Crown Jewels!'"

"The Irish Crown Jewels?" I asked, bewildered. "Did you know the Irish had crown jewels?"

"No, I didn't. But listen to this, 'The Irish crown jewels, also known as the Order of Saint Patrick, were stolen in 1907 and never recovered!'"

"The Order of Saint Patrick!" I shouted. "That nails it. Watson, you're a genius."

"Oh, so I'm Watson? Who do you think you are, Sherlock Holmes?" Olivia mocked.

"Of course. It's elementary. Look at the parallels. I'm a wealthy, depressed genius, looking for anything that will engage my supersized intellect."

"Uh-huh. Supersized ego is more like it."

"Mock all you want. The Irish Crown Jewels are as good as found. The game's afoot!"

SURPRISES

There's no way I'm going to wait until Thanksgiving to see Olivia, I thought to myself when I hung up the phone. Immediately, I formulated a plan. My next move was to walk the half-block to Tenth Avenue and hail a cab for East Twenty-Third Street and the offices of the Starr-Troutman Corporate Security firm. Starr-Troutman made the security arrangements for Philip's family, and I knew they would take my call.

"How can I help you, Mr. Howard?" asked the man who sat before me. He was thickset, not tall, but impressively large. The only hair on his gleaming white head was a salt-and-pepper goatee that secreted most of his mouth from view. Of all the people I had seen that week, he looked the most like a corporate security agent. He even had a Bluetooth earpiece in one ear.

"I would like your help to find someone," I replied. "The mother of an actress on television."

He was clearly taken aback by my request. "You'll need to tell me why you want to find the mother of an actress on TV. This is not a 'no-questions-asked' type of firm."

I smiled and said, "The actress is a friend. We met at Philip Pennfield's housewarming party and traveled to Vermont together for a weekend. She's gone back to work, filming her show in California. I want to make a surprise appearance on set, and I'm hoping her mother will be able to connect me with someone who can get me in the door."

He studied me for an uncomfortable moment or two, then said, "I know your father. Were you aware of that?"

"*My* father?" I asked, astonished.

"We handle his security whenever he comes to New York."

"I didn't know that. For that matter, I didn't know he was in the habit of

42

coming to New York."

He nodded knowingly. "It's my job to know where you are at all times when he is in town. If you don't know he's here, it makes my job that much easier."

Ignoring his last remark, I said, "My friend's name is Olivia Hunt. I don't know if her mother shares the same last name. All I know is, she lives in New Jersey. Can you find her?"

"Of course we can. What do you want, full name, address, and contact info?" he answered.

"Perfect. How long will it take?" I asked.

"Are you going home by taxi?"

"Probably, why?"

"Expect an answer before you make it back to Forty-Sixth Street."

I wasn't going to ask him how he knew my address. I preferred to be blissfully unaware of how much he knew about me. I shook his massive hand and walked outside to find a cab. True to his word, he texted while I was stopped at a traffic light at the corner of Tenth and Thirty-Eighth. 'Diane Hayward, 61 Woodfield Drive, Whippany, New Jersey,' and he included a phone number and email address. A minute later, he texted again, asking if I had made it home yet.

I didn't respond to either of his messages. Instead, I called the phone number he gave me and had a pleasant conversation with Olivia's mother. She told me that Olivia said great things about me. Over the phone, I couldn't tell if she used air quotes on the word, 'great.' She also asked when she would have the pleasure of meeting me, and I replied, "How about this afternoon?"

Within a few hours of hatching my scheme, I was knocking on Olivia's mother's front door in Whippany, New Jersey.

"I've heard so much about you, young man," she said as she relieved me of my backpack and led me to a seat by the window. The sitting room was full of antiques. Based on what I saw, Olivia's mother's antique collecting went well beyond jewelry boxes. "I think my Olivia is quite taken with you. But, oh, please don't tell her I said that. She would be mortified."

"It'll be our secret," I said. "And speaking of secrets, I was wondering if you could help with a little surprise I'm working on for Olivia."

She hesitated for a moment before replying, "Olivia is not big on surprises. Ever since that incident at college, she's become easily flappable."

"I think she'll get a kick out of this. I am going to show up on the set of her television program with a bouquet of flowers or a bottle of wine or something."

"Oh dear, are you sure about this?" asked Mrs. Hayward.

"Absolutely. She'll be taken aback at first, but I'm sure she will appreciate the gesture."

She didn't look nearly as convinced as I had hoped. Then she asked, "How will you get in? Do you know someone at Sony?"

"Not exactly," I said. "In fact, that's one of the reasons I wanted to come and speak with you. I was hoping you would connect me with someone who works for the TV show and who'd be willing to get me inside without letting Olivia know."

"I suppose I might know how to contact someone," she said with apprehension.

It was not the response I was hoping for. I wanted a name and number. The thought of going back to New York emptyhanded to sit around my home waiting for something to happen filled me with despair. However, I knew I had to maintain the image of confidence.

"It would mean the world to me," I said, "I miss her, and I'd love to see her again. In fact, why don't you come along, too? We could surprise her together. Wouldn't that be special?"

"Me?" she laughed. "I hate airplanes. Besides, I couldn't leave everything here and go to California." With this response, she waved her arms to indicate the collectibles all around her.

"This is a very impressive collection, Mrs. Hayward. Or should I call you Diane?"

"Oh, do you like it? Most of Olivia's friends can't appreciate these things."

"They all seem special in their own indescribable way," I replied, looking around the room.

"Such a sweet young man as you can surely call me Diane."

"Well, Diane, I have another item for your collection," I said as I pulled a small package out of my backpack.

Her eyes lit up like a child on Christmas morning and she unwrapped the gift to reveal the small wooden box with broken hinges I had purchased at the antique furniture store in Vermont. "It's exquisite," she beamed.

"It's a jewelry box. This box once held the Crown Jewels of Ireland," I said.

She gasped. "I've read about that. I thought they were stolen and never recovered."

"I'm impressed," I said, "Most people have never heard of the Irish Crown Jewels. And yes, they've been missing since 1907, but this is the box where they were last stored."

"I can't believe it. This is the *actual* box?"

"Yes, and as a matter of fact, I intend to take up the search to find the jewels themselves. If I find the jewels, I'll return them to their rightful owner, but I want you to keep the box."

Mrs. Hayward was bursting with excitement and for a moment, I thought she might lunge and hug me. "I must find the perfect place to display this box," she said, with a hint of panic. "Come with me, and I'll show you the rest of my collection. You can help me pick out the best location."

She gave me a complete tour of the entire house. Every room, with the exception of Olivia's bedroom, was packed with antiques, mostly jewelry boxes of various shapes and sizes. We decided that the best location for displaying the empty Crown Jewels box was the mantel above her fireplace.

"Would you like to see the garage?" she asked when we had gone through every other room.

"Do you have antiques in the garage, too?" I replied.

"Only one," she laughed. "Come and see."

In the garage was a beautiful old car. Mrs. Hayward told me it was a 1962 Chevrolet Biscayne, mariner blue with white interior. I was surprised by how attracted I was to this classic American muscle car. I had driven plenty of fast cars in Europe but never anything that looked like this.

"Does it run?" I asked.

"I suppose it would run—that is, if it had a motor," she said. She went on to explain that Olivia's father obtained it somehow, although she didn't care to speculate how, and had planned to restore it as a high school graduation present for Olivia.

"I just thought of an even better idea of how to surprise Olivia," I said. "How about I get this car fixed up, and we drive it to Los Angeles? Wouldn't that be great?"

"Oh, my goodness, you are a spontaneous young man!" she exclaimed. "Olivia needs a man like you." She looked at me, pursed her lips and tilted her head to one side, then said. "OK, I'll do it."

"You'll come with me to California?" I asked, trying to sound only surprised and not totally shocked.

"Of course not. I can't leave my collection. No, I mean I will call Randi. She is the second assistant something or other, on Olivia's show. Randi can get you onto the set, and she'll probably think it's a fun idea, too. I still have my doubts, but I like you, so…."

"I like you, too, Mrs. Hayward."

"Diane," she corrected me.

"Right. Diane, is it OK for me to get the car fixed up for her? Would you mind if I drive it to L.A.?"

"I insist. I don't know what she'll think of you showing up unannounced, but I know she will be on cloud nine when she sees this car in working order," she replied and touched the back of my hand. "Clay," she continued, "I don't know what to think of you, but this much I know. You are chock full of surprises."

FAST N' LOUD

Within a week, I was on the road, cruising west on the interstate highways that would take me to Sony Picture Entertainment in Culver City, California. The classic cars restoration garage had quoted me a price to get the car back in working order and told me it would take two weeks to complete. I told him I didn't want to wait that long, but I could pay him double what he asked for. "How about three days?" he replied.

There was a long list of items to be repaired or replaced, but the one that interested me most was the 409 V-8 turbocharged motor. When I finally hit the road and hit the gas, I discovered this old Chevrolet was a lot faster and a lot louder than any Mercedes or BMW I had driven on the Autobahn in Germany.

As promised, Mrs. Hayward contacted Randi Dunaway, the Second Assistant Director on Olivia's television show. Randi was tickled with the idea of me popping in on the set unannounced, and she promised to take care of everything. "Just call me when you're at the gate," she said before she hung up to take care of everything for everyone else.

The road trip was delightful. It was just what the doctor would have ordered, had I had the courage to see a doctor for the depression that was sapping my strength. I was exhilarated by the feeling of power darting through traffic at will. I felt like an adult pretending to run a race with a group of children. I was toying with the other cars, letting them keep up with me, but fully aware I could leave them in the dust whenever I felt like it. The car had no air conditioning, nor radio, nor sideview mirrors, for that matter. It was built for speed alone. There was a speedometer, but I didn't need it. The wind in my face and the throaty sound of the motor were all I needed to gauge my speed. I was one with the road.

The thrill of driving a classic muscle car across the country was invigorating. However, that which moved me the most—that which gave me the deepest satisfaction—was my mission. For so long, I wandered through life aimlessly. Finally, I had an objective and I had plans, and I treasured the sense of purpose they gave me.

My first day on the road, I left New York early in the morning and drove over nine hundred miles before coming to rest in St Louis, Missouri. When I climbed into bed in my motel room, my feet, my legs, and my backside were still numb from the vibration of that four hundred nine cubic inch monster hurling me across the eastern half of the country. Waking several hours later, I guzzled some dreadful coffee from the motel breakfast bar and forced down two of the driest hardboiled eggs known to man before getting back on the road for another day, and another thousand miles of driving, until I reached Albuquerque, New Mexico.

When I woke up, I was painfully hungry, and having learned my lesson about motel food, I began day three at a restaurant near the University of New Mexico that claimed to be the inventor of the breakfast burrito. Whether they invented it or only perfected it, I couldn't have said for sure, but the three scrambled eggs folded inside a flour tortilla with chicken, cheeses, and chilis, stuffed me to the gills.

My GPS told me I was only seven hundred seventy miles from the studio, so I when I pulled out of the parking lot, I fully expected to arrive at my destination by dinner. However, I didn't take into consideration the change in temperature when coming down off the plateau on which Albuquerque sits. By the time I drove the non-air-conditioned Biscayne to Needles, California, the outdoor temperature was over a hundred degrees, and inside the car it felt like two hundred.

In Needles, home to Snoopy's brother, Spike, I stopped for gas and an air-conditioned motel for the afternoon and waited for the desert to cool off before driving further. I took an ice-cold shower, then sat in front of the air conditioner.

I decided to make the most of the afternoon by continuing my translation of Louisa's book. I was in the third section, the one in which she described falling in love with Michael, whose last name I learned was Mulholland, and joining him on his journey to Vermont.

Upon disembarkation in Quebec City, Louisa learned that Michael was heading to Burlington to join a small community of Irish immigrants who had settled there. She was smitten by his kindness and compassion. They traveled together by ferry down the Richelieu River to the Canadian town of Lacolle, then walked across the border into Rouses Point, New York. They had prepared an elaborate scheme to get Louisa past the American immigration officials by pretending they were married, but to their surprise, no one challenged them as they entered the United States. After taking a train to Plattsburgh, New York, they were able to hitch a ride on a freighter sailing across Lake Champlain to Burlington. With a few months of landing in Burlington, they decided to make it official, and with the help of an itinerant French-speaking priest from Quebec, they were pronounced man and wife at Saint Mary's Cathedral on Cherry Street. Louisa Peeters became Louisa Peeters Mulholland, LPM. Nine months later, with clockwork precision, Louisa gave birth to twins, Edward and Deirdra.

It was clear from the pages of her book that Louisa loved Michael deeply. She doted on him, she cooked for him, and she looked after their modest home on Grafton Street. When the babies were born, she went right back to work making sure Michael's every wish was fulfilled. Michael was equally enamored at first. However, after the babies were born, his feelings towards her changed. He was no longer the kind gentleman who would give her his overcoat on a cold day. Instead, he became a demanding overlord who could never be satisfied with her efforts or her appearance, no matter how hard she tried.

Things were tough for Louisa in those early years, but when Michael lost his job at the lumber yard, they became even tougher. He became moody and started drinking heavily. Louisa was able to find work teaching French to the children of some wealthy families who had moved down from Canada, but most of what she earned went toward quenching Michael's increasing thirst for whiskey. Before long, when Prohibition became the law of the land in the early twenties, Michael was forced to take his drinking underground. He would disappear for hours, even days, in the speakeasies of Burlington and Poughkeepsie. Then one day, he reappeared with an odd request.

Michael had been away drinking somewhere in New York, she recounted. *He said he met a man who wanted to hire us. 'Us?' I asked. 'Yes,' Michael said, 'he wants both of us to do something for him, and he'll pay us more in one week than I made in the lumber yard in three months.' The man wanted us to ride a horse-drawn carriage from Poughkeepsie across the border to Canada, and then ride back again to the place where we started. He wanted me and the children to make the trip, so if anyone questioned us, I could say in French that I was going to visit relatives in Lacolle. Michael wouldn't tell me why he would pay us so much money for such a simple task, but I knew it had something to do with Canadian whiskey.*

Louisa went on to write that she insisted she and their children should have nothing to do with smuggling alcohol into the United States, but Michael insisted even harder. He threatened to sell their daughter to a wealthy couple in New York if she and the children would not go along. Feeling helpless, Louisa agreed to make the trip one time, but one time only.

"Good luck with that, Louisa." I said aloud as I closed the book and crawled under the covers to take a nap until it was cool enough for me to drive the final two hundred seventy miles to my destination.

It was well after midnight before I arrived at the valet parking ramp of the Biltmore Hotel in downtown Los Angeles. The valet was perturbed when I woke him up to park my car, but he brightened when he saw what I was driving. I let him see me take a picture of the odometer, just in case he had any ideas of cruising the streets of L.A. while I slept.

Upstairs in my room, however, I didn't get much sleep. I wasn't worried about the car, but I was anxious for my surprise visit to see Olivia. Furthermore, I was completely baffled by my feelings for her. Only a few months ago, I had promised myself I would never get involved with another person who could hurt me, and even though I hadn't known Olivia very long, I had fallen harder for her than I had fallen for any woman before. I was doing the exact opposite of what I wanted to do, and yet I sorely wanted to do it.

In the morning, I showered, shaved, and put on some fresh clothes that weren't covered in dust and didn't smell like the desert. While I enjoyed the Biltmore's breakfast, which was luxurious but not nearly as filling as my Albuquerque burrito, I instructed the concierge to have someone bring the Biscayne to be washed and waxed. And so it was that at ten in the morning of the fourth day, after driving nearly three thousand miles, I came within a few hundred yards of reaching Olivia. I stopped at the gate of Sony Picture Entertainment and instructed the guard to call Randi Dunaway.

SURPRISED

"You're here?" said Randi into the phone handed me by the studio gate guard. "I didn't think you would really do it." The gate was an ornate yet imposing wrought iron affair framed with carved stone posts and an arched lintel. Thick groves of tropical trees hung over the gate on both sides.

"I did it, and I'm here." I said, "Call me crazy, but I just drove three thousand miles to see Olivia. Please tell me she's here."

"She sure is, but I wouldn't call you crazy. I'd say you're romantic."

"There's not much distinction between those descriptors," I said. "I thought it would be amusing to surprise her."

"I told no one about this, so unless her mother spilled the beans, she has no idea you're coming," said Randi.

With Randi's blessing, the guard clipped a large, unsightly visitor's pass to the collar of my sport coat and instructed me to never remove the badge under any circumstances. He gave me directions to the place where Olivia's show was being filmed, and when he swung open the gate, I fired up the motor and immediately hid the visitor's pass in my jacket pocket.

I parked the car in an empty space that indicated it was for cast members only, and I walked to the sound stage door where Randi was waiting for me with a broad smile and holding a clipboard. She was short and plump with red hair. A pair of reading glasses hung around her neck.

"Nice car," she said after I shook her hand and thanked her again for her help.

"It's for Olivia," I said. "Another surprise."

She took me through a narrow corridor full of black and chrome equipment cases, lighting stands, and furniture. In several places, we had to step over large bundles of wire. When we emerged from the passage, we were standing behind a row of people with headsets, staring into one of the three large television cameras pointing at the set, which was a tastefully furnished office I recognized as belonging to the university president. Three actors were on the set, going over last-minute instructions from people Randi pointed out as the showrunner and the director. Standing between the actor who played the university president and another character who I didn't recognize was Olivia. When I saw her, my heart leaped.

"I'm so glad I came," I whispered to Randi.

"This will be fun to watch," she said in a low voice, then said, "Gotta go," and walked away.

They shot the scene over and over, repeating the same four lines about ten times. Each time they shot it, the director engaged in a lengthy discussion with the showrunner, then gave the actors new instructions on how to say their lines. After it felt like no humans could say those few words with any other inflection or intensity, the director finally told everyone to take a break. An inaudible sigh of relief was felt throughout the room.

I walked towards Olivia, and she stepped down off the set just as I was emerging from the shadows. She took a step forward before looking at me, then she lurched backwards.

"You're here!" she exclaimed. Heads turned in our direction.

"In the flesh," I said, holding my arms open wide.

"How did you get in?" was her reply. More heads turned in our direction.

"Randi let me in."

"How do you know Randi?"

"Your mother gave me her number."

"My mother?" she shouted. "You spoke to my mother?"

"I called her, and I visited your house. I saw her impressive collection of jewelry boxes, and other antiques. There are antiques in every room of the house, except your bedroom." I said, enjoying the moment.

"My bedroom?!" she yelled, even louder this time. "Who gave you my mother's phone number?"

I hesitated before answering. For some reason, I hadn't prepared myself to answer that question. "Uh, I hired an investigation firm," I stammered.

"What are you, some kind of stalker?" she shouted at me. "When I was ready for you to meet my mother, I would have invited you home myself."

"Hey, Olivia, I just wanted to surprise you, that's all. You said you were looking forward to seeing me again, and I was going crazy all alone in New York. You're too busy to come to me, but I've got nothing else to do, so I figured I'd just come on out here. I couldn't think of another way to get in the door, so I reached out to your mother. The tour of your home was your mother's idea. I didn't ask to see your bedroom, or anything creepy like that."

"No, not creepy. You just hired a detective to locate my home, then talked my mother and my coworker into sneaking you onto the set behind my back. Nothing creepy at all," she said, and then she turned around and ran off behind the set and out of sight.

Randi returned with the showrunner and introduced us. "This is the guy from New York she's been talking about."

"Monica Simon," the other woman said, reaching out to shake my hand, "and that's David Hanson, director for the season finale." She tilted her head to indicate the person behind her who was talking to a camera operator.

"I'm Clayton Howard. Thanks for letting me crash your party."

"'Crash' is aptly put," said Monica. "Not the reaction you were hoping for, huh?"

"I'm positively flummoxed," I said. "For the past four days on the road, I've been playing and replaying in my head how I expected this scene would pan out. Not once did I consider anything close to what happened this morning."

"You drove here from New York?" the director asked, turning towards me for the first time.

"Another part of the surprise," I said. "When Olivia was in high school, her father started restoring a classic car for her to drive. A '62 Chevy Biscayne. It was still in her garage, unfinished, so I brought it to a shop, and they did it up. They put in a 409 V-8 and replaced the front end, brakes, and shocks. It drives like a rocket. It was a blast to drive it out here."

"It's outside," Randi said, "in Rod's parking spot."

"Who's Rod?" I asked.

"Don't worry about it. The car is fine where it is," said Monica.

Other cast members, some I recognized from watching the show, and others I did not, came over to introduce themselves. I told them I had watched all the episodes currently available online, and although I wasn't usually a fan of television, I thought their performances were of the highest quality. They all thanked me and said they had heard a lot about me. *All good, until today,* I imagined they were saying to themselves to complete the thought. The guys all wanted to know what it was like to drive the Biscayne across the entire country.

Monica was looking at me strangely while I was talking with the others. After the conversations died down, she approached me and said, "We need to get back to work, Clayton, but I'm wondering if you would be interested in helping us out."

"What kind of help do you need?" I asked.

"The next scene takes place at a table in the faculty dining hall. We need some extras to sit at the other tables who look like they could be university professors eating lunch. Our agency sent a bunch of kids who look more like students than faculty. You, on the other hand, look like you just stepped out of a lecture hall in NYU."

"Harvard, please," I said.

"It doesn't pay much," she said, "but it'll be a fun thing to tell your friends at cocktail parties."

"I'll do it," I replied, "on the condition you don't pay me. I can't get rid of the money I already have. The last thing I want is more of the stuff."

"Deal," she said.

"But don't you think I should try to go and talk to Olivia. It would seem that I need to apologize for totally misreading our relationship."

"You should not try to talk to her right now," said Randi. "I've known Olivia for a long time. She will come around, but she needs a little time to be alone."

"Besides," Monica said, "Olivia's character is in the scene we're about to shoot. She won't have time to talk to you now, anyway."

They sent me to wardrobe, but the guy who lived in that closet told me my own attire was the perfect costume. Next came makeup, and the people in that department had the opposite response. They wanted to style my hair, add a thick layer of base, and paint around my eyes. When the makeup folks finished re-creating my face, they sat me at a table near the main characters' table. I was told to read the book that was placed before me and pretend to drink the coffee from time to time. "Don't drink it, though," they warned. "You're going to be sitting there a long time, and we don't stop so extras can take potty breaks."

The book was a collection of Sherlock Holmes mysteries, and I was only too eager to dive into it. I sat there a long time while other extras were brought in to replace the puerile actors they had already sent back to the agency. I recognized Randi seated at another table with someone else from the crew I had spotted earlier. After a long time of preparation, Olivia came onto the set. When she saw me, she smiled for just a second, then she turned away and asked someone for a tissue to dab her eyes.

The conversation between Olivia's character and a reporter who was threatening to bring down the university with some juicy piece of information was shot and re-shot from even more angles and with more variations than the one I had watched earlier. I was thankful I didn't drink the coffee, and I was thankful the book I had been given was over nine hundred pages. Another sigh of relief went out, this one audible, when the director said 'cut!' for the last time.

I was about to get up to stretch my legs, but Olivia spun around and sat down at the empty chair across from me.

"Clayton Howard, acting as an *extra* on a *television* program. Tsk, tsk. How ever did you fall so far from Harvard?"

"I'm sorry for surprising you, Olivia," I said. "I realize now that I was being selfish. I just wanted to see you, and I didn't take into consideration how it would make you feel. Your mother tried to warn me. She didn't think it was a good idea, but I wouldn't listen."

"You know how hard it is for me to be a public personality, Clay," she began. "And you know what I went through in university. When you said you tracked down my mother's house and went there, it scared me. I thought, 'If he could do it, any kidnapper could do it.' That's why I ran."

"I'm so sorry. It was wrong of me to come without asking you. I'll leave if you want me to."

She reached across the table and touched my hand. "I don't want you to leave, but there is something I need to tell you."

"What?" I asked.

Looking around, she noticed there were still several people milling around the set. "Not here," she said. "Let's remove our makeup and take a walk outside."

It felt great to get all the goop off my face, although when the process was complete, my skin felt like it had been treated with sandpaper. I waited for Olivia near the door where she told me to wait. I was eager, yet filled with a little trepidation to reveal the one remaining surprise I hadn't sprung on her yet. The car.

"Before we go outside," I said when she finally appeared. "There is one more surprise I need to tell you about."

She looked at me askance. "Did you bring my mother, too?"

"No, although I did invite her to come along. She said she couldn't leave her collection."

"Yes, that's exactly what she would say. So, what's the other surprise?"

"Your mother showed me all around the home, including the garage."

Her brow furrowed. "The garage?"

"She showed me the car your father started working on for you."

"The car?"

I opened the door that led to the parking lot and said, "Let me show you the surprise."

She bound out through the door into the parking lot and looked from side to side. When her eyes settled on the blue 1962 Chevrolet, her jaw dropped. "That's my father's car?"

"No," I said. "It's your car. Your mother told me he was restoring it for you. In fact, the title and registration are in your name."

"But it doesn't run. It never has. How did you get it here?" she asked, walking over to the car and running her hand along the fender lines.

"It runs now," I said with a smile, opening the hood to reveal the four hundred nine cubic inch motor. "If it had wings, it would fly."

"Did you drive it here?" she asked.

"All the way from New York," I said. "It's a great car. Very fast. Although, if I were you, I would consider having an air conditioner installed."

"This is my car?" she asked again, amazed. "I don't know what to say."

"Say you'll forgive me for visiting your mother before you were ready, and for scaring you with the private investigator thing."

She turned to me and kissed my cheek. She started to tell me how much the car meant to her, how her father had promised to do it up for her but left before making good on his promise. She loved the car, but sitting in the garage, unfinished, it only reminded her of her father's departure from her life.

"But you brought it to me," she said, putting her hand on my shoulder. "You finished the work my father started."

"Would a man who does that win your heart, just like a man who would give you his coat on a cold day?" I asked.

"Yes," she said, smiling, crying, and nodding her head. "Even more so."

"Do you want to take it for a spin?" I asked.

"Can I?" she beamed.

"Of course you can. It's your car," I said as I handed her the keys.

Olivia grabbed the keys out of my hand and jumped into the driver's seat. I got in on the other side and for the first time realized only the driver's side had a seat belt. She looked around the interior of the car and ran her hands along the dashboard. She fingered the number twelve pool ball her father had installed on top of the spaghetti shifter on the floor and frowned.

"I graduated high school in 2012. He promised the car would be finished by then."

"Start it up," I said.

She fired up the motor and hit the gas several times. The deafening roar of the motor reverberated through the narrow passageway between the buildings. The anti-theft alarm of a nearby car rang out the way a small dog would join the barking of the alpha dog.

She turned off the motor and smiled. Her eyes were wide, and her head was nodding slightly. "You did good, Clay. You did good," she said, still looking forward. Then, she turned to me and said, "All is forgiven." Her eyes lowered toward my lips, and she started to lean toward me slowly.

"Someone is coming," I said, pointing behind her. A man was approaching the car, looking important and irate.

She turned and gasped, then said, "Remember I told you I needed to talk to you about something?"

As he drew near us, the man was shouting something to the effect that we were parked in his space, but when he saw Olivia, he stopped in his tracks and said, "It's you! Whose car is this?" he asked but didn't wait for an answer. "No matter," he said and popped his head through the open window and kissed Olivia on the mouth. While kissing her, his eyes landed on me. "Who's that?" he asked, but again didn't wait for a response. "No matter," he said. "I'll wait for you in your dressing room. Don't be long. We have reservations for dinner tonight."

"Rod, wait," Olivia started to say, but the man stopped and wheeled around.

"I got it," he said, pointing at me through the windshield. "You must be the fellow from New York she's been talking about. Frankly, I've been starting to get a little jealous of the way she speaks about you." Moving closer to the window, he asked Olivia, "Should I be worried about this one, too?" Then, he walked to the door of the sound stage and left us alone in the front seat of the car.

"Looks like the surprise is on me," I said. I was too numb to think of a sharper response.

"Clay, it's not what you think," she said.

"I'm sure there's a perfectly reasonable explanation, but the man who just kissed you is waiting in your room for you to change your clothes because you have a date for dinner and who knows what else. We mustn't keep him waiting any longer."

"I can explain. There's something you don't know."

"Nor would I want him to be worried about me, the way he was worried about all the others."

"He had no right to say that. He's playing mind games. He's an actor; that's what he does."

"So, actors are skilled at playing mind games? Bravo!" I said. "You're very good at your craft." Then I opened my door and stepped out of the car.

"Clay, please listen to me," she pleaded.

I closed the door and said, "Enjoy your car." Then I walked through the front gate without looking back.

THREAT LEVEL

The events that followed were a blur. I was too dazed to think, too numb to speak, and far too dejected for my brain to make a record of any memories. I don't recall how or when I made it home. The next thing I remember I was sitting on the third-floor bedroom porch at my home in mid-town Manhattan, watching Broadway crowds on their way to catch a show. Under any other circumstances, I would have been down there with them, but my melancholy was so dark that even the prospect of a night at the theater brought no delight.

Philip and Stephanie were kind enough to stop by and check on me the next day. I could tell they were concerned that I might do something crazy and harm myself, but I assured them that was the furthest thing from my mind. I intimated my life was so utterly pointless that there would be no point even in ending it, but it did little to assuage their fears.

"You need a hobby or something," Stephanie said. "Or a cause. Isn't there something you can get involved in?"

"Sure," Philip jumped in. "Why don't we go to my parents' place and talk to Mum. She used to feel the same as you. Then she started doing all kinds of charity work. Now she can't get enough of it."

"Money is not the answer, Philip," I replied. "Whether you buy stuff with it or give it away, it's just meaningless mammon. It's a curse if anything. I mean no disrespect to your mother, but to give my money away would be subjecting others to the same torture that's afflicted me."

"What about that book you found at the antique shop in Vermont?" he replied. "You were so absorbed in that book when you found it. I haven't seen you that excited in years. Perhaps you should take that up again."

"I left it in the car."

"The car you drove out to Los Angeles?" Stephanie asked.

"My briefcase was in the backseat when I walked out of her life. It's gone. Besides, that whole venture would remind me too much of her."

"Time heals all wounds," Stephanie said, probably because she could think of nothing else. In truth, although I didn't admit it out loud, their concern helped lift my spirits a little.

A day or so after their visit, I received a call from the investigator who helped me locate Olivia's mother.

"This is Nigel Smith from Starr-Troutman," he began. "We need to talk."

"Do you expect me to believe Smith is your real name?" I asked.

"Would I choose an alias that sounds like an alias?"

"Fair point. What do we need to talk about? Did I forget to pay you?"

"When did you last see your brother?" he replied, ignoring me.

"Grayson?" I asked.

"I know you only have one brother, so, yes."

"I haven't seen him since the pandemic."

"Do you know where he is?"

"I have no idea. I thought that was your department. Aren't you the one who knows my whereabouts at all times?"

"Only when your father is in town," he said, causing my heart to skip a beat.

"Are you saying he's coming to New York?"

"Of course I wouldn't say that. I'm only saying I need to know where you and your brother will be tomorrow and the next day."

"I'll be right here on my porch."

"You've been spending a lot of time on your porch lately," he said. "I take it things didn't go so well with your television star?"

"I learned she was someone else's star, not mine."

"Tough break. Any idea where I can find your brother?"

"I haven't spoken to him in years, Nigel, your guess is as good as mine— better, I suspect. You have more recent intel."

"If he contacts you, I'm your first call. Deal?"

"What do you mean, 'deal?'" I replied. "A deal works both ways. What do I get out of this deal?"

"I know something you need to know, but I can't tell you."

"However, you're pretty good at giving hints," I said.

"I'd like you and your brother to stay away from the family courthouse on Lafayette Street for the next couple of days."

"Family court? Is he getting divorced?" I asked.

"If you read the news, you might be able to answer your own question. Now promise to notify me if you hear from your brother."

"Like father, like son; we know how to pick them," I replied. "Anyway, why are you telling me these things?"

"I didn't tell you anything. I can't help it if you learn things from reading the paper. I've known your father for several years now. He's made some poor choices, to be sure, but he's paid some terrible prices, too. There are times in a man's life when he needs his son by his side, even if he doesn't realize it."

"But hasn't he hired you to keep me away from his side?"

"Your threat-level is pretty low. Grayson, on the other hand, is a different story," Nigel said.

"If I hear from him, I'll let you know. And you're right. My threat-level is nil. Furthermore, I don't expect you'll see me anywhere near Lafayette Street," I said. "I haven't gone outside since getting back from L.A."

"I've noticed. I get paid for watching TV in my car outside your home. Also, I think you've been singlehandedly keeping the food delivery guys in business lately."

"Looks like I'm good for something," I said after I hung up.

Before putting the phone down, I searched online for any news about my father at family court. It didn't take long to find an article in the New York Post socialite section that described in juicy detail the contested divorce settlement between a far-too wealthy banker and his far-too-youthful ex-wife. They had already been divorced four years at that point, but the young woman claimed that the New York branch of the defendant's bank unlawfully froze the bulk of her remaining assets from the settlement. The defendant claimed she squandered the money on her lavish lifestyle and made a series of poor investments. She was suing for additional compensation on somewhat questionable grounds and even threatening to pursue criminal charges against the banker.

The sun was low in the sky, but it lined up at just the proper angle to shine down the length of Forty-Sixth Street from the direction of the Hudson River. Rush hour traffic was beginning to choke the intersection at Forty-Sixth and Tenth Avenue. I watched the brake lights of a traditional Yellow Checker Cab flash on and off as it approached the busy junction and reflected on Nigel's comments, wondering what role, if any, I should take in my father's affairs. He chose that woman over Grayson and me. He cut us out of his life in order to graft her in. Nigel said my father was paying a high price for his poor choices. So was I. So was Grayson, no doubt. It didn't seem fair of Nigel to imply that I should get involved in the life of a man who had so thoroughly and completely ruined mine.

The more I thought about him, the angrier I got, and I speculated on what sort of rage Grayson might have expressed to cause Nigel such deep concern. On a whim, I decided to call Grayson's cell phone number, but was met with an angry response from a guy who was sick of receiving wrong number calls from people looking for Grayson. So, I sent him a quick email asking for his new phone number, but my email prompted an automatic reply stating his mailbox did not exist.

My contemplation was interrupted by two sounds that occurred at exactly the same time. One came from my growling stomach, and the other came from downstairs. The doorbell was ringing, and I remembered that I had ordered dinner just before Nigel called me. *My appetite seems to be returning*, I thought as I walked down the steps. *Strange*, I thought, *these delivery guys usually call my phone rather than ringing the bell.*

When I opened the door, thoughts of dinner vanished. Standing before me was Olivia, as beautiful and radiant as ever, with a roller bag at her feet and my leather briefcase over her shoulder.

RELATIONSHIP COUNSELING

"Hello, Clay," she said as I stared at her in stunned silence. "May I come in?"

My heart was racing, and I could feel beads of sweat coalescing on my forehead. Everything inside me shouted, *No!* Everything inside me told me to shut the door and go back upstairs to my bedroom and hide.

"How did you find my home?" I asked without moving from the doorway.

"I called Stephanie from the plane. She told me where to find you."

"I don't know what to say, Olivia. I'm trying to get over you, so letting you into my home doesn't seem like such a good idea."

"You didn't let me explain, Clay. I don't want you to get over me because I'm not over you."

"Why didn't you tell me about the other guy, Olivia? We talked so many times about so many things, and you never once told me there was another guy."

Still outside on my doorstep, she pleaded, "You've got to believe me, Clay. Rod and I were never really together. We dated a few times, and I was planning to break up with him the night you showed up in California."

"You want me to believe it was a coincidence?" I asked. "The guy has no-knock privileges to your dressing room. It sounds like you two have a pretty intimate relationship."

"Rod has no more ability to get into my dressing room than I have of getting into your house. He said those things and acted the way he did because he was jealous of you."

"Was he more jealous of me or the other guys?" I asked without moving.

She closed her eyes and tilted her head back in consternation. "Clay, I'm telling you, he made that up. Think about it. When would I have had time to date him and a bunch of other guys? You're smarter than that. Now are you going to invite me inside or not?"

"I'm still trying to decide how high is your threat-level," I said, unmoving.

"Clay, I don't know where this relationship is going to go. I can't promise that we will be together forever, or that we won't ever hurt each other. But I can promise that I have never lied to you, and I will never lie to you. We have something special. I've never felt this way about another guy, and I think you feel the same way about me."

In truth, I wanted to invite her inside my home. I craved to take her in my arms and never let her go, but I was paralyzed. My arms and my voice were under the control of another force, and it was a force I could neither identify nor subdue.

Olivia saw my struggle and continued, "I want you to know something. I left the show before we were finished shooting. I knew that if I stayed in L.A. another day longer, I would regret it for the rest of my life."

"You quit?" I asked, incredulous.

"I didn't quit, but I didn't finish the season, either."

"They won't fire you, will they?"

"I don't know what they'll do," she said.

"I don't know what to say, Olivia."

"Tell me how you feel, Clay. Tell me if you feel the same way about me. If you tell me you don't feel the same, I'll leave you alone and never come back."

I closed my eyes and began to tremble. I was terrified. No one had ever risked so much for me before, and I had no idea how to handle it. I tried to picture what it would look like if I let her inside my life, but all I could see was my childhood home in Zurich, and my mother's empty chair. I opened my eyes, looked into her beautiful face, and said, "I'm sorry. I'm truly sorry Olivia. I need more time."

She took the briefcase from her shoulder, handed it to me through the open doorway, and said, "I will be at my mother's. You'll know where to find me when you're ready." Then she smiled a wistful smile, turned, and walked away.

I watched her pull her suitcase down Forty-Sixth Street toward Tenth Avenue and hail a cab. My eyes were blurry with tears, but I developed a sense that someone was watching me. I wondered if Nigel recognized Olivia on my doorstep. I half-expected a text message from him with some kind of snide remark.

No text message came, but I saw the face of a man watching me, and it was not the face of the investigator from Starr-Troutman. A man was sitting on the steps of another brownstone home on the opposite side of the street, leaning back on both elbows with his legs crossed. He was strangely dressed and yet had a familiar air. He was wearing a tailor-fitted suit, smeared with stains, and ripped at both knees. His hair was tussled, and his beard was patchy and ungroomed. His face was familiar, and there was something about his posture that I recognized. I realized he was sitting in such a way that reminded me of myself, and then it hit me.

"Grayson!" I shouted across the way.

The man smiled and waved but said nothing. I started out my door to go to him when I suddenly became aware of a large man running down the street toward Grayson. It was Nigel. "Grayson, we need to talk," I shouted. When he saw Nigel coming, he started to laugh, then sprinted away surprisingly quickly. He easily outran Nigel, who had been sitting in his car for too long and eaten too many hot dogs for a footrace.

"This is not good," Nigel panted as he passed me walking back to his car.

"What's happened to him?" I asked. "Is he homeless?"

Nigel stopped and looked at me with his eyes squinted. I could tell he was trying to decide how to answer my question. "He's not without homes; his net worth is even more than yours. However, he's not as well-adjusted as you are."

"Well-adjusted? Are you saying I'm the sane one?" I replied. "That's a frightening thought."

"He disappeared from his home a week ago and hasn't taken any medication since then, as far as we can tell."

"Do you think he's here to see my father or to see me?" I asked.

Nigel had recovered his breath and let out a long sigh. "Maybe both. But the timing tells me it has something to do with your father's court case. Look, my instructions are to keep you away from that courthouse, but I know it would go better for everyone if you were there. Your father needs the support more than he'll admit, and if Grayson shows up, you can keep him out of trouble."

"What makes you think I want to support my father? And what makes you think I can keep Grayson out of trouble?" I shot back. "Answer the first question first."

"Simple," he said. "You've been victimized, but you aren't satisfied with being a victim. You're the kind of person who wants to let go of bitterness and move forward."

"So now you're a psychologist?"

"There's a lot of psychology in my line of work," Nigel replied. "A guy who hires me to find someone's mom so he can pay her a surprise visit on the other side of the country is not the kind of guy who can abide bitterness."

"That's what you think. She came by a short time ago while you were watching the ball game or snoozing. She tried to apologize, but I sent her packing. I think I'm pretty good at being a bitter victim."

He laughed. "You sent her away, all right, but you wiped your eyes as you watched her walk all the way to Tenth Avenue to get a cab. And since she left, you've been wondering the whole time how long you should wait before you chase after her. No, you can't live with bitterness, and that's why I think you are the sensible one."

"It's one thing with Olivia, but with my father, it's orders of magnitude more complex."

"Granted," he said, nodding his head in agreement. "Grayson once told me that all his problems began with your father. The same for you?"

It didn't take long to think of a reply. "That's a fair characterization."

"So it stands to reason that if you can straighten things out with your old man, it will help you get along with other people too, including your fine-looking television star."

"It's not so simple as that," I replied.

"It's not simple at all, which is all the more reason to get started as soon as possible. Tomorrow at ten a.m., to be specific." He took a few steps toward his car then turned to me one more time and said, "Of course, you didn't hear that from me."

As I watched him drive away, I expected Grayson to reappear from around the corner, but my thoughts quickly turned to Olivia. Nigel was right; I couldn't stop thinking about her.

I turned to go back into my house and almost collided with a man who had come up behind me. "Grayson!" I exclaimed, but it wasn't him.

"Sorry. I'm Derick," the delivery man replied, holding up a bag, "Yuzu Salmon again? Second time this week, or is it the third?"

COURTROOM DRAMA

"Are you serious?" Olivia said on the phone when she heard my request. "You want me to meet you at Family Court? We're not even married, are we getting divorced? The tabloids will be falling all over themselves to get a photo of me and you in that place."

"You'd better wear the heavy-duty sunglasses, and if you have any face masks that have been laying around since the pandemic, you can wear one of those, too," I replied.

"You haven't told me why you want me to meet you there."

"Moral support," I said. "I've decided I need to face my father, but I can't do it alone."

"Your father? He's in New York? I thought he wants you to stay away from him. Why would he come here?" she replied.

"I found out that he and his embarrassingly young wife have been divorced for a few years now. It seems she might have been more in love with his money than with him."

"I'm shocked," Olivia said.

"Exactly. And now she's suing him in New York City family court, claiming he reneged on their divorce settlement. Something about an apartment here in the city."

"Did he?"

"That's no concern of mine. It's a civil case and open to the public, but I'm not going so I can listen to her argument."

"So, why are you going? Do you plan to confront him?"

"Yes, I need to." I paused for a moment, then asked, "Will you come?"

"Are you sure this is a good idea? I don't understand why it's so important to face your father all of a sudden?"

"I met a girl like no other, and I don't want to screw it up this time."

"And confronting your father is going to help you win this girl's heart?"

"Oh, I've already won her heart. However, my investigator told me I'm mad at the world because I'm mad at my father."

"Your investigator? Do you mean your therapist?"

"No, I mean the investigator my father hired to keep me and my brother out of his life. He dabbles in psychological advice. He's not bad. He told me if I don't deal with the feelings I have for my father, I'll never have normal feelings for anyone else, including you."

"He knows about me?" she asked.

"He's the one who helped me find your mother."

"And I thought my family was weird."

Once again, I asked, "So, you'll come?"

"Tell me where to find you," she said. "I'll be there."

We arranged to meet at Foley Square, a triangular plaza with a small crop of trees about a block away from the courthouse. She came right on schedule and fully prepared to remain anonymous. Her hair was tied into a neat ponytail that flowed through a hole sewn in the back of her Yankees baseball cap, and her eyes were hidden by a new pair of dark sunglasses, more stylish than the ones she had worn previously, but equally effective. The bottom half of her face was covered by a black mask bearing a Yankees logo on one side. She was completely hidden behind her disguise, and yet it was evident to all that she was beautiful.

"Aren't you that famous actress on TV?" I asked as she approached me.

"I was on TV," she said. "As we speak, the writers are furiously writing me out of the remaining scenes in the season finale."

"They can do that?"

"There is always some surprise at the end of each season. They don't even tell the cast until the last minute. They hold on to the last few pages of the script until we're ready to shoot."

"When will that be?"

"Next week, probably. By now, they would have figured out a way to make my character disappear."

"A car accident?"

"No, it'll be something more imaginative."

"Will she be kidnapped by crazed fraternity pledges?"

Olivia fell silent for a moment, then mumbled, "God, I hope not."

"I'm sorry, that was insensitive of me. Old habits die hard. Let me just say how much I appreciate what you've risked for me. I know that what I'm doing today is a small thing compared to what you did for me, but your courage inspired me."

Olivia hugged me and said, "It wasn't only for you. I'm not sure the life of a celebrity is for me. I thought I would get used to the attention and that it would be easier. But, I think it's getting worse."

Her embrace was electrifying, and my knees became weak. "We'd better talk about something else," I said, taking her by the hand and moving toward Lafayette Street. "I'm trying to steel myself for an intense encounter with my father, but you're turning me into jelly."

"Let's talk about Louisa Peeters," Olivia said. "I read your notes on the translation of her book during the flight from L.A. It's such a fascinating story."

"I haven't thought of her since I left you at the studio. I couldn't bring myself to think about her because she reminded me too much of you."

She stopped and turned to me, "I've been thinking. Let's look for the jewels together, Clay. Now that we are both unemployed, we've got plenty of time on our hands."

"Holmes and Watson are back on the case?"

"What do you say, Watson?" she replied,

"I love it," I said. "However, if you are going to be Sherlock, I think you should keep your magnifying glass on the shelf. We need more modern techniques."

"Such as?"

"I've been reading a plethora of articles lately about social media."

"Social media," she said tersely. "I should think you'd be the last person to suggest social media. Social media has done more to dumb down culture than television."

"Sadly, this is true," I began. "However, desperate times call for desperate measures."

She laughed. "So, now we're desperate?"

"We are searching for jewels that have been missing for over a hundred years, and all we have is the name of a woman in hiding and her daughter, last seen in a small town in Vermont around 1920."

"Wait a minute," Olivia mocked. "Aren't you the one who said that we have clues no one else has ever had, and that we could find the jewels with just a little detective work?"

"I was trying to persuade you to join my quest, and I might have overstated my case."

"You think?"

"The little I know about this social media fad is that it's a great way to get a message to a large segment of the population. Isn't that right?"

"You crack me up," Olivia said. "Do you really think it's a fad?"

"OK, maybe it's not just a fad. Craze, shall we say? Anyway, something tells you have more fans than you know what to do with. Probably more than the readership of The New Yorker magazine."

She laughed. "I'm over two million followers now."

"Well then let's ask all two million of your followers if they have heard of either Louisa Peeters or Deirdre Mulholland."

"And what should I say is the reason for my interest in those two women? People are going to ask."

"Tell your inquisitive followers that those two women can help lead you and your boyfriend to the lost Crown Jewels of Ireland."

Under her baseball cap, I could see one raised eyebrow. "Boyfriend?" she asked.

"Shall we say 'Friend'? … 'Acquaintance'?… 'Stranger you met at a party'?"

"I'm not sure it would be wise to mention the jewels at this point. We might garner unwanted attention."

"We can handle it," I said dismissively, as we passed through the double doors of the courthouse and waited in line at the metal detectors. "Remember, we're desperate."

The guards took our keys and phones like automatons programmed to appear as bored as mechanically possible. But when Olivia removed her disguise to reveal the beauty beneath, they became human again. I had seen the reaction several times before. First came the doubletake, then came the smiles, followed by charmed deference. "Here you go, ma'am," they said to her as they handed back each item, one-by-one, from the plastic bin. To me, they said nothing as they handed me the tray without taking their eyes off Olivia.

"Yes, I can see why you don't like going out in public. Such fawning must be tiresome."

"That part, I like," she said with a smile as she covered up again.

We found the correct courtroom and took our seats in the last row, which was reserved for the curious public. The proceedings inside the room were as boring as the security line outside. Hardly any words were spoken. Papers were passed around. Lawyers stood up and entered documents into the record while the judge sleepily looked at each one for less than a second before passing them on to someone else. Olivia nudged me when I started to snore.

"Is that him?" she said, pointing to a man who looked a lot older than he did the last time I saw him. "He's good looking."

"It runs in the family," I said.

"Probably skips a generation, huh?"

"He looks kind of haggard to me. The last ten years haven't been kind to him, I guess."

At one point, something lawyerly must have happened, because everyone before the bar stood and packed up their oversized briefcases at the same time.

"What just happened?" she asked me.

"I don't know. Either it's over, or they're stopping for lunch."

My father stood and walked with a slight limp from the front of the courtroom toward the door behind me. After he passed by me, he stopped. He turned slowly and said, "Are you going to let me walk out the door without a word?"

I was stunned. The monster was staring me down, and I melted with fear. Even though I was seated, I could feel my knees trembling. "What word would you have me say?" I finally countered.

"When I saw you come in, I had hoped you'd have the courage to tell me why you're here. How did you know where to find me?"

"I read about it in the paper."

He grunted. "I wouldn't have taken you for a reader of the New York Post."

"I'm bored a lot, thanks to you," I replied.

"Now we're getting somewhere. So, you blame me for making you rich?"

"I sure do. My inheritance wasn't to benefit me. You did it for yourself. You took away my family and you stripped away all meaning in my life."

He took a step toward me and glowered. "Your life is yours to make of it what you will. No one can take away anything, and no one can give you anything." He pointed his index finger at my chest and said, "You must decide what you will make of your life. You take what you need; you strive for what you want. Thanks to me, you don't need money. It doesn't mean you don't need other things. It's up to you to figure out what those things are. No one can give you those things, and no one can take them away."

I was no longer trembling with fear, but with rage. I stood up to him, and looked down at him, "You did. You took my mother away."

"You don't know what you're talking about. You weren't there."

"Because you sent me to boarding school."

"Your mother was sick. Just like your brother is now. Where were you then? Did you ever think to come home from England over your holidays? No, you went traveling with your friends everywhere but where your mother was. And nothing's changed, has it? Did you even know your brother had been in the hospital? You want to know who's to blame for your mother's death? Look in the mirror."

"How dare you talk that way to him?" Olivia screamed from behind me. She had taken off all her disguises; she was fierce, yet beautiful. I had never seen her so animated. "You disowned your own sons to marry her," she pointed in the direction of my father's ex-wife, who was still conferring with her lawyers. "What kind of a man could do such a thing?"

My father was clearly taken aback by Olivia's looks, as well as her assertions. "Who are you?" he asked when he finally regained his composure.

"She's with me," I said.

"I'm impressed," he said, without taking his eyes off Olivia.

"You're a creep," she replied.

"I've been called worse," he said.

"You're wasting your time, Clay," Olivia said to me.

I said to my father, "You want to know why I'm here? It's because Nigel told me that my bitterness toward you is hurting the other people in my life—and it's hurting me, too. He said I need to face you and get rid of the bitterness."

"Hmph, Nigel," he said, dismissively. "How's his advice working out so far?"

"I expected more contrition from you," I replied.

My father backed away a few inches and looked at the ground. "What do you want me to say? Am I sorry about your mother?"

"That would be a good start."

"I am. I am sorry about your mother. I'm sorry about a lot of things, but I won't get stuck in the past. I've made a lot of mistakes in my life, but I've learned from them. I've learned to move on and not be hampered by regrets."

"You sent me away, Dad. Have you moved on from that one, or do you have any regrets?"

At the sound of the name, 'Dad,' he winced. The granite façade started to crack, tears welled up in his eyes, and he choked out the words that followed. "More than you'll ever know," he said, and he turned and walked out of the courtroom.

WATSON AND HOLMES

Olivia held my hand as we walked together in silence to the garage where she had parked her mother's car, an unremarkable import.

"I love the Biscayne," she said as she was handed her mother's keys by the attendant. "Although I think it needs some modern upgrades."

"Like air-conditioning?"

"Yes, and power steering. Driving to the gym is a better workout than the gym itself."

I gave her bicep a squeeze and said, "It shows."

"I'm having it shipped to New Jersey, you know," she said while pretending to flex. "It's due to arrive soon."

"We should drive it to Burlington," I said.

"Burlington? Why?"

"Clues, Watson. Remember, we are desperate for clues. I want to see the house where Louisa and Michael lived. The house where the construction workers found her book."

"First of all," Olivia said, "you're Watson, not me. I'm the famous one, and you're the writer. It's elementary."

"But I'm moody, depressed, and bored."

She ignored me and continued, saying, "And secondly, we don't know the location of the house—only that it was in Burlington."

"Wrong!" I shouted; my reply being punctuated with a raised finger pointed to the sky. "If you had read my translation carefully, you would know that they lived on Grafton Street."

"Wrong, yourself," Olivia shouted back, poking me mid-gloat, hard in the stomach. "There is no Grafton Street in Burlington, Vermont.

"A trivial hindrance. In fact, if you were Sherlock Holmes, that detail would not be an impediment at all. No, my dear Watson, I intend to inquire of our seller of antique furniture."

"The odd man with the glasses?"

"The odd man with the glasses knows all. At least, he undoubtedly knows the address of the house. The house of James-something, as memory serves."

"Watson, Watson, Watson," Olivia replied. "You are obviously suffering from some sort of delusion amnesia. The man's name was Jake Salus, and I already searched for his address. He owns several properties because he flips houses for a living. We still won't know which house to visit."

"Impressive. Nonetheless, I still want to visit the antique shop." We stared at each other, surprised and amused. "I can't believe I just said that last sentence."

"You want to go to an antique shop? Maybe Nigel was right," Olivia replied. "Now that you've faced your father, you're a changed man."

"I hope you're right," I said as I opened her car door.

"Get to work on finishing that translation. I'll pick you up in a few days after the car arrives."

"Uh, Holmes is supposed to give the orders to Watson," I said.

"That's right. And Watson does whatever she tells him to do," Olivia said, smiling and twirling her fingers as she waved goodbye and pulled away.

I walked all the way home to Forty-Sixth Street with a spring in my step. It took me ninety minutes, and although there was a light drizzle and I had no rain gear, nothing could have dampened my spirits. I had gone toe-to-toe with my father, and I saw a fleeting glimpse of his true remorse over abandoning me and my brother. I had no idea why, after all those years, it meant so much to me to know that he cared even a little, but it did. Olivia was right; I felt like a new person. I felt free.

Late in the week, early in the morning, Olivia drove up to my house in the Chevy Biscayne. She didn't have to honk the horn when she double-parked in front of my door. She revved the engine so loudly it sounded like a plane was about to take off from Forty-Sixth Street. We made the three-hundred-mile trip in just under six hours. Heavy traffic and winding lanes on the Taconic State Parkway made it impossible to let the car run without bit and bridle, nonetheless it was a joy to drive it and thrilling to be alone with Olivia again.

I took the wheel as we made our way slowly through the streets of Manhattan. Olivia told me how she used her social media platform to get out the word that we're looking for Louisa Peeters and Deirdre Mulholland, two women mentioned in an antique book we purchased in Burlington, Vermont. A day or two had gone by with no solid leads, so she reluctantly added a small comment about the Irish Crown Jewels.

"Then what happened?" I asked. "Did anyone respond?"

She just looked at me and rolled her eyes. "Are you kidding? I got thousands of comments. You're welcome to read through them later, if you want."

When it was her turn to drive, I read aloud the highlights of my notes from Louisa's book. With the windows open, she couldn't hear me from my side of the car, so I happily slid over to the middle of the front bench seat with my hip touching hers, adding to the joy of the journey. I picked up the story from the last point Olivia read. Louisa had relented, agreeing to take the children in a horse-drawn carriage from Canada to Poughkeepsie, New York. She knew the carriage would be laden with Canadian whiskey, which was illegal during Prohibition, but she was willing to risk it because Michael would be paid so well and he promised she would only have to do it this once.

Her excursion went off without a hitch. No one challenged Louisa and the children as they crossed back across the border at Rouses Point, and the horses merrily trotted to the warehouse where Michael, drunk, was waiting with the bootleggers. Not surprisingly, they didn't pay him nearly as much as they had promised, but they assured him they would make up the difference next time she made the trip. Michael lost his temper and demanded to talk to a man whom Louisa surmised was the boss of the operation.

The men coolly brought Michael into a back room and closed the door behind them. She could hear Michael shouting at someone but couldn't hear the replies from the other side of the wall. While this was going on, Louisa was questioned by another man who seemed to be someone of importance. Rather than summarize their conversation, I read it aloud to Olivia as Louisa related it.

"You're French," the man said to me.

"No, I'm Belgian," I replied, holding the children close. I did not like the look or manner of the man.

"Your husband said you were in England before sailing to Canada."

"That's right. It was during the war. I fled to England because it was safer there," I said.

"So, you must have spent a long time in England, then huh?"

I didn't know why he was asking me so many questions, so I tried to change the subject. "Who is my husband talking to? Will he be paid what you promised him?"

The man smiled wickedly. "He's going to get what's coming to him," he said.

"I'm sorry. I don't understand that expression. Does that mean we will be paid?"

The man ignored my question and asked, "When did you go to England?"

I was worried about Michael, so I answered him without thinking, "August 1918."

His eyes widened at my response. "The Channel was a dangerous place to be at that time. How did you get to England?"

"I secured a seat on one of the last passenger ferries from Brest."

At this, he took me by the hand and led me out of the hearing of others. "You are a very important person; do you know that?"

His words frightened me even more, and I held the children so tightly they complained. "What does that mean?" I asked him.

"I work directly for Hugh Murphy. The Hugh Murphy." Waving his hand at the warehouse behind us, he said, "These morons have no idea who I am or what I'm doing here."

"I don't know any Hugh Murphy," I said.

"Of course you don't. A proper, innocent young lady like yourself wouldn't be acquainted with the rough and tumble world of business."

"Smuggling business?" I said, defiantly. I didn't like the way he was talking to me.

"We deliver goods and services to paying customers. That's all you need to know. But Mr. Murphy is more than a businessman. He is a powerful man who loves the home country, and he wants to rid Ireland of the English once and for all."

"What does that have to do with me?" I asked.

"Mr. Murphy sent me to collect the Irish Crown Jewels."

At once, I thought of the dazzling jewels in the box I took from the back of the car we were driving when my father died, but I tried not to let him see it.

"I know nothing about Irish jewels," I said.

He studied my face for moment, then continued, "A British nobleman pinched the jewels and planned to sell them to a German agent in Brest, France. In August 1918, a young Belgian woman grabbed the jewels and then brought them to England. Neither the girl nor the jewels were ever found. A witness claims to have seen the woman board a vessel for Canada."

"There were plenty of Belgian women in Brest at that time, Monsieur."

"Are you sure you don't know where I can find these jewels? Mademoiselle? They are also known by the name, The Order of Saint Patrick."

When he said Saint Patrick, I gasped.

"Mr. Murphy will pay handsomely to recover those jewels. Far more than what these fools are paying you to carry their whiskey."

"I don't have any idea what you are talking about," I said. This man disgusted me, and I wanted nothing to do with him or his boss. "Now, if you'll excuse me, my family and I must be going before it gets dark."

As if on cue, Michael came out of the warehouse limping badly and holding a bloody handkerchief over his nose.

"Michael!" I shouted. I started to run to him, but the other man grabbed me by the arm and pulled me toward him roughly.

He spoke into my ear in a hoarse whisper. I could smell his putrid breath as he growled, "Take a good look at your husband. That's nothing compared to what Mr. Murphy will do to you and your children if we find out you're hiding those jewels."

Olivia pulled the car over onto the grassy shoulder of the Taconic State Parkway, too upset to continue driving. "So that's the reason she fled? Who was Hugh Murphy?"

"I looked him up online. Seems he was an Irish mob boss in the early twentieth century with ties to the nationalist movement in Ireland. He was known for being a sadistic psychopath."

I drove the rest of the way to Burlington. Olivia slid over close to me so we could talk about Louisa and her plight, and she kissed me on the cheek.

"I wish she had just given Murphy the jewels," I said as we pulled off US Highway Two and onto Main Street. "It's such a shame to split up her family over some diamonds."

"It wasn't the diamonds, Clay," Olivia replied. "She obviously wasn't planning to benefit personally from them. It was the principle. She didn't want to give that foul criminal what he wanted. I understand why she ran."

I parked at a meter near Church Street, and we walked to the antique furniture store where I had purchased Louisa's book. It was a clear autumn day, but the sun had started to slip down behind the shops on the west side of the street. Small whirlwinds of leaves greeted us as we approached the shop. There was a sign on the door, written hastily with a marker by a shaky hand, and it read simply, 'Closed Now.'

"How odd," Olivia said, looking up and down the street. "Why would he be closed today? The other shops are all open. See all these people?"

"Indeed, it is a mystery," I said with my face pressed against the front window. "And speaking of mysteries, why did you kiss me while I was driving?"

"Do you see anyone inside?" Olivia asked without answering my question.

"It's dark in there. All I see is your reflection."

"Strange."

"Did anyone ever tell you your face is perfectly symmetrical?" I asked.

"I think you might be the first," she said, then she reached into her purse to take out her sunglasses. Before she could put them on her face, she raised a hand to her ear. "Wait! Did you hear that?"

From inside the shop there was the unmistakable sound of glass breaking. Suddenly, the front door opened, and the shopkeeper came bounding onto the sidewalk. When he saw Olivia standing there, he said, breathlessly, "Closed. I'm closed," and turned to run away, nearly colliding with me. Startled, he looked at me through his Coke-bottle lenses, his eyes larger than ever, and said, "You! You did this. Get out of here."

He made as if to run away, but I grabbed him by the arms and said, "Hold on. I just want to ask you a few questions."

He struggled to wrench himself out of my arms, but I held on tight. He shouted, "Leave me alone. They're coming. Ask *them*, if you're as dumb as you look. Let me go!"

"What are you talking about? Who's coming?" Olivia asked.

"That book I bought. Where is the house where it was found?" I asked him.

"You stay away from that house!" he shouted all the louder, tugging against my grip and craning his neck to peer into the store window.

Shoppers along the street were beginning take notice of us, so I said, "Look, I'm going to let you go, just tell me where I can find the house."

"Fool! Hickok Place, near Greene Street. Maybe you'll get what's coming to you. Now let me go."

I released my grip and watched him run with an awkward gait down the street away from his shop.

"From the looks of it, he's not a recreational jogger," I said with a smirk.

"I think we should leave, too, Clay," Olivia said, looking worried. "He's so frightened, he didn't even close the door to his shop before running away."

"So strange," I said, poking my head through the open door. I couldn't see much because my eyes were still adjusting to the darkness, but I could hear papers shuffling in the back of the store. "There's definitely someone in there," I said.

Olivia tried to pull me out, but I bounded inside and shouted, "Who's there? What d'you think you're doing?"

"Clay!" Olivia called out in hoarse shout. "Are you crazy? Get out of there."

Immediately, the shuffling sound stopped, and I heard the clang of a small bell. I jumped back and gave a small cry, which Olivia amplified greatly from her location outside the door. Two cats scurried toward me and made hairpin turns—one to the left, the other to the right—when they saw my figure standing in their way.

"I found the intruders," I shouted back to Olivia, who had her phone to her ear, presumably calling the police. "Just a couple of cats."

"Cats?" she asked, incredulous. "That guy didn't look like he was running from cats."

"Come inside, I'll show you. There's nothing here to worry about."

She hung up on whoever she was calling and turned on her phone's flashlight. I took her by the hand and led her toward the back of the store. Pointing to a glass vase that had fallen from a shelf near an open window, I said, "This is where the intruders gained entry. Probably running from the K-9 unit."

"They must be cat burglars." Olivia replied with an impish smile. She was visibly relieved.

"They were obviously planning to break into the kitty."

"Ugh," she groaned. "Although it makes sense. I heard recently some nut paid a thousand dollars for a French woman's diary."

"Belgian," I corrected.

"*Excusez-moi*," she replied. "I still don't understand why the shopkeeper was so scared. Do you really think he ran away because of those cats?"

"Who knows with that guy? He's an odd fish. First of all, the last time we came here he acted like he was *expecting* us to come looking for a jewelry box. Then he seemed surprised when I asked him about the guy who sold it to him—as if I should know who he was."

"I guess you're right. And it is strange that he would run down the street just now with the front door wide open."

"In a few minutes, he'll probably forget why he ran away and walk right back inside like nothing happened," I said.

Olivia was still looking around with her flashlight when she found something on the floor. "Look," she said. "The cats must have knocked this bell over when they jumped off the desk."

I picked up the small service bell that was lying on the floor and placed it back on the counter. I rang the bell and called out, "Waiter, table for two!"

"What type of table would you like, sir?" Olivia replied, mimicking a man's voice and gesturing to the furniture. "We have Victorian, Chippendale, and Queen Anne. Can I interest you in this wonderful demilune?"

"I'll take one of each. Have them shipped to my home on Hickok Place, near Greene Street, wherever that is. Mine is the home with the secret compartments in the walls," I replied.

"Very well, my good sir. Shall we go there now?" she said in her regular voice, extending her hand.

I took her hand, kissed it, and said, "Yes, I think we shall, m'lady. As soon as I figure out where in this fine town I might find Hickok Place."

We closed the front door as we walked back onto the sidewalk, but just before the door closed, from deep inside the store, I thought I heard the voice of a man speaking.

RENTERS

"How did anyone find anything before they invented GPS?" I asked Olivia, as we parked at the corner of Hickok and Greene.

"I guess they had to ask a human for directions," she quipped.

"How sad."

"Do you have something against humans?"

"Let's just say I've had some bad experiences," I said as we began our search for the house. Hickok Place was a small lane with large old homes lining both sides of the street. I wasn't sure what we were looking for, but I was hoping we would recognize it when we found it.

Olivia had the same thought. "How will we know which is the right house?" she asked.

"I guess we are looking for a house with some obvious signs of construction. Didn't the shopkeeper say the owner was knocking down some walls?"

The road was free of traffic; the only sign of life was the raking of leaves by one of the residents. He eyed us suspiciously as we passed his lawn, which was half green and half buried in a thick carpet of leaves.

"Good morning," I said with an inobtrusive wave.

He acknowledged my presence by raising two fingers off the handle of his rake and nodding his head imperceptibly.

"Where are you, Jake Salus?" Olivia murmured.

We walked all the way to the end of the street, but we didn't see any homes bearing the name Salus or showing any indication of construction activity inside. The only home that stood out was a freshly painted Queen Anne with an inviting porch and a realtor's advertisement signifying the home was for rent. I called the number on the sign.

"Hello, my name is Wilson Granite, and I would like to inquire about the home for rent on Hickok Place."

The realtor introduced herself as Theresa Lahey and immediately launched into a monologue covering every detail of this 'glorious' home. By the time she began describing the septic system, I interrupted her to ask, "Is this Jake's place? I heard he bought a place at auction and wants to rent it out."

She paused for a moment, then admitted, "Yes, however, Mr. Salus rents all his properties through me. You see—"

"Can I check it out on the inside?" I interrupted her again.

"When can you be there?"

"In about seven seconds. I'm standing on the street in front of the home now. How about you?"

"I live nearby, and I can drive right over there. Make yourself comfortable on that glorious porch."

I assured her I would be comfortable and climbed the stairs to the porch, where Olivia and I sat on the Adirondack chairs facing the street.

"What do you hope to discover inside?" she asked.

"Who knows? Maybe there's another hiding place where she kept the jewels."

"I suppose that's possible," Olivia said, although I knew she didn't believe it.

"At least, I hope we can learn something about Louisa and the children that might give us a clue as to where she went," I countered. "And furthermore, I'm dying with curiosity to see inside the home where so much of her diary was written. Hopefully, Jake didn't make too many alterations."

"But this isn't the same house. They lived on Grafton Street," Olivia said.

"It's got to be this house. I have a good feeling about this place."

I got up from my chair and looked out onto the street. It was still deserted, except for two beefy men who were walking by the house and looking at the screens on their phones.

Scanning up the road toward the intersection where we parked, I said, "I don't see any sign of that realtor."

"That's because you're looking the wrong way," Olivia replied. "Look the other way, I see a car turning the corner. I bet it's her."

She was right. The ebullient Theresa Lahey leapt from her car to greet us and asked us if we didn't enjoy resting on the glorious porch. Inside the home, she showed us many other glorious qualities of the home, as well as some that were splendid, magnificent, brilliant, and marvelous.

Touring the home, I was convinced that this was where Louisa and Michael lived in the early years of their marriage. It was marvelous to walk through the rooms I had read so much about in her book. The kitchen, where so many meals were prepared, still contained an old stove that looked as if it might have been the very stove on which Louisa tried to prepare meals to suit Michael's Irish tastes. The hearth around the fireplace in the living room almost certainly was the same setting where she massaged and warmed his feet at the end of the day.

"These hardwood floors are exquisite, aren't they?" Theresa asked.

"Why is the wood different in this section?" I asked her as we explored the bedroom.

"There was a wall here, but the homeowner knocked it down to combine the master bedroom with the room next door. Isn't this such a grand space?"

"There was a wall here?" Olivia asked. "It seems pretty wide for a wall."

It was, indeed, wide for a wall. The marks on the floor outlined a wall that would have been almost two feet wide. No doubt, it was the wall in which the book and the letters had been discovered.

"They don't build 'em like they used to," the realtor affirmed. "How long would you two be thinking of living here? We can do a one-year lease or a multi-year lease. I recommend the multi-year lease to lock in the super-low rental price."

"We're taking it one step at a time," I replied to her with a wink. "We're still dating."

"Well, you make a gorgeous couple," she replied. Then, turning to Olivia, she asked, "Have we met before? You seem very familiar?"

"I get that a lot," Olivia said, then she left the room to examine the bathroom.

"Is she at the university?" Theresa asked me.

"Yes, that's right. You've probably seen her at the university. Tell me, this is such a splendid home, who owned it before Jake? Is it true Jake bought it at auction?"

"The house sat empty for several years, but don't worry, the homeowner spared no expense with upgrades to the electrical wiring and the plumbing. It's all up to code now."

"I'm sure it is. I can tell the contractor did a great job. Say, who was the contractor? I'd like to know, in case I ever need to hire him for something myself."

"Oh, uh. Well, the homeowner would be the one to hire contractors for any work that needed to be done. You wouldn't have to worry about that."

Olivia came back into the bedroom and asked, "The home exudes history, doesn't it? What can you tell us about its backstory?"

The realtor seemed conflicted. I could tell she loved to talk and wanted to share a good yarn, but something was holding her back.

I pressed the matter, saying, "I've heard there were Irish families in this section of town. In fact, didn't this road have another name years ago? I'm part Irish, you know. It would be wonderful to tell my Irish grandmother I'm staying in an Irish home. Is it Irish?"

"Your familiarity with Burlington's history is quite impressive, Mr....," she paused to think, "Stone, did you say?"

"Granite. Wilson Granite. The Irish part is on my mother's side. And yes, I've been doing my homework. So, there were Irish folk here?"

"There were many Irish families in this neighborhood. And yes, this road used to be known by another name. It was called Grafton Street. The new name, Hickok Place, was adopted in the past sixty years or so."

"Is that so?" Olivia asked. "What was the name of the family who lived in this particular home? Do you know?"

"Yes, I know it, I grew up not far from here. But it's not a terribly pleasant story, so maybe it would be best to wait for another day."

I put my hand gently on the back of Theresa's shoulder, smiled, and said, "Don't worry, Theresa, nothing you could say could change my mind about renting this magnificent home."

She looked at Olivia and said, "You'll need to watch this one, dear. He's not only charming, but smart."

"He's a real catch," she said, "and he loves history, pleasant or unpleasant."

Theresa relented and shared, "The last person to live in this home was Mr. Mulholland. Edward Mulholland. He lived here all his life. Never married."

"He lived here all his life?" I probed.

"People say he was born in this very room, which is fascinating when you consider he died in this room, too."

"He died in this room?" Olivia asked.

"Yes," Theresa said. "But don't forget your promise, Mr. Granite, that you won't let that affect your decision about the home."

"Of course not, Theresa," I assured her. "I find that fascinating. Tell me all you know about Edward Mulholland. The more I know, the more intrigued I am."

"Mr. Mulholland was born in this home and was raised by his father here. His mother and his twin sister disappeared when he was quite young. Folks aren't in agreement about whether she died or took the girl and went back to Europe."

"What was Mr. Mulholland senior's first name?" I asked. "And what happened to the sister?"

"I don't know Edward's father's name," Theresa said. "And no one knows the whereabouts of the sister. That's why the county had to put the house up for auction."

"Because Edward Mulholland died with no heirs?" Olivia asked.

"That's correct. Oh, it's a terrible story, and I'm really not comfortable sharing it—here of all places."

"What happened, Theresa?" I asked.

"Burlington is a very safe town. This kind of thing just doesn't happen here," she stammered.

"What happened?" I repeated.

"There was a break-in a little over ten years ago. Mr. Mulholland was in his nineties. The thieves broke in and tore the house apart. They smashed holes in the walls and tore up parts of the floor, and they killed poor Mr. Mulholland. Died of a heart attack in the very room in which he was born."

"That sounds dreadful," Olivia said.

"Awful," I concurred. "Did they ever catch the scoundrels?"

"The police had no clues, whatsoever. Who would want to do that to a poor old man in his own home? It made no sense. So, there was an exhaustive search for the twin sister, or any of her relatives, but they never found anyone eligible to inherit this home. Then, after an allotted time, the county put the home up for auction."

"What an amazing story," I said as we began to make our way to the front door.

Back on the porch, Theresa added, "The whole town was thrilled when Mr. Salus invested so much money into fixing up the home. For ten years, it was an eyesore, but you could never believe that today. Look at this place. Isn't it glorious?"

I replied with all sincerity, "Indeed, it is a most fascinating home, and you, Theresa, are an exemplary realtor and local historian. You have given us a sterling introduction to the merits of this wonderful home. Bravo!"

After saying our goodbyes and assuring Theresa that we would call with our decision, we walked back to the corner where we had parked. I was replaying the intriguing conversation from inside the home when a man's voice interrupted my reflections.

The man who had been raking leaves was now relaxing in a lawn chair on a carpet of green grass. He was looking straight at me.

"I'm sorry," I said. "Were you talking to us?"

He looked to the left, and then to the right, saying wordlessly that there was no one else around to whom he might have been talking. Then he spoke again, "I said, 'Did they find you?'"

"Did who find us?" I asked.

"Your friends," he answered. "The two fellows who were asking after you."

"Are you sure they were looking for *us*?" I asked.

"They said they were friends with the attractive woman and a grumpy-looking man who passed this way a few minutes ahead of them. I'm pretty sure they were referring to you two."

We quickened our pace and got into the car.

"Cats, huh?" Olivia said to me as she quickly slammed and locked her door.

"Maybe the man with glasses is not so crazy after all," I said, driving away with a long look over my shoulder.

ALONE

We drove to Robert and Roberta's bed and breakfast, checking frequently to make sure no one was following us. Robert was waiting for us in the sitting room.

"Roberta told me you two were coming to Burlington together to shop for antiques. I didn't believe it, so I had to see for myself."

"Which is more surprising," I asked, "that I would want to go back to an antique store or that Olivia would be willing to travel with me?"

"Both," he replied. "I lost the bet and now I need to do dishes solo for a week. How many rooms are you wanting?"

We looked at each other awkwardly. We'd both been thinking about this question, but neither of us had the courage to bring up the topic earlier.

"Two rooms," I said.

However, at the exact same instant, Olivia said, "I guess one room is OK."

I responded, "You think one room is OK?"

While she replied simultaneously, "Two would be better."

Robert was thoroughly enjoying our embarrassment as he looked back and forth between as someone watching a tennis match.

"Two rooms," Olivia and I said together.

"You got it. The only two vacant rooms I have are in the back, opening into the dining room. We use them for overflow. It's very quiet back there at night, but it can be a little loud in the morning. Our breakfast cook comes through the back door, which is right next to your rooms."

"No problem," I said. "But speaking of the back door, would it be OK for me to park my car out back?"

"You're not in Manhattan, Clay. Burlington is boring, but it's safe. Your car will be fine on the street."

"That car is easy to spot, and I don't want people to know we're here," I said cautiously.

Robert looked at me askance. "What have you gotten yourself into, Clayton? You didn't come here to shop for antiques, did you?"

"We'll tell you all about it, but first let us get the car out of sight and put our things in our rooms."

He handed us keys to our rooms and the back door, and he told us to meet him and Roberta in their private family room after we got settled.

After moving the car, I changed into an old pair of sweats and a T-shirt for the night, then I heard a gentle knock on the door. It was Olivia. She had changed into soft blue cotton pajamas that looked both elegant and comfortable. They were at the same time modest and incredibly alluring. Seeing her dressed for bed awoke in me a craving that had lain dormant for several years. I was reminded of my younger days when I would rush headlong into physical relationships with reckless abandon. I was thrilled, but I was scared.

"Are you OK?" she asked, waving her hand in front of my face.

I'm in love, is what came into my mind; "I'm thinking," is what came out of my mouth.

"I'm hungry," Olivia said in reply.

"Me, too," I agreed, although I was pretty sure we didn't mean the same thing.

Roberta welcomed us in their family room and presented us with a tray of finger sandwiches. She apologized that Robert hadn't thought to get us anything to eat.

"I was too shocked by the sight of you two together," he said.

"I had a feeling about you two all along," Roberta inserted. "Sometimes it's the ones who argue the most at first who end up together the longest."

"That bodes well for us," I said, smiling at Olivia.

"Now," Robert said, "I want you to tell me the real reason you're here and why you needed to hide your car out back."

I was in the middle of chewing my first sandwich, chicken salad with apples and walnuts, so Olivia started. "Last time we were here, Clay bought a book."

Olivia went on to tell them about Louisa and her father, how they recovered the Crown Jewels of Ireland from the man who stole them, and how they planned to return the jewels to their rightful owner, but that proved to be more difficult than planned. She told of Louisa's journey to Burlington and her marriage to Michael, which produced two children, Deirdre and Edward. Then she recounted in impressive detail the encounter with the bootleggers and the threats from Hugh Murphy's henchman.

"It was at this point, we believe," said Olivia, "that Louisa chose to take her daughter and flee."

"Just the daughter?" asked Roberta.

"Just the daughter," I said. "Apparently, she felt Michael couldn't live without his son, and the son would be better off living with his father."

"With the Irish Mob breathing down their necks?" she asked.

"I'm trying to withhold judgment."

Olivia continued, we think she took the jewels and fled, but the book doesn't say where she was planning to go. There's just an apology to Edward for leaving him behind and a plea for forgiveness.

"Such a sad story," Roberta replied, closing her eyes in palpable sympathy.

Robert nodded, but he asked skeptically, "So, why are you hiding your car? Do you think Hugh Murphy is after *you* now?"

Olivia answered, "We don't know who is after us. Obviously, Murphy is long dead, but the jewels are still out there somewhere. Someone scared the daylights out of the antique dealer. We went in there and saw a broken window. We thought it was cats at first, but now we know there were people inside the shop. We believe those people overheard us talking to each other, then followed us to the home where Edward Mulholland was born and where he was killed."

"He was killed?" Roberta asked.

"About ten years ago," I replied. "Edward was ninety-something years old. There was a burglary, and he apparently died of a heart attack. The place was torn apart, as if the attackers were looking for something hidden in the house."

"The book?" she asked.

"Maybe the book. Maybe the jewels themselves," I answered. "Police investigated, but they had no clues. I don't think they knew anything about any of this."

"Let's say you're right," Robert continued, still not convinced. "Let's say that Edward Mulholland was murdered in Burlington ten years ago because a new generation of mobsters suspected the jewels were in the house. How do you explain why those people happened to show up at the furniture shop today, after so many years?"

Olivia and I looked at each other, puzzled. We hadn't asked ourselves that question. Then, her eyes widened, and her jaw dropped. "Instagram!" she shouted.

"What about it?" Roberta asked.

"Yesterday, I wrote a post on my Instagram story saying we found a book at an antique furniture store in Burlington that has information about the lost Crown Jewels of Ireland."

"You posted that on Instagram?" Robert asked.

I squirmed and admitted, "My idea."

"Not your best," said Roberta.

"I think we'd better call the police," said Robert.

"And say what?" asked Roberta, "They are being chased by guys searching for jewels stolen over a hundred years ago?"

"I don't think the Burlington Police Department would have any idea what to do about this. They'd lock us up for psychiatric evaluation," I said.

"Maybe so," said Robert. "But I know someone in City Hall who works in the building department. I can introduce you, so they'll know you're not a nutcase; maybe they can help us. Try to get some sleep, then tomorrow morning, I'll go downtown with you."

We said good night to our hosts, walked through the empty dining room, and locked the back door. I walked with Olivia to the door of her bedroom, my mind racing with thoughts of what might come next. She put her hand on the knob, then stopped and turned to look into my eyes.

I held her tightly and gave her a lingering kiss on the lips, then asked, "Are you going to be OK?"

Her eyes were locked on mine as I stroked her shoulders. "I'd feel safer if I wasn't alone," she answered.

"Me, too," I said and kissed her again. The warmth and softness of her pajama top weakened me in the knees.

She reached behind her and opened her door, then wrapped both arms around my neck and pulled my lips onto hers as she stepped backwards, dragging me into her darkened room.

"OK, I'm coming," I tried to say as her lips pressed against mine.

Suddenly, the lights came on, and strong hands yanked us apart. A burly man, one of the two we saw on Hickock Street earlier in the day, threw me back and stiff-armed me against the wall. He was shorter than me, but he was built like a tank. With my back to the wall and his hand on my chest, I felt like I was being crushed in a vise. His companion, who was taller and even more beefy than his counterpart, grabbed Olivia by the neck and had her in a headlock with his oversized hand covering the bottom half of her face. Her eyes were bulging in fear.

"No!" I shouted and slipped sideways to get away from the man holding me against the wall. I dove at the man holding Olivia, but my attacker pulled me back like a rag doll and punched me in the gut harder than I had ever been punched before. I doubled over in pain, then I tried to shout, but I couldn't breathe. I lunged at Olivia's attacker again, and he kicked me in the groin, sending me to the floor, writhing in pain.

The taller man spoke first, "Stay on the floor. I'm going to talk, and you're going to answer my questions."

I tried to get up again, but the shorter man kicked me in the ribs. "This one's not very smart," he said.

I looked up at Olivia. She had stopped struggling. Her eyes were closed, and she was whimpering with tears streaming down both cheeks. Without loosening his grip on her neck, the man said, "You know why we're here. Give us what we want, and no one gets hurt."

Pain was radiating through my body, but my abdominal muscles were beginning to relax, and I was able to take shallow breaths again. "You can have it," I mumbled. "Let her go. The book is in my room. I'll go get it."

As I stood up to get the book, the shorter man punched me in the gut again, and I thought I was going to pass out. My vision narrowed and I felt myself swaying uncontrollably from side to side.

The taller man kept talking, his voice sounding as if coming to me through a long tunnel. "Did I say anything about a book? Where are the jewels?"

"I have no idea," I said, as if in a nightmare.

"Wrong answer," said my attacker, as he jabbed my chest with what looked like small black flashlight. Searing pain like fire burst through my whole body, and every muscle locked up in cramps tighter than I would have thought possible. I tried to scream, but I could feel the muscles in my throat squeezing my airway shut. The man smiled and pressed his stun gun harder against my chest, causing me to begin shaking involuntarily. Finally, losing all control of my legs, I fell flat on my face, and the pain stopped.

"Where are the jewels?" asked the man with Olivia's head in the crook of his arm.

I could feel the warmth of blood that had started running out of my nose as I got up on all fours. "We haven't found them yet," I said.

The shorter man kicked me again, but the other said, "That's enough. We need him alive for now."

I crawled on my knees to the man holding Olivia by the throat and said, "Please, you've got to believe me. I don't have the jewels, but I have the book. You can use the book to find the jewels."

He looked at the shorter man and said, "You're right. This one's not too bright." Then, looking at me, he said, "I thought I told you; I don't care about the book. Are you both deaf and dumb?"

"I'm just trying to help you get what you want," I replied.

"You want to be helpful? Get up off the floor and get me those jewels," he said in return.

"Look," I said, standing slowly. "We can talk about this, but you need to let go of her. She can't run anywhere. You don't need to hold her like that. You're hurting her."

"Hit him again," the man said.

Without hesitation the other henchman pounded me, once again, in the gut, sending me to the floor for the third time.

When I regained the ability to speak, I said, "Look, those jewels are worth two million dollars today. I will give you five million dollars if you let her go right now."

"Did I say I wanted money?" the man replied. "Do I look like I need your money? Is that what you're saying? You think I look poor?"

"He's not only stupid, he's disrespectful, too," said the other. "Can you believe this guy?"

"Zap him again."

The shorter man pulled out his stun gun and moved toward me, but I sprang back in fear, "No!" I shouted. "Stay away from me."

Ignoring my plea, he pressed me up against the wall and hit the button, sending current through both of us. Within seconds, he jumped backwards, stunned.

The other henchman sneered at him and said to me, "I don't need your money, and I don't want any books. I only want the jewels, and you're going to give them to me."

"I'll give you whatever you want; just let her go."

"You'll bring me the jewels?"

"Absolutely. Let her go, and they are as good as yours. I'll bring them to you myself," I told him.

"Just like that?" he sniggered. "You've suddenly become Mr. Cooperative, huh? Or, do you take us for fools?"

"We'll need some kind of collateral," the shorter man said, having regained his composure.

"Like a deposit?" I asked.

"No," said the taller man, now stroking Olivia's hair. "We don't need a deposit. We've got all the collateral we need right here."

"No! Please, no!" I shouted, louder this time.

"You bring me the jewels; I give you back your girlfriend. It's that simple."

Olivia started screaming from behind the man's massive hand. Though muffled, I could hear the fear in her voice and see it in her bulging eyes.

"No!" I screamed. "Take me. She's the only one who can find the jewels. She's Sherlock; I'm only Watson. I can't find them without her help. Let her go, and I'll be your hostage."

"Who would care if we took you?"

I wasn't sure anyone would.

"This one, on the other hand," he said, grinning. "When people find out she's missing, s**t will happen. You ever heard of Missing White Woman Syndrome?"

Olivia's muffled screams became louder and more urgent. She started twisting and kicking, trying to break free, but the more she struggled, the tighter he squeezed her neck with the crook of his arm.

"Let me zap her," said the shorter one, approaching them with his stun gun in his extended arm.

"Stay away from me with that thing!" the taller one shouted, backing away in fear with his eyes fixed on the man's weapon.

I took the distraction as my opportunity to open the door of Olivia's room and scream into the dining room as loud as my pummeled chest could manage. "Help!" I shouted. "Call the—"

Before I could say the next word, I could feel the prongs of the stun gun in my back, followed by searing pain pulsating through my body. I shook uncontrollably, and started to fall, although it felt more like floating than falling. I felt like I was treading water in a pool filled with shards of broken glass. How long it lasted, I have no idea because I eventually lost consciousness. The next thing I could remember was waking up on Olivia's floor. The room was dark. I was alone.

ANSWERS AND QUESTIONS

I could hear voices in the dining room outside the door. I tried to stand, but my legs were too stiff from the effects of the stun gun. Opening the door and crawling on all fours, I limped into the dining room like a dog that had been beaten and left for dead. Every muscle in my body tried to resist any movement. I was bloody and bruised, and I smelled of urine, having wet myself during my convulsions.

At the table closest to Olivia's bedroom door sat a large, round woman who was talking ceaselessly with a fork full of pancakes swinging inches from her mouth. Her equally corpulent husband, meanwhile, was wasting no time devouring his own pancakes as he nodded in complete agreement with whatever she was saying. I lurched toward them and clambered to my feet, grasping the edge of their table.

As I stood over her, the woman turned, dropped her jaw, and stared up at me with eyes as wide as the saucers on her table. She made no sound at first, but seconds later, her plump face turned pink, and she emitted a piercing screech that turned every head in the dining room. Her husband dropped his forkful of pancakes, and with surprising quickness, he jumped to his feet and ran away. As he vaulted out of his chair, his belly lifted the table, spilling pancakes and coffee all over his screaming wife and knocking me off my balance. I began to teeter toward the woman and would have fallen on top of her, had Robert not come up behind me and held me upright.

Robert pulled me away from the screaming woman and led me through the open door to Olivia's bedroom. He scanned the room, looking for Olivia, but before he could ask, I answered in a hoarse whisper, "Call the police."

"What happened in here?" he asked.

"They were waiting for us. They took Olivia."

"Who was waiting? Where did she go?"

All I could say was, "So stupid. How could I be so stupid?"

Roberta came into the room laughing, "Mr. Kennealey called the police. He thinks a homeless man tried to steal his breakfast." When she saw the condition of the room and realized Olivia was not there, she stopped laughing, and she asked the same questions Robert had just asked.

"We need to find her, now!" I said. "She's scared out of her mind."

They looked at each other, stunned. Roberta spoke first, "Are you saying Olivia has been abducted?"

"Yes!" I shouted, then instantly regretted it, holding my sore ribs. "They told me they'd let her go when I give them the jewels."

Robert shook his head and said, "None of this makes any sense. You don't have any jewels. I mean, who ever heard of these jewels anyway?"

"The police will be here in a few minutes," Roberta said, "they'll know what to do." Then looking around the room, she said, "We'd better not touch anything, including you, Clay. They'll need to see things as they are."

"He stinks, Roberta," Robert said. "Can we at least change his pants?"

"I don't need to change clothes right now," I said. "With every minute that goes by, Olivia will be harder to find. I need to talk to the police now!"

They walked me out to one of the tables in the dining room, which had been quickly vacated by the guests I scared away. The police arrived a few minutes later, accompanied by the rotund Mr. Kennealey, who warily pointed out his alleged homeless attacker. They found me at the table, wishing I had never heard of Ireland or its crown jewels.

Robert sat down alongside the officer who had come to investigate. He was a young man with a thin, patchy beard that gave me the impression he had not yet started shaving. Because he was new to the force, he didn't know Robert or Roberta. "In fact," he admitted, "this is my first week on the job."

He was not surprised to hear Robert say that Mr. Kennealey was mistaken and that I was, in fact, just another guest. "The sergeant figured there was some mistake," he smiled. "That's why he sent me." His expression turned decidedly sour, however, when I started speaking.

"There's been an abduction," I interrupted. "Olivia Hunt was taken by two thugs—the same two guys who did this to me."

"Olivia Hunt? The actress?" he asked.

"Yes, the actress. She was a guest here last night. We were in that room," I said, pointing to the room where the men were hiding. "Two men were waiting inside and grabbed her. I tried to stop them, but they punched me, and kicked me, and shocked me with a stun gun. I passed out. When I came to, they were gone."

"The actress and the two men?" he replied, pulling a notebook out of his shirt pocket with shaky hands. "Where did they go?"

"I don't know, but the longer we sit around here and talk, the farther it will be," I answered.

"Who else saw these two men?" he asked while scribbling more notes in his book.

"We were alone."

He stopped writing and looked up at me. "There are no witnesses to corroborate your story?" he asked.

Robert spoke next. "The inn was full; the only two rooms I had available were these two overflow rooms off the dining room. There are no other rooms out here, and the rest of the guests are too far away to see or hear anything."

The cop asked Robert, "They had separate rooms?"

"That's right," he answered.

"And you didn't call for help? Didn't think to call the police?" the officer asked me.

"It's a little hard to call the police when you're getting beat up by two gorillas—one of whom is wielding a stun gun."

"That's one explanation," he replied. Then passing me his pen and notebook open to a blank page, he said, "I'm going to need your full name and phone number." While I was writing, he turned to Robert and asked, "Do you have any surveillance cameras here? A doorbell camera? Anything?"

Robert looked at me sheepishly and said, "We bought a system, but I never got around to installing it. Sorry, Clay."

"Mr. Howard," the officer continued, reading my name out of his notebook, "tell me about your relationship with Ms. Hunt."

"What do you want to know?"

"Close, were you?" he asked, scrutinizing my expression. "Intimate?"

"We were close."

"Sleeping together?"

"We had two rooms," I said. "Mine is next to hers."

"I see that," he began writing in his notebook again, "but you say that you were in her room when all this happened."

"She invited me in as we were saying goodnight."

"Did she? Or did you invite yourself in?"

"If you must know, she had her arms around my neck and pulled me into her room. Once we were inside, the lights came on, and the two guys pulled us apart."

"She was choking you," he replied.

"No, her arms were around the back of my neck—playfully."

"You two were roughhousing, and now she's gone."

"It's not like that. I'm telling you; we were embracing each other when we came into the room, but these hoodlums attacked us. We're wasting time.

You've got to call the State Police and start looking for them before they get too far."

His pen and notebook were back in his pocket, and he looked at me as if he had already cracked the case. "I'm going to call this in," he said, rising to his feet. Pointing at me, he said, "Don't leave this room."

"I think you might need to call a lawyer," Robert whispered when the officer stepped away.

"I need Nigel," I said. "This idiot suspects I'm the cause of her disappearance. We're wasting time. They could have taken her anywhere by now."

"Who's Nigel?" Roberta asked. She had finished cleaning up the Kennealey's mess and joined us at the table.

"Nigel is a private investigator with a corporate security firm. He'll find her faster than these clowns, anyway." I told Roberta how to contact Nigel and asked her to tell him what happened to Olivia and that I need him here right away.

The young officer came back and told us that a detective was on the way.

"Have you alerted the State Police or the FBI?" I asked.

"Detective Larkins will do that if she deems it necessary," he said. Then he pointed toward the back door and said, "There are no signs of a forced entry. Did you let these guys in?"

"Seriously?"

"How could there have been two men in your room if they didn't force their way in, and you didn't let them in? Can you explain that?"

"Why don't you find them and ask?" I said.

Roberta came back into the room and said, "Nigel's on his way. I called Philip, too, and he'll bring Nigel in the plane."

"Is that your lawyer?" the police officer asked with a sneer.

"Nigel is a detective. An actual detective, not a peach fuzz flatfoot."

"You want me to arrest you right now?" he shot back.

"That won't be necessary, officer," interjected Roberta. "Mr. Howard's been through a lot this morning and just forgot his manners."

"Actually, I'm always like this," I said.

"That's the first thing you've said that I believe," replied the young cop as he walked through the door into Olivia's room. "This is where you say the men were waiting?"

"That is where they were waiting, yes."

"No sign of forced entry here, either."

"We didn't lock the door."

"Convenient," he said, returning to the table where I was sitting. "Did these kidnappers say anything about ransom?"

"Ransom?" I responded. I had been hoping to avoid that question as long as possible. I was certain Officer Peachfuzz had never heard of the Crown Jewels of Ireland.

"Why did they kidnap her and not take you, too?" he asked. "It seems to me they would get twice as much ransom if they took both of you. Can you explain why she's gone and you are still here?"

"They said something about 'Missing White Woman Syndrome,'" I replied.

After an attempt at an intimidating glower, he said, "Why don't you save us a lot of time and tell us the truth?"

The back door opened and in walked a trim woman, mid-forties with short hair. She was wearing dark pants, a white blouse, and a tan jacket that was bulkier under one arm than the other. She was carrying a large briefcase, which she set on the floor near me as she introduced herself. She was Detective Judy Larkin of the Burlington Police Department.

The young officer pulled out his notebook and began to rattle off his observations, but midway through his account, Detective Larkin waved a hand and said, "Write it up, officer. I'll read it later."

"What should I do now?" he asked her.

"Do I look like your mother? Don't answer that. I suggest you get back to your desk and start typing."

"He told us he's new," said Roberta, as she offered the detective a cup of coffee.

Taking the cup, she replied, "The chief's nephew. Good coffee."

"So, you're the man who was with Olivia Hunt last night?"

"Yes," I replied, "I'm Clayton Howard, of New York City, and I will answer all your questions to the best of my ability if you will first notify the State Police and FBI, or whoever needs to be on the lookout for the two guys who kidnapped her. It's killing me that we're sitting here talking while they are getting farther and farther away."

She nodded slowly as she scrutinized my appearance from top to bottom. "You say there were two men here last night, besides yourself, is that right?"

"Yes, and I went through all this with Officer Peachfuzz," or whatever he's called.

"That's not his name, but I like it."

"When we entered her room last night, two men, both built like gorillas, attacked us. The bigger one kept Olivia in a headlock while the other one kept beating me and zapping me with his stun gun."

"Can you provide evidence that anyone besides yourself was in the room with Ms. Hunt last night?"

I pointed to the burns from the stun gun and the blood on my face. "Aren't these evidence enough?"

She folded her hands and leaned her chin on her thumbs, her eyes locked on mine. "I'm not seeing the injuries of someone beaten up by a large, violent man. They seem more consistent with resistance of a woman who carried a stun gun in her purse for protection."

Roberta gasped. "That's nonsense, detective. Clay and Olivia were getting along fine last night."

"Last night. So, you've seen them fight at other times?" she asked.

"I didn't mean it like that," Roberta said. "I just can't believe anyone could suspect Clay did this."

"Did what?" Larkin probed.

"Caused Olivia to go missing," answered Robert, who was sitting at the table next to Roberta.

"Detective Larkin," I said, "I understand why you suspect me. I read the news. I know about the guy in California who reported his fiancée missing, even though he had killed her. But even in that case, the police also carried out a missing person investigation. I don't care that you suspect me because I know what really happened. She really is missing, and I want—no I need your help to find her. I need the FBI, the State Police, even Officer Peachfuzz to search every car or storage facility or wherever someone can hide a kidnapped television star."

"You'll cooperate with my investigation, so long as the FBI searches for a missing person?" she asked.

"Yes, please notify the FBI."

"Then you'll be relieved to know I have already notified the FBI, and if a body isn't found within twenty-four hours, they will take up the case."

I took a deep breath, leaned back in my chair, and told her everything that happened between Olivia and I since we met. If she had had trouble believing any of it, she didn't let on. She listened quietly, took notes, and asked a few clarifying questions along the way.

"You say they didn't want money, only jewels?" she asked when I finished my story.

"Not just any jewels, but a specific historical piece. I offered them far more money than those jewels are worth, but they wouldn't take it."

"And you have no idea where those jewels are now?"

"None. Olivia and I had just begun searching for them, more as a lark than for any other reason. I've never needed to work a job, and she recently walked away from her TV show, so we thought it would be a fun project to pursue together. If we were successful, we planned to return the jewels to their rightful owner."

She looked at me intently, and I could tell she was sizing me up, trying to figure out if my entire story was just a fabrication. "Can you stand?" she asked as she produced a camera from her briefcase.

I stood, and she examined my injuries, taking pictures of various parts of my body, including the urine stain on my sweatpants. She pointed to the three pairs of holes burned in my T-shirt where I had been attacked with the stun gun. "Do these still hurt?" she asked, snapping away.

"Not as much as my ribs where the guy kept kicking me."

"You should see a doctor and get some X-rays," she replied as she pulled a small box out of her bag. "I'm going to check her room for prints. Are you willing to be fingerprinted now?"

"Why would I not be?" I asked.

"You need to say yes."

"Yes. Why would I not say yes?"

Without answering me, she opened her fingerprinting kit and made impressions of all ten of my fingers on both sides of a large white card.

"Can he change his pants now?" Robert asked. "The smell is making me sick."

Detective Larkin handed me a large plastic bag and said, "Take off your clothes and place them in here." Then she stood up and entered Olivia's room to take pictures and dust for prints.

I went to my room and placed my soiled clothes in the evidence bag and washed up in the sink. Every muscle in my body ached as I changed into fresh pants and a shirt. The bed I never slept in looked inviting, but even though I was exhausted, I wouldn't be able to sleep thinking of Olivia and the horror she was experiencing.

There was a knock on my door. I opened it to see the detective wearing latex gloves and holding a small phone. "Does Olivia Hunt use a flip phone?" she asked. "This was on her bed."

"I've never seen that phone before," I answered.

"There are no prints on the phone, so undoubtedly someone wiped it after it was last used." She flipped it open, and the small screen indicated there was an unread message from a private number.

"Read it!" I shouted.

She pressed the button with her gloved hand and the following message appeared, 'In ten days we will call this phone. If you have what we want, we will tell you where to find her. If not, you will never see her again.'

KING

Nigel arrived several anxious hours later, accompanied by Philip, Stephanie, and a lawyer I had never met before. Detective Larkin had completed her examination of the crime scene and left with her evidence and her suspicions. She told me I was not going to be arrested at that time but warned me not to leave Burlington. "If you try to flee, it will only make matters worse," she said.

"Robert briefed me on the situation," Nigel began, "and told me we have ten days."

"We don't have ten days. She can't last that long, we need to find her now!" I said.

"You need to prepare yourself, kid. There are no guarantees in cases like this."

"I cannot accept that, Nigel. You don't know Olivia. She suffers distress when fans get too close; can you imagine what she's going through in the grip of kidnappers? She'll be traumatized for life!"

Stephanie hugged me and said, "Turns out you're human after all, Clay. We're here to support you in any way we can."

"Hundred percent, Clay," said Philip. "We're going to get her back and punish these guys. Whatever it takes, you've got it."

Nigel spoke next. "It doesn't work that way, folks. I know you two are accustomed to buying your way out of problems, but I'm warning you not to get your hopes up. Cases like this don't always turn out the way we want them to, no matter how much money we throw at them."

"So warned," I replied. "But I won't rest until we find her."

"I'm going out to check surveillance cameras in town," Nigel said. "Chances are these two guys stopped in a bar, a 7-Eleven, or some place with video. We might be able to get a look at them. Maybe even see what kind of wheels they have."

"Too bad Burlington's finest didn't think of that," I replied as he was leaving. "Of course, they already have their man."

As if on cue, the lawyer came over to speak with me. He was a tall thin man with graying hair, wearing a pinstripe three-piece suit. In his hand was a yellow legal pad and a pen. As if there could have been any doubt that he was a lawyer, he approached me and introduced himself as a criminal defense attorney. He said his name was Tobias Rendelman, and he made the trip to Burlington at the request of my father.

"My father?" I asked.

"Nigel notified your father, and your father called me. He's very concerned about you."

"I don't know if I believe you," I said. "My father has never been concerned about me."

Ignoring my comment, he produced a folded contract from his jacket pocket and said if I signed on the dotted line, he would do everything in his considerable legal expertise to keep me out of jail.

I signed.

"The police have requested you voluntarily turn over your cell phone. They want to look for any evidence that you sent the text message to the flip phone found on Ms. Hunt's bed. I advise against it."

"Wouldn't that make me look guilty?" I asked.

"You already look guilty, otherwise they wouldn't have asked."

"If they search my phone and realize I didn't send the text, might they not redirect their investigation to try and find the kidnappers?"

"If they gain unlimited access to your phone, they will pull out their fine-tooth comb and spend days looking at every message, phone call, email, location pin, contained therein. I strongly advise against complying with their wishes. Furthermore, I want to know what you have already given them. Is it true that you already made a statement and voluntarily surrendered your fingerprints and the clothes you were wearing last night?"

"Yes, I suppose I did."

"You suppose you did? Or did you?"

"Detective Larkin asked if I would consent to being fingerprinted. I said yes. Then she told me to take off my clothes and put them in the bag, which I did."

"Did she tell you to do that, or did she ask your permission to confiscate your clothing?

"She most certainly told me to take off my clothes. I remember because I was going to make a wisecrack, but I decided not to."

Robert spoke up, saying, "I heard it, too. It was not a question. She told him to take off his clothes. Knowing Clay, I was waiting for the repartee."

Rendelman wrote a long note to himself on his legal pad, then said, "They will use the clothes to collect DNA evidence from you. Evidence you did not consent to give them. From now on, you don't talk to the police without me being there, understood?"

"Understood," I said. "However, as far as I'm concerned, they can have my DNA, but they can't take my phone. I need it to make a call that I'm loath to make."

"Who are you calling?" asked Philip.

"Diane Hayward, Olivia's mother. She needs to hear about this from me, not from the news."

I went to my room and made the call—the toughest of my life—and came back into the dining room an hour later. Nigel had returned while I was on the phone, looking pleased with himself. He and the others were enjoying Roberta's coffee and home-made scones.

"You talked to the mother?" he asked. "How's she taking it?"

"She blames herself. Diane said she never wanted Olivia to take the job on the television show. She said she had a feeling something like this would happen, but Olivia insisted on doing it because she wanted to provide for her."

"She expected Olivia would be kidnapped? How can that be?" Philip asked.

"Mothers know," said Stephanie. "Does she have anyone around her to support her?"

"She's alone. It's just her and her collection of antiques."

Stephanie turned to Philip and said, "We need to bring her here. She shouldn't be alone at this time; she should be with others who are concerned for Olivia's safety."

"She can stay in the Kennealey's room," said Robert. "They checked out early, due to indigestion after their breakfast today."

"Sorry," I said.

"They won't be the only ones to check out," said Roberta. "We should have plenty of room to make this our base of operations to find Olivia."

"I really appreciate your support, folks, but I'm afraid it's not much of an operation. We don't even know who took her."

"About that," Nigel said, tapping his index finger on his phone, which was lying on the table, "We have a lead. I think I found our guys on the surveillance video at the convenience store on Main Street."

"Champlain Farms?" Robert asked.

"Right. They bought gas at the Shell Station, then went inside to buy snacks," Nigel replied.

"When were you going to tell us this? And how do you know it was them?" I asked.

Ignoring my first question, he answered the second. "Two guys their size, obviously from out of town by the way they're dressed, tend to stand out in a place like this, but just to be sure—." He handed me his phone on which he had recorded the video. The shock of seeing those two men again nauseated me, and I felt like I might faint. Nigel watched me, and seeing my reaction, he continued, "That's what I thought."

"When was the video taken?" Philip asked.

"Yesterday, shortly before Clay and Olivia went to the furniture store downtown."

"What kind of car were they driving?" I asked. "Maybe the State Police can track it down."

"Can't see the car on the video, only the tires. Black."

"That's helpful," I said.

Roberta was in the kitchen, but she poked her head into the dining room and asked, "Did they pay with a credit card?"

"Cash only," replied Nigel. "But I'm hopeful we will be able to ID these guys. I sent a screenshot of our boys' faces back to my office. There's a good chance they'll match with a mugshot or two in the database. I expect to hear something soon."

"Soon is not soon enough," I said. "I'm going crazy just sitting here. We need to get her back now!"

Nigel gave me a knowing look.

"Clay," Robert said, "we're doing all we can right now. You need to come to terms with the fact that we're not going to find Olivia today. And probably not tomorrow or the next day. It's going to take time."

Nigel put his hand on Robert's shoulder. "It's alright. I've seen this reaction dozens of times in missing person cases."

"But not all your cases involve people who had already been traumatized by a faked abduction. This is going to crush her," I said.

"People are tougher than they look," said Nigel. "I've seen guys who are the biggest fraidy-cats you've ever seen turn into superheroes under—." He never finished his sentence because his phone signaled a message coming in. "OK, folks. We have names," then after a pregnant pause, he said, "but you're not going to like what we found."

"Who are they?" I asked.

"Their names are Joey Kilbane and William 'Big Bill' Donahue. Although, I don't suppose those names mean much to you."

"I take it Donahue is the one who had Olivia in a headlock, and it was Kilbane who knocked me out with his stun gun."

"Sounds about right. But their names aren't as significant as who it is they work for. They're in the employ of the most notorious crime family in

Boston."

"You're kidding," I said. "The Irish mob is still after the Crown Jewels? Hugh Murphy can't possibly be alive still."

"Not Murphy, and they're no longer in league with the Irish Nationalists, as Murphy was. The new boss is named King, Danny King, and he fancies himself to be royalty. He's a ruthless, psychopathic narcissist. It doesn't surprise me that he wants the Irish Crown Jewels. He probably thinks if he had them, he could ascend to the throne of Ireland."

"He's that crazy?" Stephanie asked.

"I'm afraid so," Nigel answered.

Philip pounded the table. "Then we need to take him out!" He pointed his finger at Nigel and said, "There are still some things money can do."

"Philip!" said Stephanie, staring at him in disbelief.

"What does this mean for Olivia?" I asked Nigel.

"King can't be killed, and he can't be bought. King gets what King wants. There is only one path to getting Olivia back. We need to find those jewels."

"Oh no!" cried Stephanie.

"Oh yes," I replied. "And thanks to Detective Larkin, I know just where to start."

SEALED AND DELIVERED

I pulled out my phone and called Brian. It went to voicemail. "I need your help," I said. "SOS. Olivia's missing. I need you to get something from my apartment and call me, ASAP."

"You want to fill us in?" asked Nigel.

Brian texted a response before I could answer. 'OMW.'

"He's on his way," I said. "When they found Louisa's book hidden in the wall, there were some other items hidden with it."

"What items?" Philip asked.

"There was an old key and a bundle of rejection letters."

"Rejection letters?" he asked. "What do you mean?"

"There was a bundle of letters tied with a string. When I first started reading them, they seemed like a random collection of mail that had been sent to him. I couldn't figure out why he chose to save those particular letters. There were letters from women who weren't interested in dating him; there were letters from employers who weren't interested in hiring him; there was a letter from a publisher indicating they weren't interested in his book— Louisa's story, I presume; and there were several letters from his mother. All the letters were from people who rejected him."

"His mother sent him rejection letters?" said Stephanie.

"His mother disappeared with his sister and left him behind," said Nigel. "It must have felt like she rejected him."

I turned to look at him with one eyebrow raised.

"I skimmed your translation of the book," he said. "I was trying to figure out why you were so engrossed in this story, until I came to that part. Then I understood."

"Nigel is not just an investigator," I said to the others, "he's also my shrink."

"So, his mother took the jewels and the sister, and they all vanished, is that right?" asked Philip.

"Right. His mother wrote him, apologizing over and over for leaving him and asking his forgiveness, but none of the letters told him where she was."

"Postmark?" Nigel asked.

"They are postmarked from various small towns in upstate New York, but she wrote in each letter that she had to keep moving because she was afraid of being caught by the men who were after her."

"But you found something in the letters that will help us?" he asked.

"Not the letters—the envelopes."

Stephanie cocked her head and said, "But you just said the postmarks aren't helpful."

"Not the postmarks," I said. "Think back to the episode of Olivia's show we watched together, last time we were here."

"What about it?" asked Philip.

"DNA!" Stephanie said.

"Yes. Remember what Olivia said? She said that if you have someone's DNA, it's possible to track them down if any of their relatives are in any DNA database."

"That might work," Nigel said. "Not bad, kid. Not bad."

"I'm still not tracking with you, Clay," said Philip.

"Brian said if a DNA sample in any database—be it law enforcement or private ancestry websites—comes within a certain number of centi-somethings, you can track down that person or their family members."

"Centimorgans," Nigel said. "If Louisa's daughter, or any other children she had later, or any of their children, are in any of the DNA databases, we should be able to find them."

"Find the children, find the jewels," I said.

"Possibly," said Nigel.

"But those letters are almost a hundred years old. Do you think you'll be able to get a useable DNA sample from a hundred-year-old envelope?" asked Philip.

"It depends on the storage conditions," said Nigel. "If the letters have been hidden away in the wall of a New England home, in a cool, dark environment for all that time, there's a pretty good chance we can collect some decent samples from the letters. Of course, the more letters, the better chance of collecting enough genetic material."

"Wait a second," said Stephanie. "Are you sure people licked their letters to seal them in the 1920s? When was that kind of envelope invented?"

I gasped; I felt like I had been kicked in the chest again. Closing my eyes, I said, "I hadn't thought of that."

"I'm on it," said Philip, who was looking it up his phone. "According to multiple sites online, the adhesive envelope was in commonplace usage by 1850. There should be plenty of good DNA in those envelopes."

Nigel said, "Have your man bring all the letters to my office. We'll see to it the samples are extracted and analyzed."

"How long will that take?" I asked.

"If he gets us the letters today, we'll know by the end of the day tomorrow whether the lab is able to find enough intact DNA to enter into the database."

My phone began to ring. "This is probably Brian, telling me he's in my house," I said before looking at the screen. In fact, it was Olivia's mother.

"Do you have any news?" she asked. From her voice, I could tell she'd been crying. "I know we just spoke a little while ago, but I'm going crazy staring at these walls. And I can't bring myself to look at that box you gave me. I'm so sorry to be ungrateful, but I can't bear it."

I wasn't sure the best way to respond to her question. In fact, we had news, but I didn't think it would be helpful to tell her the men who abducted her daughter were known to be vicious killers. "We have the beginnings of a plan, Ms. Hayward" I said. "It's rudimentary, but it's a start."

Stephanie walked over to me and signaled that I should give her the phone. "Can I talk to her?"

I muted the phone before handing it to Stephanie and said, "Don't tell her about Big Bill. She doesn't need to know who he is." She rolled her eyes and said without words that that was one of the most unnecessary and condescending comments she'd ever heard.

"Mrs. Hayward, this is Stephanie. We've met before; I'm the one who introduced Olivia to Clay. I can't even begin to imagine what you must be going through, but I don't think it's good for you to be alone right now. There are several of us up here in Burlington, Vermont. We're working with a private investigator to find Olivia. We're going to get her back."

Taking the phone back, I said, "We found a picture of the guys who did this. We know their names and who they work for. We can get her back; we just need to find those jewels."

"How can you possibly find the jewels?" she asked, continuing to weep.

"We have a plan. It's a longshot, but it's our only shot. I can send a car to bring you to the airport in Teterboro, and the Pennfield's plane can bring you here. Stephanie's right. You shouldn't be alone right now."

"Oh, I don't know," she said, her voice trailing off. "I'm not good with airplanes."

"Then I'll have the driver bring you here. Diane, please." I began to cry, too. Stammering, I continued, "It's not just for you. I… I have to admit that I need you here. Would you come?"

"I'll come on one condition," she replied after a long pause.

"Name it."

"Promise me you will do everything you can to find my Olivia, no matter the cost. I don't want to live if I have to live without her."

DREAMS BITTER, WAKING WORSE

Sleep was hard to come by that night. Robert moved me out of my overflow room, into the bedroom I occupied on my first weekend with Olivia. Although I was exhausted and lying in one of the most comfortable beds on the planet, yet every time I closed my eyes, I couldn't get past the visage of a smiling Big Bill Donahue's hand over Olivia's mouth, her eyes wide with fear. In the silence of that room, the memory of her muffled screams echoed relentlessly throughout the night. Even in the brief stretches when I was able to fall asleep, Olivia's nightmare filled my dreams.

One of those dreams was especially vivid:

I'm driving the '62 Biscayne over a hundred miles an hour down the New York Thruway; police cars with their lights flashing and sirens blaring are in hot pursuit. I can see Olivia up ahead, reaching out for me, but she is tied to a tree. Suddenly, I am no longer in the car. I'm standing right in front of her, trying to reach her but my hands won't move. Olivia's once beautiful face is streaked with cuts and bloated from her wounds; she's almost unrecognizable. Tears are streaming down both sides of her head and in a strained voice she is calling to me. "Hurry Clay, hurry." I'm trying to reach her and pull her away from the tree, but my arms are still frozen at my side. At this point there is an abrupt change in our location. We are in a house, and I realize it's the house on Grafton Street. The tree to which Olivia is bound is growing through the middle of the bedroom. Her mother is there, standing to my right. She doesn't seem to notice Olivia, because she is looking at me with tears in her eyes. "How could you?" she repeats over and over, "How could you?" I try to point out Olivia, who is tied up just a few feet away, but I still can't move my arms. "Hurry Clay," Olivia repeats with increasing desperation. "I'm coming Olivia," I say. "I'm coming. I'm doing everything I can, but I can't move." My hands feel as if they are tied behind my back, and when I turn around to see what's wrong, I see Detective Larkin and the young police officer locking their handcuffs and wagging their heads at me. "How could

107

you?" they repeat, "How could you?"

And then I woke up, tearful and soaked in sweat.

When morning came, my nightmares turned to waking reality. Olivia Hunt was gone because I mixed her up in the story of Louisa Peeters Mulholland. At sunrise, I walked to the park that coursed along the edge of the lake and found the bike path where Olivia and I had ridden together on our first visit. Several bikers passed me on the path as they enjoyed the cool, crisp air so common for a morning in New England. My mind was racing with thoughts of losing Olivia and what would happen to Diane if Olivia was never found. From time to time, I would think of my own mother, and for the first time, I realized how much I missed her. I thought of my friends, Philip, Robert, and Brian, and I wondered what I had done to deserve such loyalty from them. I could not remember ever being as kind to them as they were being to me at that time in my life. Finally, my thoughts turned to my father. I wondered if the lawyer was telling the truth when he said my father was concerned about me, or if Nigel had told him to say that.

I walked as far as Rock Point Open Air Chapel, where Olivia and I had stopped to rest and to talk. Cyclists on the path passed me occasionally. One couple stopped not far away to drink from their water bottles. Watching them reminded me of Olivia. I yearned to see her face, hear her voice, and to feel her touch. Sitting on the cold stone bench, I could still feel the softness of her body and the warmth of her lips as she held me outside the door to her room, just before the nightmare began. I had promised myself I would never fall in love again, but I went ahead and broke that promise, to the ruin of two lives besides my own.

"What have I done?" I shouted aloud. The couple who had stopped near me turned their heads to look. They had finished drinking and seemed to be working on some mechanical issue with one of their bikes. I considered making a wise crack about nosy neighbors, but I thought better of it, so I turned around to face the other direction.

My thoughts turned to our plan to use DNA to find descendants of Louisa Peeters Mulholland. It was beginning to seem like a waste of precious time. Before I had gone to bed, Nigel told me Brian delivered the stack of letters to his office, and his people were working on the extraction of genetic material from the envelope seals. However, he told me that even if we found a potential hit from a database, we would need to confirm it with a direct sample from that individual before we could know if they were related to Louisa. The longer I thought of it, the less feasible it seemed.

My stomach began to growl, and I started thinking of food for the first time in a long time. "It's hopeless," I said as I stood up. When I turned around, I noticed the nosy couple was now standing much closer to me. They had been joined by another cyclist and seemed to be tinkering with another mechanical issue on another bike.

Then it hit me. They weren't random people who happened to stop near me. They were watching me.

I approached them and demanded, "Who are you?" No sooner had the words left my mouth than I recognized the third member of the party was the young police officer with a peach fuzz beard who had interrogated me the day before. "Why are you following me?" I asked him.

"Why don't you answer your own question, Mr. Howard?" he said. "What have you done?"

"It's none of your business."

"What's hopeless?" asked another member of the threesome.

"You have no right to harass me," I said. "You don't care at all about finding Olivia. You just want to pin the blame on me."

"We care a whole lot about finding Olivia," said Officer Peachfuzz. "We're launching a major search today, in fact. Why don't you save us all a lot of time and tell us where the body is buried?"

"You're an idiot," I replied. Then I remembered my dream and said, "You wouldn't see her if she was right in front of your face."

"Right in front of our face, huh? Are you saying this is where she is buried? Is that why you walked here this morning?" asked the other male member of the party.

The woman must have decided to attempt using empathy. "If you're having regrets about what you have done, Mr. Howard, the best thing you can do is tell us where to find her. She deserves better than to be buried in an unmarked grave."

"That's right," said another. "You owe it to Olivia. And think of her mother. She deserves better, too. She deserves closure."

"They deserve better all right," I replied. "They—we deserve a professional police force who's intelligent enough to investigate a kidnapping, rather than mindlessly pursue a trope they've seen on worthless television police dramas."

As I started to walk away, the empathetic one placed her hand on my shoulder. "You know, we can offer a lot of leniencies for folks who cooperate with us. We know you're an upright man with a clean record. If you help us out, we can be a tremendous help to you later."

"Take your hand off me," I said, glaring at her. "You are wasting my time. I have no use for any of you."

As I walked away from the trio, I could hear Officer Peachfuzz say, "Go back to the inn, but don't even think about leaving Burlington."

"I'll go wherever I need to go to find Olivia," I said without turning around. "You're welcome to follow my lead, but you'd better bring your badges and your guns. You're going to need them when I find the people who did this."

THE GAME'S AFOOT, AGAIN

When I returned to the bed and breakfast, coffee and pancakes were flowing copiously. Roberta said, "Clay hasn't once been on time for breakfast at our inn."

"I'm sorry I'm late, but I can't tell you how thankful I am for all of you. This morning, I was reflecting on how little I have done to deserve such fine friends as you."

"Who are you, and what have you done with Clay?" asked Robert.

At that moment, I noticed Brian was there, and so was Olivia's mother. "When did you get in, Ms. Hayward?" I asked.

"Diane," she scolded. "You promised to call me Diane. Brian and I arrived last night. That car you sent to pick me up was very comfortable. I'm sure I would have slept the whole way here, if the circumstances were any different."

"Mercedes van with Airmatic suspension," Brian said. "Rides like a dream. I would have slept the whole way here if I hadn't been driving."

"Sit down, Clay," said Philip, pointing to a seat across from him and Stephanie. "Where have you been?"

"I went for a walk."

"Alone?" asked Stephanie.

"I thought I was alone, but Officer Peachfuzz and company followed me."

"Did you speak with them?" asked Nigel.

"I did, but let's not tell Mr. Rendelman. He's not going to be at all happy with the way things went down."

"The only thing that makes me happy, Mr. Howard, is winning cases and getting paid for my services. And not in that order, because I get paid whether we win or lose." I hadn't seen the lawyer sitting in the back of the room. He continued, "Clients who hide things from me are the only people who end up in the second category. We will talk this morning before I fly back to New York."

"You might need to postpone that flight, Tobias," said Nigel. "The FBI is coming this morning, but they didn't say what time."

"Maybe they will take this case seriously," I said as Roberta placed a heartwarming stack of blueberry pancakes in front of me. "Where are the other guests?" I asked her with a mouth full of pancakes.

"Most checked out on their own, and we relocated the holdouts to other inns," Robert answered, "and we canceled all reservations for the time being. This inn is now home base for Operation Olivia."

"It's also an active crime scene," reminded Nigel. "Please be sure to stay out of Olivia's room. I notice the police tape is down."

"That's my fault," said Diane. "I needed to see the room for myself. I promise I didn't touch anything."

"You'll be happy to know, Clay, that my people worked through the night and said they recovered quite a bit of genetic material from those envelopes. They are comparing her genetic profile with data in both CODIS and GENmatch. We might have results as soon as this afternoon."

Diane turned toward me and asked, "Is this the plan you were telling me about?"

"We got the idea from an episode of Olivia's show," I replied. "We are going to use DNA from the woman who wrote the book to locate her descendants. If we can find any of them, we might find the jewels."

She closed her eyes and took a deep breath. After a minute or two, with a trembling voice, she uttered, "I wish we had a better plan."

Nigel said, "The FBI has a different plan, but if you ask me, it's even worse than ours."

"I'm open to any and all proposals," I said. "For now, this is the only plan we have, and even though it seems hopeless, I'm going to do everything in my power to make it work."

"And I will do everything I can to help you," Diane affirmed. "I don't mean to be a Debbie Downer; I'm just worried for my little girl."

"Of course," I said.

"Tell me more about how all this works. What are CODIS and GENmatch? How did you get DNA from the woman who wrote that book? And how do you expect to find her relatives?" Diane asked.

"CODIS is the name for the government's Combined DNA Index System," Brian answered, "and GENmatch is a private-sector index of genetic information compiled from samples submitted to various ancestry search engines, like Twenty-Three Dot Com and many others. Law enforcement agencies can access both databases to locate people associated with criminal activity." Then to Nigel, he said, "Private investigators are not supposed to have access to these data. How did you gain access to that sort of private information?"

"I don't care how he does it," I said. "As long as it can help us find those jewels and get Olivia back."

Nigel ignored Brian's stare and said to Diane, "When Clay bought the book from the antique dealer, he also acquired several letters that were written by Louisa Peeters Mulholland to her son, Edward. The letters were cut open at the top, but the seals where Louisa had used her tongue to wet the surfaces before closing the envelopes were intact."

"And you were able to find her DNA in those seals?"

"Fortunately, we were able to gather quite a few cells from those envelopes, which produced more than enough snips for us to use in a database query."

"Snip stands for single nucleotide polymorphism, or SNP," Brian added. "It's an irregularity in the DNA of an individual that causes their genotype to stand out from the crowd. If two people have enough snips in common, you can be sure they're related."

"Well, that all sounds very scientific, but do you really expect to find a match with Louisa's DNA?" Diane asked. "They didn't have any of this technology in her lifetime, or most of the time her daughter was living. It seems impossible that either her or her daughter's DNA would have been submitted to any database."

Nigel responded, "This is true, but it's possible that Louisa's daughter, Deirdre, had children and grandchildren of her own. If so, then it's possible that one of them could have submitted a cheek swab to any one of the ancestry websites, or been implicated in a criminal investigation."

"Think about it," I added. "Louisa would have been tight-lipped about where she came from and why Deirdre didn't have a father or any siblings. Deirdre's children and grandchildren wouldn't know their roots, so they'd be the perfect target market for ancestry services. If any one of them ever submitted a sample, we'll be able to drive right up to their home and beg them to sell us those jewels."

"I suppose there's a chance," admitted Diane, "but I wish our chances were better."

"We'll know soon if there are any matches," said Nigel, waving his head, "but it's not likely we'll get a name and address."

"What are you talking about?" I asked. "What good is a match if we don't get the name and address of the person who submitted the sample?"

"If the hit is on CODIS, we'll get all we need to know. The government data is complete. However, if the hit comes from the private-sector database,

GENmatch, there might not be as much personal information attached to the sample. Most people who submit their own samples volunteer only their email address, and maybe their city or region."

"The clock is ticking, Nigel," I said.

"And I told you, kid, we need to be patient. Olivia is tougher than you think. She will be able to hold out, and as long as there is any hope of our success, King's people will see to it she remains alive."

"How will King's people know anything about our hope of success? We are no longer in possession of the burner phone they left us. We couldn't give them an update if we wanted to."

"Believe me," Nigel said in an ominous tone, "Until he has those jewels in his hands, King's people will never be as far away as we'd like them to be."

As if on cue, a shadow streaked across the blinds on the back door window. "Did you see that?" Stephanie shouted.

Philip sprung to his feet, opened the door, and peered outside. "There's nobody here. All I see is Olivia's car."

Robert came running into the dining room and said, "You're never going to believe who is in the front yard."

My heart was pounding. "It wouldn't happen to be Big Bill Donahue, would it?"

"No," said Robert. "I'm not completely sure who he is, but by the looks of him, I would guess he's your twin brother."

"Grayson!" Nigel and I shouted simultaneously.

"You have a twin brother?" asked Diane.

I heard Philip answer her as I ran to the front door. "He's several years older, but people mix them up sometimes."

I made it to the door shortly after Nigel did. He was shaking. I'm pretty sure he was more excited to see Grayson than I was. In the yard outside the house, we watched Grayson pace back and forth, muttering to himself. His beard was gone, but he was still wearing the same torn suit I had seen him wearing in New York City.

He gave no indication that he had seen us at the door yet, so I told Nigel to stand back out of sight. I was afraid Grayson might be spooked if he saw him.

Once Nigel was hidden, I called out, "You picked a fine time to come for a visit."

He stopped in his tracks and looked straight at me. In a nonchalant tone, he said, "I heard about the girl," then he walked past me into the living room without another word.

CALL ME ORPHEUS

Grayson would say nothing coherent about where he had been or how he found us. In response to our many questions, he would get agitated and ramble in what was either his own gibberish or a Turkic language that was unknown to me. The only intelligible words we could catch were 'drugs,' 'doctors,' and 'sleep.' The latter was spoken most frequently. Although he was clean shaven, he smelled as if he hadn't bathed in quite a long time.

"You're the wannabe psychologist, Nigel," I said. "What do you think we should we do with him?"

"Give the man what he's asking for." Nigel turned to Robert, who had followed us to the door, and said, "Give the man a room and let him sleep."

"And let him shower," Robert said, leading Grayson up the stairs.

I spent the rest of that morning in my own room, my head was spinning from the events of the past few days. Olivia, Officer Peachfuzz, Diane, and, of all people, Grayson. I was agitated and anxious, pacing and reading to calm my nerves.

I read Ovid's Latin account of Orpheus and Eurydice in his *Metamorphoses*. I knew it didn't end well for those lovers, but I related to Orpheus, whose bride, Eurydice, was taken from him so soon after they began their life together.

Orpheus' mother was a muse, and his father was a king. Orpheus was a lyrist, a singer, and a poet. His music was so beautiful that he could seduce animals, rocks, trees, and sometimes gods to do his bidding. He fell in love with the nymph, Eurydice. They were married, but they did not live happily ever after. In fact, most tales from Greek mythology didn't end favorably for the protagonists, which is probably why I was drawn to them. I took comfort in reading stories about individuals whose lives were far worse than mine.

As the story goes, on their wedding day, while walking in the grass with her bridesmaids, Eurydice stepped on a poisonous snake, and she died. Orpheus was devastated, but because he loved Eurydice so much, he decided to brave a journey to the Underworld to find his lover and bring her back to the land of the living. With his song and his poetry, he told the tale of a love that was ended too soon and a life that was cut short too cruelly, and he entreated Hades and his wife, Persephone, to 'lend' Eurydice back to him, until the 'span of her years is full.' Orpheus' music was so powerful, Milton would write centuries later, that he 'drew iron tears down Pluto's cheek and made Hell grant what love did seek.'

There was a catch, however. In Ovid's account, Orpheus would be permitted to lead Eurydice back to his world only if he trusted Hades' promise to release her. Orpheus had to go in front and trust she would be allowed to follow. If he ever looked back—even for a moment—to ensure she was on the road behind him, the offer would be rescinded, and she would be taken back to Hades for eternity. So, he made the long, dark journey with her walking silently behind him, but when he had almost reached daylight, he became anxious to see her again. He turned around, only to see her instantly slipping away, back to the Underworld; she was gone forever.

Why did I read that? I asked myself as I heard a firm knock on the door of my room. It was Nigel.

"Clay," he said, opening the door without waiting for me to respond, "the FBI is here, and they're ready to talk to you. Rendelman, too. Let's go."

Nigel led me down the stairs and into the living room, where three men were waiting in silence. Tobias Rendelman, the lawyer purportedly retained by my father, was facing the other two men. All three were stern-faced, and all three wore dark suits, in stark contrast to the relaxed New England décor of the Vermont bed and breakfast. To say they looked out of place would have been a gross understatement.

"I'm Special Agent James McClurg," said the older of the two agents in a raspy voice. He was balding with a reddish complexion and a red, bumpy, somewhat swollen nose. "This is Russell," he said, pointing his thumb at the man seated to his right on the floral loveseat they shared.

"First name or last?" Mr. Rendleman asked. He was taking notes on a yellow legal pad.

"Last," said the other agent. "I'm Special Agent Eldon Russell, of the Albany Field Office. Agent McClurg is from Boston."

"I'm Tobias Rendelman, and I represent Mr. Clayton Howard in this matter. He is participating in this interview of his own free will. You may ask him questions regarding the disappearance of Ms. Olivia Hunt, but he will only answer if I approve. Is that understood?"

"Crystal clear," said McClurg. "We love it when lawyers get involved.

Makes things go so smoothly."

Rendelman ignored the sarcasm and reminded me to keep my mouth shut until he told me I could speak.

Agent Russell spoke first. "Mr. Howard, we are aware that the Burlington police have already begun an investigation into the disappearance of Ms. Hunt and that you are a person of interest in their investigation."

"Have you taken over the investigation?" asked Nigel. "Kidnapping is a federal crime. You boys should be taking the lead on this."

"The Burlington Police are ruling this a homicide and are taking the lead. We have not yet decided whether to open a kidnapping investigation," said Russell. "That is why I asked for this interview."

"I'm here because Nigel told me this case involves King," said McClurg. "My person of interest is King."

"Mr. Howard," began Agent Russell, "would you tell me in your own words what happened here the night before last?"

"He will read a detailed statement I prepared after speaking with him at length," said the lawyer as he handed a printed sheet of paper to me and each of the agents, drawing a chortle from Agent McClurg.

After hearing my statement, McClurg said, "You're lucky to be alive. There aren't many who had dealings with 'Big Bill' Donahue and that idiot, Kilbane, and live to tell about it."

Agent Russell looked at McClurg and said, "The Burlington Police found no evidence that anyone else was in the room."

"No evidence? What about Clay's bruises? And the stun gun scars?" asked Nigel.

"The police have a theory, and they are tracking it down," Russel said.

"Donahue and Kilbane were spotted on surveillance video in town. I assure you, they didn't come to Burlington to enjoy the fall foliage," said Agent McClurg. "King only lets those pit bulls out of his kennel when he has something important to get done."

"And what about the phone?" I interjected, drawing a stern look from Rendelman.

"We have not yet seen the phone," said the agent from Albany. "We're waiting for the police to turn it over to us."

"And when you're finished looking over the phone, we expect its timely return to us," added Rendelman.

"Does it belong to your client?" Russell shot back.

"It does not, however, it was found in Ms. Hunt's room, and Mr. Howard wants to be sure we don't miss a message from her kidnappers."

"If we decide to investigate a kidnapping, we will monitor the phone twenty-four hours a day and follow up on any contact."

The lawyer looked at me, and I nodded in agreement.

"Very well," he said. "When will you formally decide whether to open a kidnapping investigation? As you are aware, time is of the essence."

"I would like to speak with the victim's mother, Mrs. Hayward," said Agent Russell. "I understand she is staying here, too?"

"I'll bring her," Nigel said.

"No need," said the agent, who was staring at me. "Tell me where to find her. I want to speak with her privately."

When he left, Agent McClurg took off his jacket and loosened his tie. "I thought he'd never leave," he said. "Listen, Mr. Howard, I'm sorry about your girlfriend. I hope she's OK, but it's highly unlikely; they're animals, every last one of them. But I'm not here for her. I'm here to find King and nail him to the wall, and you are going to help me do it."

Rendelman jumped in, "My client will do nothing of the kind, so long as he is considered a person of interest in Ms. Hunt's disappearance."

"That's a matter for the local police. Sadly, the FBI has no authority over them."

"The same can be said for my client. You have no authority to compel his cooperation."

"Any man would jump at the chance to get back at the guy who hurt his girlfriend," said McClurg. "What'd you say, Mr. Howard? Are you game for a little retribution?"

"My only concern is to get Olivia back. If you can catch the guys who attacked us, I'm all for locking them up, but that comes a distant second to securing Olivia's safe return."

"How do you propose to do that?" he asked. "Assuming she's still alive."

"I intend to find the jewels and make a trade." The idea sounded more foolish when I said it out loud.

McClurg squinted at me and pursed his lips, as if sizing me up for something. "Our goals might be different, but our plan has something in common. I think we can work together."

"Not while the police are threatening to arrest him for murder," said my lawyer. "You will have to convince them first."

I raised my hand toward Mr. Rendelman. "I'd be open to hearing about this commonality of method."

McClurg looked at Nigel and asked, "You haven't told him?"

Nigel shook his head.

"It's like this," the agent began. "The Brits have a replica of the Order of Saint Patrick in a museum in London. If we can guarantee its safe return, they are willing to loan it to us as part of a sting operation."

Nigel continued shaking his head. "This is a stupid idea," he said.

"Go on," I replied to Agent McClurg.

"It's not stupid. It's simple. You tell them you have the jewels, and when they arrange the drop off, you deliver them."

"How does that help either of us?" I asked.

"If the girl is still alive, and they are inclined to do so, they will release her. Although, I don't think that was ever part of their plan. They'd kill her before they let her testify against any of them."

"What's in it for you?" I asked him, ignoring his last remark. "I don't see how handing him fake jewels brings you any closer to getting your hands on this guy."

"In addition to delivering jewels, you will be carrying tracking devices—several of them. All I need is his location. We have more than enough on that guy to nail him with the death penalty many times over, and he knows it. We just don't know where to find him."

"You think they're going to give Clay an audience with King, himself? He won't get anywhere near King. Some lackey will examine the jewels, find they're fake, and kill both him and the girl. Game over."

"You're wrong, Nigel. I know King. I've been hunting him my whole career, which, by the way, should be over by now. As soon as this guy is sitting on death row, I'm done."

"Nigel makes two good points," I said to McClurg. "It seems unlikely that I'll be face-to-face with the boss. Furthermore, there's a pretty good chance they will be able to spot the fake."

"You're both wrong," the agent replied, pounding his fist on the edge of the sofa. "King is obsessed with these jewels, but for some reason, he has not made it known to his criminal network. It's a secret he is holding very close to the vest."

"Why?" Nigel asked.

"I wish I knew," said McClurg, "but his behavior makes him vulnerable. It's one of very few weaknesses I can exploit."

"You don't think he'll have someone check to make sure the goods are authentic?" Nigel continued.

"The Irish Crown Jewels have not been seen in over a hundred years. To authenticate the jewels, they will be using the same photographs and drawings the Brits used to make the replica. No one knows exactly what the real ones look like, so how can they spot a fake?"

"Did the Brits use all the same types of gemstones?" I asked. "The materials are well documented in detail."

"Rubies, emeralds, and Brazilian diamonds, Sterling silver, the works. Scotland Yard has some of the world's best forgers at their beck and call. All they need to do is knock a little time off a sentence, and presto, they have a Mona Lisa hanging in their office."

"If there is any chance this will bring Olivia back, I'll do it," I said.

"A word with you, Mr. Howard?" said the lawyer.

"No, sir. I appreciate what you're trying to do for me. But those fools on the local police department aren't going to back down. They won't believe I didn't kill Olivia until she is safe in my arms."

"A romantic?" McClurg, thumb pointed at me, asked Nigel. "There is the matter of insurance," he continued.

"Insurance?" I asked.

"Even fake jewelry is worth a lot of money when it's encrusted with diamonds, rubies, and emeralds, et cetera. The Brits tell me the replacement value is about a million bucks."

Nigel, who still seemed unconvinced, asked, "Is the United States government going to put up the money for a bond?"

"No insurer worth his salt would ever take that bet," McClurg replied. "We will need to self-insure it. And by 'we,' I mean 'you,' Mr. Howard. Uncle Sam is a little strapped for cash these days."

"Preposterous," exclaimed the lawyer. "You want everything from us and offer nothing in return."

"Not true," said the agent. "I offer retribution and the possibility of getting the girl back."

"What do you want to do, kid?" Nigel asked me. "It's your call."

I closed my eyes and tried to think. I could still see Olivia's pleading face from my dreams as she cried out, *'Hurry, Clay, Hurry!'* I opened my eyes and saw all the three men staring at me, "I agree with Nigel that this is a stupid idea."

McClurg let out an irate sigh.

"However, even a stupid plan is better than no plan. If we can't find the real jewels before the remaining eight days are up, we'll have no other recourse but to risk it."

"You could be killed," said Mr. Rendelman.

"I should be dead already, according to Agent McClurg," I said. "Olivia made me feel alive for the first time, and if I need to march into the pit of Hades to get her back, then that's what I'll do."

GRAYSON

Just then, Agent Russell came back into the room with Olivia's mother, who was looking apprehensive. He was carrying her suitcase, and he called out to Agent McClurg, "It's time to go."

"Go where?" he asked.

"Burlington PD called and asked to speak with the victim's mother. They feel it's best that she doesn't stay in this house, and I concur."

"Clayton," said Diane, "did you ever threaten to hurt my little girl? Why would she be afraid of you?"

"Olivia was never afraid of me, Diane. What in the world makes you think that?"

"The police told me so."

"That's enough, please, Ms. Hayward," interrupted Agent Russell. "There's nothing more we can say at this time." He put his arm around her shoulder and walked her to the front door. She looked small and defeated, and she left me without saying goodbye.

"I'll be going, too," said Agent McClurg to Nigel. "I'll work with my contact in England to get the replica shipped over."

When he had left, Nigel walked over to the lawyer and whispered in his ear.

"I was thinking the same thing," said Rendelman, who immediately started texting someone with his phone.

"What was that all about?" I asked Nigel.

"We're trying to keep you out of the Pit of Hades."

"Pit of Hades?" Grayson said, bounding down the stairs. "Count me out. I've been there before, and I have no desire to go back again."

"I thought you were sleeping," Nigel said.

"Maybe I am. Maybe you're just a specter in my nightmare," he replied. Grayson had cleaned himself up. He had showered and shaved and had changed clothes. The torn suit was gone; he was wearing faded jeans and a dark blue polo shirt.

"Where did you procure that clothing?" Mr. Rendelman asked. "You weren't carrying any bags when you arrived."

"I noticed that my pants were torn, but I seem to have misplaced my luggage. I found these clothes in the room next to mine. They fit remarkably well; don't you think?"

"He's wearing my clothes," I said. "Grayson, where have you been? How did you get here?"

"Here and there, there and here, thither and yon," he said, whimsically.

Nigel and Rendelman exchanged glances.

"I came at once I knew your need; I walked."

"Does he always talk like that?" the lawyer asked. "It's rather odd."

"It's iambic pentameter," I said. "As far back as I can remember, Grayson would break into a meter whenever he is under stress."

"Is it stress that drives me to speak in rhyme? Or does rhyme bespeak my unsettled mind?"

Nigel waved his arms in the air and said, "Enough of this nonsense. We've no time for this." Then he looked at me and said, "Clay, we need to take you away from this place."

"What are you talking about? I'm not going anywhere until we get some news about the search for Olivia. Furthermore, Grayson just showed up on my doorstep. I haven't talked to him in years."

Nigel grabbed my shoulders and said, "There's no time for talking, you need to go."

"Go where?" Grayson asked with surprising lucidity.

"France," Mr. Rendelman answered, showing Nigel a text message on his phone.

"France?" Grayson and I replied simultaneously.

Phillip and Stephanie ran down the stairs and into the living room, shouting, "A TV crew is setting up on the street in front of the house!"

"Back door it is, then," said Nigel with a nod of his head in that direction.

"France does not extradite prisoners who could potentially be tried in a case involving the death penalty," the lawyer answered. "Your father's jet is waiting at the airport in Albany. The pilots are preparing to take off as soon as you get on board."

"This is ridiculous," I said. "Why are we panicking all of a sudden? I didn't hurt Olivia. They can't possibly find any evidence against me because I didn't do it."

"The police have something, Clay," Nigel began. "I don't know what it is, but they wouldn't have alerted the media if they weren't planning to take action against you. And you saw the way Diane left. She was rattled. Furthermore, Tobias' associate has been hanging around the courthouse, and she just informed us that the police are in chambers with the judge."

"No doubt seeking a warrant for your arrest," Rendelman added.

"Don't let them arrest you, brother," Grayson said. "Don't let them take you alive."

"Grayson," I said. "I don't want to leave."

Grayson cupped my cheeks in his two hands and looked me directly in the eye. Then he began to speak in gibberish again. His face was stern, yet compassionate. I felt like he was offering needed words of advice from a loving, older brother.

"I can't comprehend a word you are saying," I replied, "but I think I understand your meaning."

A pounding on the door interrupted the moment. Stephanie looked out the window and said with astonishment, "There are four police cars on the front lawn. I'm so sorry, Clay."

"Quick! Go upstairs," Nigel whispered hoarsely in my ear.

Before I could move, and before any of us knew what was happening, Grayson opened the front door. I was pinned behind it, hidden in its shadow. Through the crack between the hinges, I could see several police officers with drawn weapons pointed at the door. Officer Peachfuzz was one of them. Clusters of reporters in the street behind them were watching and hastily trying to set up their cameras on tripods.

"Mr. Howard," said the officer who had pounded on the door, "we'd like a word with you." I couldn't see him, but his voice sounded familiar. "You don't look so good," he continued. "Trouble sleeping lately?"

I had no idea how Grayson would reply to the officer's question. The last thing I would have guessed is just what he said.

"I have COVID," he answered. Then he coughed a very convincing cough. "Would you like to talk inside, or should I go out there?"

The officer hesitated, and I heard him step back from the stoop. "Outside is better," he said.

"What would you like to talk about, officer?" Grayson said, following him. I could see Grayson's right arm and shoulder, but I couldn't see the cop.

"Tells us about Mr. Theocharides," the officer said.

"Dr. Theocharides was my Modern European History professor," Grayson said. "Oxford University, multiple PhDs. Brilliant man."

"We're talking about Vito Theocharides, the owner of an antique furniture store on Church Street. Seen him lately?"

"I've never seen him in my life."

"Really? We have witnesses who say you were outside his store just a few days ago. You were holding on to him and threatening him. You frightened him so badly that he ran away from his store with the door open."

"I don't remember doing that," Grayson said, "but I sometimes forget things."

"You then proceeded to break into the antique store, and you stole a valuable book and some jewels. Does that ring any bells?"

"I don't hear bells," he said as his voice trailed off. "I often hear birds, however. Nonetheless, if he ran away with the door open, then there was no breaking and entering. Isn't that right?"

"Your lawyer trained you well, Mr. Howard. But you're going to need more than a good lawyer. You're going to need a priest. Mr. Theocharides has been missing ever since he ran away from you, and we have reason to believe you killed him, too. Double murder means the death penalty. Do you understand me, Mr. Howard?"

"Not entirely, no," he said with a yawn. "Are we almost finished talking? I'm getting tired again."

"We're just getting started, Mr. Howard," said the voice of another officer. "Can you explain this?"

I couldn't see what he was being asked to explain, but I heard what sounded like the unfolding of a piece of paper.

"It's an email," he said, "from Amazon."

"It's an order confirmation dated last week. Ms. Hunt told her mother she was buying a few things because, and I quote, 'Clay wants me to go with him to Burlington again.'"

Grayson replied, "She bought an electric shaver for her trip to Vermont?"

"It's not a shaver, Mr. Howard. Take a closer look."

I risked pulling the door back toward me to widen the crack, which enabled me to see Grayson with his face just inches from the piece of paper the officer was holding in front of him.

"What is it?" he asked.

"It's a stun gun," replied the officer. "An electric device for women's self-defense. She purchased it because she needed protection."

"From whom?"

"We think she needed protection from you, Mr. Howard?" the officer asked. "Do you think she needed protection from you?"

Grayson looked up and scanned the sky as if he was watching a replay of the events of his life. He nodded his head and said, "She wouldn't be the first."

The officer was clearly surprised by his response. He threw the paper to the ground, reached for his handcuffs, and started to say something about being under arrest. However, as soon as Grayson saw the handcuffs, he pushed the officer, knocking him down. Then, Grayson began to run.

Another officer stepped in front of him, but Grayson, with surprising strength, punched him, knocking him to the ground as well. Then, just like he did in New York, he started to sprint with incredible quickness. The other officers pointed their guns at him and ordered him to freeze, but he kept running. When he was across the street, he stopped and turned, looked directly at the door where I was hiding, and said something unintelligible that sounded like 'so good car dash.' As he turned to run again, a single shot rang out, and Grayson fell face down on the neighbor's lawn.

"No!" I cried out and started to come around the door to run after him, but Nigel pulled me back. Covering my mouth with his hand, he kicked the door shut and wrestled me up the stairs and into a bedroom with a window looking over the street. I watched in horror as officers approached him, first with weapons drawn, then with boxes of first aid equipment. More police came and many neighbors joined the reporters lining the streets who were craning their necks to get a better look. I watched for any sign of movement by Grayson, but he was hidden from my view.

Moments later, an ambulance came, and the paramedics patiently removed the gurney from the vehicle and wheeled it toward Grayson. The paramedics' slow, deliberate action could only mean one thing. My brother was dead.

ESCAPE TO FRANCE

The irony wasn't lost on me. The story of Louisa's involvement with the Crown Jewels began in France, and France was where I was headed.

My brother had been shot dead in front of dozens of witnesses. Television reporters told their viewing audiences that cops killed the man who allegedly murdered the famous actress, Olivia Hunt, missing for over twenty-four hours. Footage of the shooting was aired on news programs across the country, preceded by a warning that some might find the video 'graphic and disturbing'—translation, 'stop what you're doing; you've got to see this.'

Getting to the plane proved much simpler than it would have been before the police shot Grayson. After the scene was photographed and his body was removed, all spectators, reporters, and even the police packed up and disappeared as quickly as they had arrived. Brian pulled the Mercedes van around to the back door, and before the dust settled, I was whisked away with no luggage and no telephone to the general aviation terminal of Albany International Airport, where the plane was waiting. The pilot filed a flight plan from Albany to Zurich, Switzerland, and submitted an electronic record to Customs and Border Protection that he was shuttling my father, Samuel Howard, back home, along with associates Nigel Smith and Tobias Rendelman.

My father's plane was larger than the Pennfield's plane, and more ostentatiously adorned. I believed it was my father's plane because Nigel told me so, but I knew beyond a doubt it wasn't he who picked out the model or its decorations. He was far too frugal for such profligate spending. On board with me, besides the crew, were only Nigel and Mr. Rendelman. The others stayed behind to deal with the aftermath of the shooting.

Shortly after takeoff, Nigel handed me his phone. "You tell him. I don't have the words."

"You want me to call my father and tell him his son is dead?"

I had never seen Nigel so shaken. His lips were trembling, and his head was twitching to one side. "He will want to know you're ok."

"My father hired you to keep Grayson and me away from him because we posed some kind of security risk. With Grayson gone, I thought you two might be happy because the threat is cut in half."

Nigel turned and backhanded me in the face.

"That's enough, gentlemen!" the lawyer shouted as he stood up and got between us. "You need to learn some self-control, Mr. Howard. You speak like a knee-jerk reflex. You have a bad habit of shooting off your mouth without the intervention of your brain."

"I've been called a jerk many times before, but never with such eloquence," I said, my face still stinging from the slap. "I apologize, Nigel, I ought not to have said that."

"You shouldn't even be thinking that," said Nigel. "That's the problem. You don't understand your father, and you haven't made any effort to try. Now, call the man. He's probably already seen the news that you were shot and killed."

I tapped the contact for S. Howard. He picked up before the second ring.

"What the hell happened, Nigel?" came the voice, familiar, yet stifled by tears.

"They killed Grayson," I said.

Silence followed. "Who is this?" he said, at last.

"It's me, Clayton," I said. "Dad, it was Grayson. He showed up at the house in Burlington shortly before the police came for me. Nigel was trying to hide me, but Grayson opened the door, and they thought he was me. When they got out the cuffs, he punched one of them and ran away. They shot him in the back."

"Cowards!" he shouted, before adding a string of profanities. "An unarmed man with severe mental illness, and they put a bullet in his back." He stopped speaking, but I could hear him sobbing. "I'm so sorry, Grayson," he said before blowing his nose. "Where are you now?" he asked me.

"I'm not sure," I replied. "Somewhere over the Atlantic, I suppose."

"Newfoundland," Nigel said, guessing the question that was asked.

"Put Nigel on," my father said.

Nigel took the phone from me and disappeared into a private bedroom in the back of the plane. I sat in the plush lounge chair across a small wooden table from Mr. Rendelman, who was furiously scribing notes on one of his numerous yellow legal pads.

"Why are we going to Zurich? I thought our destination was France." I asked him. He didn't answer me at first, so I tapped the table in front of him and repeated the question.

"I have no knowledge of the flight plan," he said carefully. "However, if you are correct, and I were to venture a guess, I would say it has something to do with returning the plane to where it belongs. Driving from Zurich to our destination in France will not take long."

After watching him fill up an entire page of legal paper and turn to a new leaf, I asked him, "If the police think I'm dead, then why did I need to leave?"

The lawyer answered without looking up or ceasing to write. "They will figure out their mistake soon enough."

"Why did I have to leave my phone and my luggage?" I asked.

"If the police ask for your personal effects, and your friends fail to turn them over, they will figure it out even sooner. I want to get you some place safe before they realize you left the country."

"Can't you get in trouble for this? Aren't you harboring a fugitive?"

He stopped writing and looked at me. "Are you a fugitive, Mr. Howard? Have you been arrested for something and failed to notify me?"

"Ah-hah," I said. "They never arrested me. They almost arrested Grayson, but not me."

"That's correct. There is presently no legal restriction against your leaving the country."

"Nigel told me the pilot recorded my name as Samuel Howard on his CBP manifest. Why didn't just use my own name?"

"I wouldn't know anything about that," Rendelman said, returning to his notes. "But if he did so, it seems like an understandable error, considering it's your father's plane."

"Plausible deniability?" I queried.

Rendelman didn't answer.

Nigel came out of the bedroom and sat down across the aisle from us. I swiveled my chair toward him and said, "You're right about one thing, Nigel, I don't understand my father. Why is he sticking his neck out for me? What's his angle?"

"I'm right about many things, kid," Nigel said. "I'm not sure I could explain it to you until you have a child of your own. He would do anything for you."

"Nigel, he hired you to keep me away from him."

"He hired me for protection. A man with that much money has a huge target on his back and faces many threats every time he leaves the house. He's made a lot of enemies, and he's worth a lot of ransom. You and your brother carry a lot of animosity toward him, so naturally, we had to consider you as threats. Grayson, more than you, though."

"Why do you keep saying that?" I asked.

"History," was all he would say in response.

"I still don't accept the proposition that he would do anything for us. He sent us away, Nigel. He chose that gold-digger over us and kicked us out of his life forever."

Nigel stared at me in silence, then shook his head and said, "Let he who has never done something stupid cast the first stone. You ever done something you later regretted?"

"Not something as bad as that," I shot back. "There's stupid and then there's horrible."

"There's regretful, and then there's horribly regretful, desperately regretful, utterly regretful. Be thankful you haven't been so stupid as to become horribly regretful, but don't for a moment think you don't have the capacity walk that same path."

His words stung nearly as much as his slap in my face. "How much longer before we get there?" I asked, unable to look him in the eye.

"About three more hours," Nigel said. "Go all the way to the back of the plane; you can use your father's bedroom. It'll be morning in Europe when we arrive."

I started to move in that direction when I heard Nigel's phone receive a text message.

"Hold on," he said. "We got something."

"Please elaborate," Mr. Rendelman said.

"We got a hit. A DNA sample submitted to GENmatch from a subscriber in Canada. There's a high probability that the subscriber is related to Louisa Peeters Mulholland."

SWISS CHARADE

"Turn the plane around!" I shouted to Nigel.

"Not going to happen," he said. "My orders are to bring you to Zurich. When we get there, we will meet with your father and formulate a plan of action. Go back and get some rest. You're going to need it."

"Not going to happen," I said. "I couldn't sleep now if my life depended on it."

"What if *her* life depended on it," Nigel said, handing me part of a pill he snapped in half. "You need sleep, and that's about three hours' worth. But get into bed before you take it; I don't feel like picking you up off the floor."

I don't know what pill he gave me, but the dosage was just right. When I awoke from a dreamless sleep, the sun was shining into the small windows of our plane. The engines were quiet; we were on the ground.

Outside my room, I could hear voices talking. Nigel was speaking in English to a man who was translating for another man in French. Through the cabin door I could tell the other two voices belonged to the Swiss border police who boarded the plane on our arrival. Nigel was explaining that Mr. Howard was sleeping in his cabin and asked to not be disturbed. The bilingual man was embellishing Nigel's remarks with assurances to the other that he knew this plane and its owner and could vouch for him. In his opinion, there was no need to wake Mr. Howard from his sleep. The other acquiesced, and they left the plane.

"Mr. Howard is awake," I said to Nigel as I opened the door. "What did you give me? I haven't slept so soundly in days."

Nigel was looking out the window, watching the border police officers drive away from our airplane. "It's better you don't know," he replied and glanced up at Tobias Rendelman, who rolled his eyes and walked away.

"Better pack your stuff, kid, we'll be going soon."

"I don't have any stuff, Nigel," I replied. "You made me leave everything in Vermont, and furthermore, the only place I want to go is on the other side of the Atlantic Ocean. We need to get to Canada."

"Patience, Clay, you need patience. Our people are already en route to Quebec City."

"Quebec City? Is that where the sample came from? That's where Louisa Peeters first set foot in North America. It totally makes sense that she would move back there to get away from Hugh Murphy's gang."

"The subscriber listed their address as Lac-Megantic, a couple hours away by car," Nigel replied. "Quebec City is the nearest airport, and that is where your friends and a couple of my staff are headed as we speak."

"Then why are we still speaking? Why aren't we headed there, too?"

"Because you don't have a passport, Mr. Howard," he replied. "And your friend, Philip Pennfield, said they need a day or two to get set up."

"Set up for what?"

"He didn't say. He just said something about Brian and Dr. Strange," Nigel replied, dismissively. "It doesn't matter. We can't go anywhere until we get you a passport that doesn't say Clayton Howard."

A familiar figure walked up the airstairs and poked his head in the front of the plane, "Hello Mr. Clayton," the man said in heavily accented English.

"Bonjour Etienne, ça faisait longtemps qu'on ne s'était pas vu," I answered my father's long-time driver and personal assistant. He had aged quite a bit since I'd seen him last, but his eyes were still bright and his face cheerful. Etienne was one of the few fond memories from my younger years.

"Long time no see," he stammered in English. "I improved, no?"

"You have, indeed."

Nigel and Mr. Rendelman trotted down the airstairs carrying their bags, and I followed, empty-handed. Etienne held open the rear door of my father's car, a Carmine Red Porsche Taycan Turbo S electric, so Nigel and Rendelman could enfold themselves into their seats.

He smiled and opened the front door for me, and said, "Or would you prefer to drive?"

I pointed to the passenger seat and said to him, "You'd better fasten your seat belt."

I silenced the protestations from the backseat, and once on Highway A51, I stomped on the accelerator, sending every loose object flying past them to the rear windshield. It had been years since I lived in my father's house on Susenbergstrasse in the elevated Zurichberg district, but muscle memory kicked in, and I had no trouble finding the inconspicuous garage built into the side of the hill under his home. The house was large by Swiss standards, although small compared to the home of billionaire bankers in America. It was a white three-story building with a red roof, the length of which ran perpendicular to the street. The top floor was mostly glass and afforded its inhabitants breathtaking views of downtown Zurich. Etienne clicked a button to open the garage door, and I turned around to see Nigel and Mr. Rendelman looking an usual shade of green.

"You fellows going to be OK?" I asked. Neither spoke, but they both nodded slightly in the affirmative. "Etienne told me this car has seven-hundred-fifty horsepower. That was quite a ride."

"Now I know what it feels like to be kicked by seven-hundred-fifty horses," mumbled Tobias.

"You're not driving us back to the airport," Nigel said.

"I'll be taking an Uber and flying commercial to New York," said the lawyer.

Etienne led us up the stairs into the house. He put his hand on the doorknob, smiled, and said to me, "Bienvenue à la maison, monsieur Clayton."

When he opened the door, I was standing face-to-face with my father in a cavernous sitting room. The walls were white and bare, except for markings left by paintings that formerly hung there. There was no rug on the wooden floor. The only furniture to be seen was a small cast-iron table with a marble top and a couple of matching cast iron chairs. The set was strikingly similar to the one on the patio of my New York townhome.

"Clayton," he said with quivering lips. He motioned as if he would hug me, but he backed off when he saw my face was cold as stone. "The Burlington police department called to tell me you were dead. I'm happy to confirm the report of your death was an exaggeration."

"No exaggeration where Grayson is concerned," I replied without emotion.

"That is regrettable. However, I'm glad you are out of reach from that moronic detective. God knows what would have happened if they had arrested you."

"I'd be in the custody of the Burlington Police Department, which is better than what I can say for Grayson or Olivia. God knows what kind of hell she is going through," I replied. "Every minute she is bound, gagged, and stuck in a closet—or worse, is a minute too long."

"I understand," he said. "And because the police still have the flip phone, we have no way of contacting the kidnappers about ransom."

"They only want the jewels," I countered. "We must find those jewels; it's our only way to save her. Nigel says we have a lead in Canada, but we need to get me a passport under an assumed name. How long will that take?"

My father and Nigel looked at each other. "We have been discussing how best to proceed, Clay," said my father. "There's a possibility, but it involves some risk."

"I'll take any risk I need to take," I said.

"That's a brave thing to say, kid, but stupid," Nigel interjected. "No offense, but if you get caught with a fake passport at the border, you'd have no chance to bring the jewels to King, even if we could find them. Everything hinges on you staying out of prison. And let's say we get you through the Canadian immigration inspection, there's still the matter of finding the jewels in Lac-Megantic. There are thousands of people who live in that town. We can't just go knocking on every door."

"Brian will think of a way to narrow the search. Life is a video game to him, and he's a genius at problems like this."

"You might be placing too much faith in that guy. He always seemed a bit odd to me," said my father.

"He is odd. But that's because he's one of the most creative game designers in the world. There is no one else like him. He started a PhD program in game theory at Princeton, but he was bored because his professors didn't know as much as he did."

"You still want to go through with it?" Nigel asked my father.

"I do."

"Is there any word on the passport?" Nigel asked.

"Nothing yet. We should know something in the morning."

"What passport?" I asked.

"Your brother's Swiss passport," said my father. "Grayson became a citizen of Switzerland after college."

"He never told me that," I said. "Why would he do that?"

"He fell head over heels in love with a woman from Central Asia. Kind of like you and Olivia. He couldn't live without her, but traveling there on an American passport brought a lot of unwanted attention. They wouldn't let him emigrate there, so he bought a place in Lugano and became Swiss."

"How does that help me?" I asked.

"The passport is a few years old, and you two look enough alike that I doubt anyone would challenge you, arriving on my private jet from Switzerland."

"Where is the passport now? Is it here?"

"I suspect he would have used his US passport when traveling to America and that his Swiss passport might be in his home in Lugano. I sent people down there to look for it."

My pulse quickened, and I immediately felt both relief that his passport might be within reach and shame for so rapidly taking advantage of the fact that my brother was dead. My father seemed to read my thoughts.

"He would want you to use it," he said. "It will buy you some time. You have seven days before the police realize the body in their morgue is not

Clayton, but Grayson Howard."

"Seven days?" I asked. "How do you know they'll figure it out in seven days?"

"Because I'm going to tell them. They asked me to come and identify your body for the record. I told them I had important business matters to attend to, but I would be there in seven days. At that time, I will tell them they killed my son, Grayson, not Clayton. Grayson deserves a proper burial, so I can't allow the charade to go on indefinitely. You have seven days to fly under the radar."

"I wish I were flying now," I said, "to Quebec City."

"I'm confident my people will find you a passport. I expect we'll be able to leave tomorrow."

"We?" I asked. "You're coming, too?"

He nodded slowly and said, "Sit down, son. It's time we talked."

GROUND TURBULENCE

Nigel and Rendelman followed Etienne out of the room, and they shut the door without saying a word.

My father and I were face-to-face across the marble tabletop, sitting in chairs that looked as if they belonged in an Italian piazza. My father, in his expensive banker's suit seemed out of place in the austere surroundings.

"I like what you've done to the place," I said.

"Save it," he replied. "She took all the furniture. I hated it, anyway. Nigel bought me this set of table and chairs for my birthday."

"You wanted to talk to me?" I said. It was phrased as a question, but I meant it more as a complaint.

"There are many things you don't know about Grayson and your mother," he began. "I take full responsibility, but it's time to set the record straight."

"Go ahead," I said. "Let's start with Roeun."

"I had to send your mother away," he began. "Her condition was getting worse, and the hospital at Normandy University was the best place in Europe offering treatment."

"You told me it was drugs."

"I lied."

"I'm shocked."

"Drug problems can be rehabilitated. Your mother's condition was untreatable," he said.

"You're telling me she had a terminal illness?"

"That's the truth."

"Why did you lie? And why should I believe you now?" I fired back.

"It wasn't exactly a lie. Your mother had become addicted to her

135

painkillers, but the real problem was the tumors."

"So, rather than tell her family she was dying, you told us she was a drug addict? You went out of your way to keep us from seeing her before she passed away? Why would you do that?"

He looked out the window, as if he was searching for an answer on the cityscape below us. "I didn't want you and Grayson to know about the cancer."

"Cancer?" I snapped. "It wasn't cancer you were hiding. You beat her up one too many times, didn't you? Everyone knows you broke her arm and her leg. What happened, did you finally go for the head?"

"To hell with you!" he shouted, pounding the table with his fists. "I should have left you in Vermont. So, any time a woman is injured, there must be a violent man in her life? That's what they believe. Is that what you believe?"

"To hell with me? To hell with *you*!" His response triggered uncontrollable fury. "I didn't ask you to send a lawyer; I didn't ask you to send a plane. I'm sitting here thousands of miles from where I want to be because *you* wanted it this way."

Searching the window again, his response was barely audible, "You're the only family I have left."

"I've found that I'm better off without family," I said.

He turned to look at me, and I could see tears in his eyes. "It all started with the broken bones," he said.

"What started?"

"First she broke her arm while cross-country skiing in Austria."

"Go on," I replied.

"It was strange because she wasn't going very fast when she fell, and she was wearing so many layers. It shouldn't have caused a broken bone."

"I remember when that happened. I was at school."

"Shortly after that, we were back here in Zurich, and she broke her leg tripping on the stairs coming up from the garage. I took her to the hospital, and when the doctors saw a woman with a cast on her arm coming to the Emergency Room with a fractured leg, they called the police."

"As would I," I said.

Closing his eyes and shaking his head, he replied, "If it hadn't been for a particularly sharp orthopedic resident, they probably would have arrested me on suspicion, just like the flatfoots in Burlington almost did to you."

"What did the doctor do?" I asked.

"He went back to the X-ray with a magnifying glass, then he ordered a bone biopsy. He figured out she had bone cancer."

It was my turn to search out the window. I took time to process this new information, then I asked, "Why didn't you tell me or Grayson any of this?"

"She didn't want you to worry. We thought it was treatable. They operated on the tumors and said chemo and radiation will keep them from coming back. But the pain was unbearable; that's when she became addicted to opioids."

"Obviously it didn't turn out that way. When did you realize her condition was terminal."

"This is where the story turns tragic," he said.

"What have I been hearing so far, a comedy?"

"Tumors started showing up in surprising places. The doctors said they didn't think the new tumors were metastatic. They were *de novo* tumors."

I stared at him harder. "What are you saying?"

"They did some genetic testing and discovered she had something called Li-Fraumeni Syndrome."

"I've never heard of it," I said.

"It's a mutation on a particular gene that causes fleshy tumors all over the body. It's rare, but it can affect people of all ages. Even young people, like your mother."

"You still haven't explained why you didn't tell us," I replied, growing frustrated with his smokescreen.

"It's a genetic disorder, Clayton. It's highly heritable."

"What are you saying?"

"We didn't want to ruin your lives worrying about whether you had it. Truth be told, not we, but me. It was my idea to keep it from you. Your mother wanted to bring you and Grayson in."

"You should have listened to her. So, what is your point, exactly? Do you think I could get this?"

"Maybe. You wouldn't be the first in your generation to have it."

"Grayson?"

"It doesn't always show up as bone tumors. Another common expression is glioblastomas."

"Grayson had a brain tumor?"

"Not one brain tumor, several tumors. His condition was terminal. In fact, no one expected him to live as long as he did."

I reflected on the short time I had with Grayson in Burlington. Even though we lived apart for so long, this was the first time I could truly say I missed him. "Is that why he acted strangely? The brain tumors caused his quirky behavior?"

"Apparently so," he replied. "However, you need to keep in mind that Grayson was always eccentric. I think the cancer only amplified his peculiarities."

"In Burlington, he spoke to me in gibberish. It sounded like a language, but if it was, it's one I had never heard before."

"Azerbaijani? His love interest was from Azerbaijan. That's why he got a Swiss passport."

"Maybe so," I said. "God, I miss him. I hardly knew him, but when he showed up at the inn and started doing his weird things, he was so lovable."

"Nigel told me he stepped outside to talk to the cops so you could get away."

I smiled and said, "You should have seen it; he was perfect. I still don't know if he was acting strange or just being strange, but the performance was priceless."

"Cost him his life," my father observed.

"I had no idea he had brain cancer," I sighed, "but that explains a lot."

"Maybe it was wrong of me to keep it from you, but I didn't want you to live your life worrying about it. It's either in your genes, or it's not. There's not a single thing you can do about it."

I closed my eyes and shook my head. "I suppose I could get a DNA test. Nigel seems to know a guy. But I just don't think I'm going to get it."

"Blind optimism works for some people," my father replied.

"Ha! I'm no optimist. My life has been so miserable that I can't imagine it ending any time soon. I envision a slow, dismal march toward the grave."

"You weren't always like this," he said. "When you were young you had visions of conquering the world. What happened to you?"

"My father told me he wished I hadn't been born. That kind of takes the wind out of ones' sails."

"I never said that," he insisted.

"Not in so many words, no. But you sent me away, paid me to stay away, and hired a security firm to keep me away. I read between the lines."

His face darkened and he sat in silence. He seemed to shrink before my eyes. I could tell he was drowning in his regrets, swirling in the torrent of decisions he could never unmake and actions he could never undo. Another person in my situation might have been moved by the pain of his struggle and stretched out a hand of mercy. But not me. Witnessing his turmoil only energized me to strike him harder.

"You're a fool," I said. "That girl you married had no interest in you, she only wanted your money. Everyone could see what you couldn't see. Everyone who knew you laughed at you behind your back and said, 'Look at the buffoon preening around with a girl half his age pretending not to notice how ridiculous he looks.'"

"As a child I looked up to you. I saw a brilliant businessman, a guy who came out of nowhere to take Europe's greatest bankers by storm. You were a superhero, my superhero, and I wanted nothing more than to be with you, to be like you. I wanted you to notice me and approve of me as your heir apparent, the Dauphin who would take over your empire. But you would have none of that. You sent me away to boarding school, making it clear you didn't want me in your life. Then you told me that my mother didn't want me in her life, either. You said she chose drugs over me. And then you put an exclamation mark on your sentence of rejection by choosing that girl over me and sending me away permanently."

My father pulled a handkerchief from a pocket in his jacket, wiped his eyes and blew his nose. "I had no idea you felt that way, Clayton," he mumbled. "All those expensive schools I sent you to, you never once expressed any interest in banking or economics. I thought you hated what I did. And during your holiday breaks, you hardly ever came home. You went traveling with your friends or visiting their homes. You spent more time with the Pennfields than you did with us."

He wasn't wrong, and I knew it. Back then, I tried to punish my parents for sending me away to school by never coming home. The logic of a wounded child.

"Look, Clayton, I made a lot of mistakes. But I've discovered that whenever I get buried in regret, the only way to dig my way out is to learn from what I did wrong."

"I don't get buried by regrets, either. I can usually find someone else to blame for my mistakes. You should try that."

"You avoid facing serious issues by making wise cracks. You think it keeps you free of entanglements, but you're kidding yourself. No one can get away from the consequences of their actions. Do you want to know what I learned from my brief marriage to my second wife?"

"Interior decoration?"

"I learned that you and your brother mean more to me than anything else in the world."

"Ha!" I laughed out loud. "Says the man who hired Nigel to keep us from getting anywhere near him."

He looked at me for a moment, expressionless, then said, "Grayson tried to kill me more than once."

"Come again?"

"I'm sure it was the tumors. Some glioblastomas grow in the frontal lobe of the brain and cause people to act with excessive aggression. Grayson shot me once. Haven't you noticed I walk with a limp? Another time, he tried to run me through with a medieval sword he stole from a museum in Bavaria. Then, he blew up my Mercedes. No one was in the car at the time, but that was when I realized I needed to keep him away."

"Assuming I believe all that, why did you tell Nigel to keep me away, too?"

"He thought Grayson would use you to get to me."

"I still don't buy this. It doesn't make sense. If I meant so much to you, why didn't you ever reach out to me? You could have called me. Apparently,

Nigel knew how to find me."

"How would you have responded?"

"I would have told you to go to hell."

He nodded in agreement. "I knew I had to wait for the right opportunity. Throughout my life, I've had to learn that timing is everything and patience is not just another virtue; patience is the queen of virtues."

"So, Olivia's kidnapping was your opportunity?"

"You need my help for the first time since you were five years old. I don't expect you to just forgive and forget the past. When this whole thing is over, you might tell me to go to hell, anyway. I get that. But you need my help now, and I'm going to give it. You were surprised to learn I was accompanying you to Canada. You'll be even more surprised to know I'm not leaving you until Olivia is back safely in your arms."

I reached for the handkerchief he had placed on the table. "You think we have a chance?"

"I'm a stubborn guy, Clayton. I've never failed to obtain what I set my mind to grasp—for good or for bad. We have more than a chance; we're going to succeed. I know it."

"Finding the jewels in Lac-Megantic will be like finding a needle in several thousand haystacks. Furthermore," I reminded him, "we only have seven days."

"God made the whole world in six," he said. "This will be like a walk in the park."

SIPS 'N SNIPS

After hours of searching, my father's people found Grayson's passport in an unlocked safe behind an original Van Gogh on his bedroom wall. So, a little over twenty-four hours after landing in Zurich, Nigel, my father, and I began the journey back across the Atlantic Ocean to Lesage International Airport in Quebec City, Canada. Mr. Rendelman, as promised, took a commercial flight to JFK.

It was late in the afternoon when we arrived in Lac-Megantic, a small town in eastern Quebec, only a few miles from the western border of Maine. The town sits on the northern shore of a long lake by the same name and is known for being the site of Canada's most serious railroad disaster.

A few years earlier, in the hours after midnight, an unattended freight train carrying millions of gallons of crude oil that had been parked atop a hill careened into town at sixty miles per hour and derailed, causing a fiery explosion in multiple tank cars. The blast radius was over a mile wide; more than half the downtown area was completely destroyed.

Events leading to the disaster had begun the night before. Firefighters had been called to put out a fire in the engine of that train hours earlier, and after dousing the flames, according to protocol, they shut the engine down. Unfortunately, they were unaware that the engine needed to be running in order to power the compressor that fed the airbrakes. With the engine off, the airbrakes slowly lost their ability to hold the train in place. Hours after responders had left the scene and gone to bed, the unwatched train began to trundle towards the city, reaching breakneck speed at the bottom of the hill.

As we approached the center of town, the devastation caused by this tragedy was still readily apparent. Whole neighborhoods were leveled. We witnessed several blocks where the only sign of habitation was a scorched patch of earth indicating it was once a family's home. There were few people on the sidewalks, and those faces we saw seemed to bear the telltale signs of post-traumatic stress.

Our driver pulled into the parking lot of a small building on Rue Papineau, near the marina. A makeshift sign read, 'A Venir: Café Belgique du Louisa.' Philip and Stephanie were the first to greet us when we emerged from the vehicle. They were wearing jeans and flannel shirts, and looked, quite uncharacteristically, as if they had been doing manual labor.

"What do you think?" Philip began, "We've been busy while you were hovering back and forth over the Atlantic."

"Louisa's Belgian Café?" I replied. "Are we opening a bistro or searching for the Irish Crown Jewels?"

"We could tell everyone this a DNA-testing center, but we thought it might garner unwanted attention. The café was Robert's idea. In fact, I think he truly has visions of relocating. Burlington has lost its charm for him and Roberta, and this place is so beautiful, except for all the burned-down homes."

Stephanie tapped me on shoulder, gave me a hug, and whispered, "Are you going to introduce us?"

I turned around to see my father carrying an overnight bag, standing next to Nigel behind me. "Stephanie," I said, "this is my father, Samuel Howard."

"Pleased to meet you, Mr. Howard," she said.

"Stephanie is my fiancée, Mr. Howard," said Philip. "It's been a long time, sir. I'm sorry for the loss of your son."

Nigel cleared his throat and said, "We should move inside."

"Right this way, gentlemen," said Stephanie. "Wait till you see what we've been up to."

Small bells above our heads rang as Stephanie opened the front door for us, and we were ushered into a square room with several small tables, each with wooden chairs stacked on top. As I surveyed the room, I was struck with a smell like burnt toast. "What are you cooking?" I asked.

"Robert has been roasting coffee all morning," Philip said, pointing to an enclosed area at the back of the shop, behind a glass display case.

"I'm confused," I replied.

Stephanie, full of excitement, jumped between us and said, "When Brian heard that we needed to figure out who in this community sent their DNA sample to the ancestry site—"

"Or more importantly, who from this community is related to Louisa Mulholland," Philip interrupted.

"Right," she continued, "Once he understood the problem, he went into a Dr. Strange-like trance, mumbling to himself and moving his head this way and that, evaluating scenarios only he could see. Literally, this went on for, like, ten minutes. Then he jumped up and said he figured out a plan that would give us the greatest probability of success."

"Uh-huh," said Nigel.

"Strange, indeed," said my father.

I glowered at them and said, "I told you, Brian is a genius when it comes to this sort of thing. If he says this is the best way forward, I believe him." Then, turning to Stephanie, I asked, "What's the plan?"

Beaming, she answered, "Free coffee samples at Food Lion."

"Free coffee samples?" I replied, second-guessing my confident stance. "That's the plan?"

"Free coffee samples *at Food Lion*. It's brilliant. Who, but Brian, could ever have thought of a plan like that?"

"For those of us not so 'brilliant' as Brian," my father said with air quotes, "can you, perhaps, give us a little more detail?"

Brian emerged from the back of the shop and said, "The Food Lion is the only grocery store in town, and on any given week is the establishment frequented by more local residents than any other."

"Hello, Brian," said my father. "It's been a long time."

Ignoring him, Brian continued, "A coffee sample gives us an easy way to capture a bit of DNA from the store's customers. Once we get them to take a drink from our marked cups, we can prep a sample and run a quick screening test in minutes."

"You're going to set up a lab outside the grocery store?" Nigel asked.

"No need for a lab," answered Brian. "The screening test is like a COVID rapid antigen test strip. Only, instead of detecting a virus, we designed it to react to snips from Louisa's DNA. In particular, it signals a match to the DNA sample submitted to the ancestry database."

"We call it operation sips and snips," laughed Philip.

"You call it that, babe," said Stephanie. "No one else, but you."

"We'll get the name and address of customers who drink the coffee, so we can follow up on the samples that turn up positive."

"Lots of false positives?" Nigel asked.

"There might be false positives, perhaps. I estimate no more than two false positives per correct hit."

"That sounds manageable," I said, "but how are you going to convince people to drink the coffee sample—and worse, how will you get them to give you their name and address?"

"Simple," said Brian. "We bribe them."

"Come again?" said Nigel.

Philip spoke up, "We give them a ten-dollar Food Lion coupon if they drink the coffee and give us their address."

"You're going to pay each customer ten dollars?" my father queried.

"Brian did the research using multiple AI chatbots and discovered how much one needs to pay the average consumer to surrender their name and address," said Stephanie.

"Eight dollars and forty-seven cents," said Brian. "Four-eighteen to get their phone number, but if you want a physical location, you need to up the ante."

"AI chatbots?" my father sighed. "This keeps getting better."

I raised my hand toward my father in a gesture for silence and asked, "Do we know if the proprietor of Food Lion will allow us to set up shop outside his door?"

"We took care of that this morning, Clay. Not to worry. Stephanie went in and charmed the guy into acquiescence," said Philip.

"Then Philip gave the man five thousand dollars for five hundred coupons," she said, producing a stack of small papers. "He's letting us put up a table and a pop-up canopy tent. We told him we need the tent for making coffee, but we'll also use it for extracting the samples and running the tests."

"Do we have enough test kits?" Nigel asked.

"We've completed a hundred, so far. There is another batch of a hundred drying in the back of the shop," Brian said. "We'll have at least five hundred by the time they open tomorrow morning."

My father looked at Nigel and asked, "What do you think?"

"Honestly, I think it might work. It's crazy, but we don't have time for a shoe-leather search. We only have five days left before you need to make an identification of Grayson's body."

"I wish I had your confidence," he said.

Nigel turned to Brian and asked, "Is there anything I can do to help?"

Brian looked at Philip and said, "You haven't asked him yet?"

"We'd like you to follow anyone who tests positive, just to make sure the address they gave us isn't fake," Philip stammered.

"What about the other thing?" Stephanie said to Philip.

"The other thing?" Nigel asked.

"Uh, Diane is coming," Philip said. "Robert let it slip that we have a lead on the jewels here in Lac-Megantic. She pleaded with him to let her come and help search."

Nigel shook his head. "I don't like it. Last time I saw her, she was believing what the police were feeding her. She thinks Clay is dead; I say let's keep it that way."

"That ship has sailed," said Brian. "She's on her way. We need you to determine how she'll respond when she learns Clay's not dead yet."

"Yet?" we asked in unison.

HOPE FOR DEAR LIFE

The next morning, my father and I were inside the pop-up tent at Food Lion, receiving instructions on how to analyze residue in discarded cups. Customers who sampled Robert's freshly roasted coffee from Café Belgique du Louisa handed their cup to Stephanie, who gave them a coupon and watched them write their name and address next to an innocuous-looking reference number that matched a barely visible number on the bottom of their cup. While they were writing their address, Stephanie casually passed their cup to Philip, who secreted it to us in the tent.

Inside the tent, our job was to prepare the sample and develop the test strip. We first used a permanent marker to accurately transcribe the cup's reference number onto the small plastic strip. Then we dipped a clean swab into an activating agent, wiped the rim of the cup, and soaked up the coffee backwash. Next, we dipped the swab into a small pipette containing a pale-yellow solution, agitated it for fifteen seconds, and placed four drops of the solution onto a circle on one end of the plastic strip. Then, we placed the sample to the side and moved on to the next coffee cup while the test strip developed. After seven minutes, if the circle on the opposite end of the strip turned pink, we would know the coffee had been sampled by a descendant of Louisa Peeters Mulholland.

"How's it going in here?" Brian asked us after we completed our first few cups.

My father replied before I had the chance. "It's been a long time since college biology lab, but I've done enough COVID tests to make me an expert. How about you, Clayton?"

"I'm going to need a whole lot of that coffee to stay awake."

Nigel seemed to be enjoying himself. "It does the heart good to see billionaires working for a change."

My father smiled and said, "I'll give you a thousand dollars to take my place."

"Not a chance," said Nigel. "My skills are needed elsewhere."

The samples began coming in at a rapid pace. The people of Lac-Megantic must have been true fans of coffee—or free groceries—because it seemed like the whole town was converging on our table that morning. By lunchtime, we had used up more than half of our five hundred test strips and ten-dollar coupons. Unfortunately, despite the rush, none of the test strips turned pink. Things slowed a bit in the afternoon, and we still had a handful of coupons remaining on the table at the end of the day, but still no positive test results in the tent.

I stood up, stretched my back, and groaned. My father had gone back to his hotel a few hours earlier, once the testing slowed down. Roberta came into the tent to fetch me and bring me back to the café.

"Looks like you survived your first day of manual labor," she said. "How does it feel?"

"When I close my eyes, all I can see are cotton swabs, like a forest of menacing trees converging on me to soak my head in a bucket."

"And to think, some people thought you couldn't manage it without going crazy."

"If I can find one pink spot, it will all be worth it. Every time I started feeling sorry for myself, I thought of Olivia and the horror she must be going through," I replied.

"Speaking of Olivia," Roberta said, "there is someone back at the café who is anxious to see that you're not really dead."

"Diane is here?"

"She is. When she got here, we told her about Grayson. She's shocked but relieved you're OK."

I nodded and said, "She must have assured Nigel she wasn't going to call the Burlington Police Department with the news."

"She's as angry with them as we are. They treated her horribly. In fact, they threatened her if she didn't sign a statement against you, they would name her as a person of interest in their investigation."

When we walked through the door of the café, Diane ran to me and threw her arms around me. We cried in each other's arms for several minutes while Roberta poured us glasses of sparkling water.

"I knew you were alive, Clay," she said. "I don't know how I knew, but I just knew."

"You have great intuition. What about Olivia?" I asked. "Do you have any insight about her?"

She paused for a moment, then nodded her head. "Yes," she said, wiping a tear, "she's alive. I can feel it. But we have to hurry."

"We're close, Diane. We're close. Somewhere in this town is someone related to Louisa Peeters Mulholland, and I believe they will know where the jewels are. At least, I have hope that they'll know."

"If hope is all we have, then we'll hold on to it for dear life," she replied. "I'm just thankful to be out of Burlington. That place is a madhouse."

"Stephanie has been watching the news and giving me updates," I said. "It seems like they're digging up the whole town looking for Olivia."

"They practically destroyed your friends' bed and breakfast," she sighed. "Did they tell you what the police did after they got a warrant?"

"No, they didn't say anything. They brought me my clothes and my briefcase, but they didn't say anything about a search warrant."

"We thought you'd been through enough already, Clay," said Roberta, handing me my glass. "We didn't want you to burden you with the goings-on at our inn."

Diane continued, "The night they shot you—I mean, your brother—they came back to the house with a warrant and kicked everyone out. They smashed walls and tore up floors. They threw clothes and furniture out into the front yard, then left the place in ruins when they found nothing."

"They're as desperate as we are to find Olivia, only for vastly different reasons," I said.

Diane nodded in agreement, then said, "They even impounded your car. Apparently, someone heard you—I mean, Grayson—say something about the dashboard of the car."

"He did," I replied. "He looked right at me as I was hiding behind the door, and he said, 'So good, car dash.' But he had been talking in gibberish the whole time he was there. My father thinks he might have been speaking Azerbaijani."

Roberta laughed. "Clayton Howard, master linguist, is flummoxed by the Turkic tongue. Your father's correct. Earlier in the day, I had asked Grayson what language he was speaking. He looked at me as if I was nuts, and said, 'Azerbaijani, of course.'"

"Those were his last words," I said. "I need to figure out what he said."

"Sogul Qardash," replied Roberta. "I looked it up. It means, 'Goodbye, brother.'"

"Goodbye to you, Grayson," I muttered after a moment. "I wish I had known you."

"It must have been quite a day working side-by-side with your father," Diane said. "I was told the two of you analyzed hundreds of samples together."

"Every once in a while, I looked over at him. He was always flustered, trying so hard to keep up the pace and make sure he didn't mix up the samples

147

or drop any pipettes. He was a wreck."

"You weren't the picture of calmness, either," added Roberta.

"True. But whenever I saw him so agitated and uncomfortable, I thought to myself that he wasn't there because he wanted to be there. He was only there because of me. He was suffering, and even though there was nothing in it for him, he showed up anyway."

Diane raised her right eyebrow and asked, "How did that feel?"

"It was… indescribable."

"Most kids experience that throughout childhood," Roberta said with a wistful smile.

"First time for me," I said.

"That's something you share with Olivia," Diane said. "Her father made so many promises to show up for recitals, concerts, and school plays, but something always came up. Sometimes, I think she took the job on television so her father could watch her perform."

"I wasn't very kind to her about acting on television," I said.

"You were an absolute cad," said Roberta.

"She told me so," said Diane, "but she couldn't stop talking about you. That's how I knew she was falling for you."

"It hurts so bad, Diane. I miss her so much."

"Clayton," she said, putting her hand on my arm, "if we don't find her, I don't want to go on living."

"Then let's find her," I said. "Tomorrow, we'll be back out there with another five hundred coupons and five hundred test strips. Hope is all we have, so we will hold on to it for dear life."

PINK

Word got out that some crazy promoters were giving away free coupons for groceries. The value of the giveaway seemed to increase as rumors spread. On our second day in front of Food Lion, many patrons were disappointed to find out our coupons were only good for ten dollars. Some were expecting fifty dollars, a hundred dollars, or free groceries for a year, but everyone seemed to recognize the value of a ten-dollar coupon was 'better than nothing.'

I was thankful that Brian anticipated the crowd to swell because we had already given away four hundred coupons by lunch time. He and Robert had prepared over eight hundred test strips the day before. I was also thankful for the addition of two other helpers, Diane and Roberta, who helped share the burden of analyzing samples. Nigel had told me that when my father returned to his hotel room the night before, he drained the minibar and fell asleep with his clothes on. As I watched him work, he looked as if he could have used a few more hours of sleep, or a few more bottles in his minibar.

At the end of day two, we looked even more haggard than we did the day before. I hugged my father for the first time in memory before he climbed into Nigel's rented car for the ride back to the hotel. "I'm thankful you are here. It means a lot to me," I said as he got in the car.

"I'm going to be a more generous tipper from this day forward," he said. "I never realized there were people who worked harder than me."

Food Lion's manager came out and brought us sandwiches from the deli. "You're coming back tomorrow, eh?" he said. I wasn't sure if it was a question or a request.

"You bet," said Roberta.

"You all work at the café?" he asked. He seemed puzzled by how many of us came out of the tent.

"It's a family business," Roberta said. "A real opportunity. We're excited about the future of this town."

"These people have been through a lot. Many are still living in temporary housing, trying to rebuild what was lost in the fire."

"Were you here during the fire?" she asked.

"No. I'm from Calgary. I came out here after the fire. The former manager lost his life in the fire, and I was hired to replace him. The people of this town really appreciate what you're doing—myself most of all, I guess. I don't know if you'll ever recoup the cost of all these coupons, but I can promise we'll never forget."

"Thanks for that," she said. "My husband and I aren't going to forget either."

Roberta was deep in thought as we drove back to the café, and I could tell she had taken the manager's words to heart. Once inside, she found Robert watching the coffee roaster, and they began a serious, quiet conversation.

"Something tells me the bed and breakfast will never reopen," I said to Diane.

"What are we doing here, Clay?" she asked. Her eyes were brimming with tears. "Two days of this, and over a thousand people tested. Are we sure they live in this town? Are we even sure the test works? I feel like we are wasting precious time."

"Let's give it a couple more days, Diane. I trust Brian's ability to work out solutions to complex problems. This was the solution that had the highest likelihood of success. I don't know any other way to find the person who sent in that sample to the ancestry website."

"How high was the highest likelihood?" she asked.

"He didn't say, and I didn't ask."

"I don't know how much more of this I can take."

The next day came with another flood of testing, but another drought of the sought-after results. By the end of day three, we had tested almost a quarter of the population of Lac-Megantic and given away almost a hundred fifty thousand dollars' worth of groceries.

Day four of our testing began with my father announcing he would be flying to Albany so he could identify the body of his son in the morgue at Burlington. In the parking lot of the hotel, I hugged him for the second time in my life. We were both weeping. Mourning the loss of a son and brother, mourning the loss of countless years. I tried to pull away, but he wouldn't let me go. He just held on to me, shaking.

"I wanted to be with you until the end. I wanted to be here when you found the jewels, and I wanted to be there when you found Olivia," he said as he wiped away tears. "But I need to take Grayson's body back to Switzerland. Any other course would raise too much suspicion."

"I understand, Dad," I said. "You're right. You're doing it to protect me. I get that."

"I'll come back as soon as I can," he said.

"I know you will. We still have a few days before the kidnappers are supposed to contact us, we'll find the jewels. They are somewhere in this town; I know it."

"Any idea how they will contact you? The police have their flip phone locked away in some evidence box."

"Nigel thinks they've been following us. He has no doubt they know how to reach us."

"Well, that's good. I guess. You be careful; these guys are killers," my father said.

"Yes, Dad. And I'll be sure to look both ways before crossing the road."

He got into the Uber without another word and sped off to the airport where his private jet was waiting to whisk him to Albany. For Grayson, it meant a proper burial, but for me, it meant the end of flying below the radar. I knew that within hours, the Burlington Police Department would discover I was no longer dead.

I arrived at the Food Lion well past opening. The morning rush was in full force, and Diane and Roberta were frantically trying to keep up with the analyses. When I entered the tent, they didn't look up. Roberta said, "About time," but that was all.

I organized my workstation and was about to begin tackling the backlog of sample cups when I happened to notice something out of the corner of my eye.

"Diane!" I shouted and pointed to the completed sample strips on her table.

"What?" she hissed without looking up from her work.

"It's pink! Look at it. It's pink. It's a match!"

I must have been talking loudly enough to be heard outside the tent because Stephanie came stomping in.

"What's going on in here?" she asked.

"Number 1623," I said, holding up the small plastic strip with a pink circle on one end. "Find the address and find Nigel!"

CUSTOMER 1623

Work inside the tent ground to a halt, and we stared at each other in wonder at what had just happened. Outside, Stephanie and Philip continued serving Robert's coffee and passing out coupons to Food Lion customers, so as to not arouse suspicion. Nigel, after looking at the video footage to see who drank out of cup number one thousand six hundred twenty-three, gathered his team and waited to follow the customer home.

Hours later, he returned with his report. "The address checks out," he began. "She didn't go straight home, but after running a few errands, she led us right to the duplex on Rue Lemieux. It's currently being rented by Maxime Tremblay and his wife, Emilie. The husband is thirty-seven years old, and Emilie is thirty-four. They have a twelve-year-old son named Olivier."

"You do good work," Philip said, nodding his approval.

"We're professionals," said Nigel.

"What happens next?" Stephanie asked him.

"We pay them a visit," I said. "Let's go."

"Wrong," Nigel shot back. "How do you think that would play out? 'Good afternoon, Mme Tremblay, we served you coffee at Food Lion, so, naturally, we'd like to ask you about your treasured family heirlooms.' She'd slam the door in your face and call the cops."

"Then, what do you propose?" asked Philip.

"Rendelman."

"Rendelman?" I asked.

"Rendelman calls them and follows up by FedExing a letter on his stationery. He tells them he represents a client with interest in antique jewelry, and his sources tell him they might know the whereabouts of a valuable piece. The client would be willing to pay handsomely, of course."

"How long is that going to take?" I asked.

"It could take a day or two."

"I like my way better. We could have the jewels in hand tonight."

"That's because you're not thinking straight, Clay," Nigel replied. "Look, I know you want to get Olivia back yesterday, but if we screw this up, the jewels might be out of our reach for good. It might take extra time, but it's the best way to get the outcome we're looking for."

"What do you think, Diane?" I asked.

"Nigel seems to know what he's doing, Clay. I think he's right. We can't just show up and ask for the jewels and expect her to hand them over."

"What if I show up and offer to hand over two million dollars in cash? Or three million, if that's what it takes. Don't you think that might persuade them?"

"I agree with Clay," said Philip.

"Of course you would," replied Nigel. "I keep telling you boys, not every problem can be solved with money. Not everyone can be bought and sold. You trusted Brian with this coffee-tasting scheme—"

"And it worked," I said.

Nigel continued, "And it worked. Now I'm asking you to trust me. I know what I'm doing, but you need to give me a few days to make it happen."

"Call in Rendelman," I said, "but I'm only giving you one day. If he gets nowhere, I'm marching up to the Tremblay home with a suitcase full of cash."

BOUGHT AND SOLD

News broke early the next day that the police in Burlington shot the wrong man, and the alleged murderer of the illustrious actress was still at large. Theories abounded as to where I might have gone. Tips began pouring in immediately from people claiming to have seen me or claiming to be me. The news reported on rumors that I had fled to Europe, or that I might have escaped to Canada. In a hurried press conference, the Burlington police chief tried to distract attention from these speculations by coyly implying they suspected I was at my home in New York City. He said he couldn't say too much because he didn't want to tip off the alleged killer. A worse acting performance, he could not have given.

"They totally know you're not in New York," said Robert, who was watching the news with me at the café.

"Europe and Canada, not bad detective work," I replied.

"Canada's a big country," he said.

I turned to him and asked, "How did you pay for all the supplies you needed for the coffee-tasting?"

"What do you mean?"

"I mean, the cups, the pens, the tent and tables—all the stuff we used at Food Lion."

He shrugged his shoulders, "I don't know. We bought the stuff at Walmart. I guess we used our credit card."

"Thought so."

"Wait," he shot back, "you don't think they traced you to Canada through my credit card do you?"

"I don't know, maybe. When they realized I wasn't dead, they would have gone to your bed and breakfast to ask if you'd seen me. When they realized you were gone, they might wonder if your absence was related to my disappearance and start digging around. If they found out you've been shopping at Walmart in Lac-Megantic, Canada, they might think it worthwhile to pay a visit."

Robert grew red in the face and shouted, "What are you saying? Are you blaming me for trying to help you?"

"Take it easy, Robert. I'm just pointing out the possibility of police tracking us here. I'm not blaming anyone."

"It sounds like blame to me. Now I know how your father feels."

"My father?"

"Yeah, you're always whining about the way he cursed you by handing you a couple billion dollars on your twenty-first birthday. I wish my father had been in the position to curse me like that."

Roberta came into the room as he was speaking. "What in the world is going on out here?" she asked.

"Robert is telling me I should be thankful for the way my father has treated me," I said.

"Clay is telling us we screwed up by paying with our credit card for the supplies we needed to keep his butt out of jail and help him find Olivia," Robert countered.

"All I was trying to say was that the police might now be aware that I am here in Lac-Megantic."

"The police? Here?" she asked, astonished. "How could they find you here?"

At that moment, Nigel came through the front door of the café. "Bad news, kid."

Robert and I looked at each other. "What now?" I asked.

"You probably heard that your father identified the body of Grayson Howard in the morgue at Burlington. So, the police are aware that you are alive, and a warrant has been issued for your arrest."

"Saw it on the news, yes." Robert answered.

"Well, I just got word from one of my people that the FBI has been in contact with the Sûreté du Québec and have been given permission to look for you in this province."

Robert was speechless. He slammed his fist on a table and marched behind the curtain into the back of the store. Roberta followed after him.

"What was that all about?" asked Nigel.

"He's mad at me because I said the police could track me from his credit card purchases at the Walmart down the street."

"That's called projection. It's blaming others for your mistakes in order to protect your ego," Nigel said, craning his neck to see past the open curtain. "However, in this case, it's a misplaced emotion."

"Meaning?"

"Meaning that's not what led them to Quebec."

"Are you sure?"

"A border control agent at Quebec City Airport's General Aviation Terminal made a notation in the record that the appearance of a Swiss citizen named Grayson Samuel Howard, arriving with his father on a private jet from Zurich, had changed significantly since his passport picture was taken. When Grayson's death was reported to Interpol, the Canadian system issued an alert."

I found the nearest chair and sat down. "I feel like a noose is tightening around my neck."

"A couple of months ago, I bet you never thought you'd be the subject of an international manhunt," Nigel said.

"A couple months ago, I was complaining my life was boring and had no purpose. Now, I'm engrossed in a struggle just to stay alive."

"And to rescue a dear friend," Nigel added. "While we are on the subject of your life being turned upside down, I have more news for you."

"I can't wait to hear it," I said.

"You once told me that the fortune your father gifted you sabotaged your life because it took away all meaning for your existence. Is that a fair summary?"

"Something like that, yes. More importantly, why do you ask?"

"The FBI has frozen your assets," Nigel answered. "You're currently broke. Unless you happen to have some cash in your pockets."

I grabbed the arms of my chair with sweaty palms. The room was spinning out of control, and I could taste bile in the back of my throat. "I can't breathe," was all I could utter.

What happened next was a bit of a blur. I recall hearing Nigel shout out for help, but the next thing I remember after that was lying on the floor looking up at the ornately crafted copper ceiling of the café, surprised I had never noticed it before.

"He's coming around," said Roberta as Robert put the cap back on a bottle of ammonia.

"Welcome back, Clay," said Robert. "You gave us quite a scare."

I sat up on the wooden floor and said, "Nigel scared me first. He told me I'm broke."

"I heard," said Robert. "I'm sorry for what I said earlier. I had no idea about any of that."

"I know," I said. "And I'm sorry I implied you were responsible for the police finding me. Nigel told me that's not what happened."

"Are you going to be OK, Clay?" asked Roberta.

"Robert was right when he chided me for disdaining the resources given me by my father. For the time being, I will have the opportunity to experience life without the safety net of abundant, instant money."

"Glass half-full, Clay?" Robert replied.

"I'm growing partial to the concept of optimism."

"Once this whole thing is over, and you're no longer hiding from the authorities," Robert said, "I'm going to post that quote with your name on it."

"Something tells me that once we find Olivia and my life is restored, I am going to have a new appreciation for undeserved blessings."

Nigel, who had been talking quietly on his phone, hung up and said, "We're in no position to claim victory yet. Rendelman just arrived. The Tremblay family agreed to meet with him this afternoon, but he doesn't share your newfound penchant for optimism."

"Your plan needs to work, Nigel," I replied. "I no longer have any suitcases full of cash to offer them."

CAN'T BUY ME LOVE

I spent that afternoon setting up a bedroom for myself in a windowless closet at the back of the café. Nigel's people cleared out my room in the hotel and brought my overnight bag and briefcase to me in my new accommodations. It would have been easy to feel sorry for myself for becoming suddenly penniless, but I knew, in my case, that would have been blatant hypocrisy. Try as I might, however, I couldn't shake the feeling of desperation that came over me when all my money was abruptly pushed out of reach. I suddenly found myself deep in the bottom of a well and powerless to climb out of it.

Opening Louisa's book for the first time in days, I read through her incredible story again and marveled at the bravery she displayed. She had no fortune to rest upon, in fact she struggled daily just to feed herself and her children. Through no fault of her own, her drunken husband led her into an association with criminals and they forced her to choose between life and death, between son and daughter.

"A life filled with challenges is not the utopia it's purported to be," I told Robert when he came to my closet to check on me.

"You were the only one who claimed it to be so," he said. "When Roberta and I bought the bed and breakfast, we had to sell everything we owned just to make the downpayment. Our first two years in business, we had the bankruptcy lawyer on speed dial. Things got so bad, I remember one time I wanted to buy a pack of gum, and I had to stop and ask Roberta if we could afford it. It was hell not knowing if I would be able to provide for my family."

"It must have been difficult to have me around," I replied.

"You didn't notice we never invited you to our Thanksgiving parties?"

"I noticed; I just figured you knew I wouldn't have come. I didn't think I had anything for which to be thankful."

Robert nodded and smiled. "Nigel told me you should come out front. He wants to talk with all of us."

When I walked through the curtain to the front of the shop, I saw Philip, Stephanie, Diane, and Roberta seated around one of the larger tables of the café. Brian was seated by the window, game console in hand, once again. Nigel was seated alone at one of the other tables, looking grim. "Good news is, we found them. This was no false positive. They do, in fact, have the jewels."

"There must be bad news, or you wouldn't be looking like that," Stephanie said.

Nigel continued, "Bad news is, they told Tobias to leave and never come back," he said. His voice was breaking as he said it. "I'm sorry."

I was shocked. Tobias Rendelman, Esq., of New York City exudes gravitas. If anyone could convince Emilie and Maxime Tremblay he was a trustworthy man, a man to be taken seriously, it was him. "Where is he now?" I asked.

"Anywhere but here," Nigel answered. "A warrant for your arrest has been issued, so he would be compelled to report to the police any and all contact with you. In fact, his official recommendation to you is to turn yourself in to the authorities for processing."

"What's the message, unofficially?"

"He received another burner phone in the mail from an anonymous sender," Nigel replied, removing a flip phone from his pocket that was identical to the one Detective Larkin found on Olivia's bed.

"Is there a message for me?" I asked, taking the phone from Nigel's hand.

I didn't wait for a response but turned on the phone and read a text message from an unknown number. 'You are more stupid than we thought. We told you no cops. You have two more days. When I call you better have what we want. Or else you'll never see what you want. Try to stay out of jail. Idiot.'

"This message was sent yesterday," Nigel said, "which means we have until this time tomorrow."

"Assuming the FBI doesn't find us first," said Robert.

"It's time I pay a visit to the Tremblay family, myself," I said. "Rue Lemieux is only a mile from here. I'm sure I can get there without the Feds spotting me."

"I'm coming with you," added Diane.

"They're not at home," said Nigel. "We're watching the place. They went out and locked the doors. They're probably out to enjoy all the Friday night life Lac-Megantic has to offer."

"Why did you mention the locked doors, Nigel?" Philip asked. "Are we considering helping ourselves to what we need?"

"Just for the sake of completion, young man," he answered. "It's the way we work. We have no plans to break the law at this time."

"We don't need to steal those jewels," I said. "I just need to reason with them."

"I'm pretty sure that lawyer tried reasoning, Clay," said Philip. "He's pretty good at it. No, I think now is the time for other methods."

Stephanie looked at him askance. "Philip Pennfield, sometimes you scare me."

"What would you have us do? Those jewels are practically within reach. The only thing between us is a lock that I posit Nigel could open blindfolded. Should we let Olivia die and Clay get the blame, all because we don't want to break into a shoddy duplex in Canada? That's absurd."

Brian spoke for the first time. "Philip's plan is feasible in the short run, but there are downstream consequences that make it untenable," he said, without stopping his gameplay.

"Clayton is right," said Diane, ignoring Brian. "You know I want my Olivia back with all my heart, but I know breaking in and stealing those jewels is not the right thing to do. There must be another way."

"We tried your way, Nigel," I said. "Now it's time to try mine."

He nodded thoughtfully and answered, "OK, kid. We'll do it your way. As soon as the family returns home, I'll let you know."

HEIRLOOMS

Nigel knocked on my closet door early the next morning. "It stinks in here," he said.

"It's a bit musty, but better than a jail cell," I replied. "Did they come home?"

"They were at a bar in Laval-Nord and stumbled home pretty late last night. Go ahead and get dressed. Breakfast is served. We'll give them a little time, then catch them before they decide to go out again."

When I walked out to the front of the store, the tables were laden with plates of crêpes, dusted with confectioners' sugar and smothered in maple syrup. "Courtesy of the manager at Food Lion," Roberta told me. Robert had brewed some of his home-roasted coffee, and he served it in paper cups with the numbers one-six-two-three written on the bottom.

"Here's to a successful visit to the Tremblays," Philip said, standing and raising his cup. "If that doesn't work, smash and grab is always a useful plan-B."

Nigel asked me, "Speaking of plans; what's yours?"

"I'm going to ring the doorbell and play it by ear," I replied with a mouthful of crêpes.

Diane asked Nigel, "Why did they refuse to do business with Mr. Rendelman? Did he tell you anything?"

"He said they weren't interested in selling—it wasn't a question of money; they simply don't care to part with the jewels."

"There's a difference between the promise of money and the sight of money. I like Clay's idea. Bring suitcases full of cash," said Philip.

"Which is no longer an option, thanks to the FBI," I said. "No. We need another strategy."

"Well, you better come up with one quick," said Nigel, looking at his phone. "They're up."

I suddenly felt like I would vomit, and the thought of all the crêpes I had just eaten didn't help. Diane saw the color leaving my face and said, "You can do this, Clay. There's no one I trust more to fight for my little girl."

I whispered in her ear, "I don't know what I'm doing."

"Sure, you do," she said in a hoarse voice that reminded me of Olivia. "You're going to ring the doorbell and play it by ear."

"Bring your stuff, kid," said Nigel. "Leave no trace. With Feds on the loose, you have to be ready to pivot."

"You mean he might not be able to come back here?" asked Stephanie.

"One of my guys spotted an outlier at Food Lion," he said.

"What's an outlier?" asked Robert.

"A person who looks out of place. Could be nothing; maybe just an officious local. But this individual acted in a manner consistent with your stereotypical FBI agent."

"If the FBI is at Food Lion, it's only a matter of time before they come looking for our café," said Roberta.

"Therefore, we want no indication that Clayton Howard was ever here."

I grabbed my overnight bag and my briefcase and darted into the back seat of Nigel's car. Diane sat in front for the short drive to Rue Lemieux. Once there, Nigel waited in the car while Diane and I approached the front door on the left side of the duplex.

The lighted doorbell was warm to my touch. Before pressing it, I said to Diane, "Of all the houses in the world, we found the one that contains the Crown Jewels of Ireland. For over a hundred years, people have been searching for them, and against all odds, we found them."

"Kind of boosts your confidence, doesn't it?"

"There's no way we came this far, only to fail now," I said.

I rang the doorbell.

The heavy front door opened with a swoosh of air, and a forty-something woman clad in yellow gingham pajamas with fluffy rabbit slippers stared at us through the glass storm door. She was not fat, but not especially thin either. Her hair was tousled, and her eyes were red. "Bonjour, que veux-tu?" she said.

"Bonjour, Madame Tremblay," I began, then shifting to English for Diane's sake, I said, "My name is Clay Howard, and this is Diane Hayward. May we come in? We have something important we need to discuss with you."

"It's not a good time," she replied in accented English. "Come back another day." Then suddenly, as if a thought occurred to her at that moment, she started looking behind us and around us.

Assuming she was searching for Tobias Rendelman, I smiled and said, "There's no one else here. Please, Mrs. Tremblay, may I call you Emilie? It's vital that we talk to you. I'm sorry to bother you at this hour. We wouldn't have come if it weren't critically important."

A man appeared behind her. Maxime, I surmised. He was wearing boxer shorts and a tank top tee shirt. "Is this the guy?" he asked her in French.

"Je ne suis pas lui," I told him. "I know that guy. I told him not to come here, but he came anyway. Please, let us in. It's a matter of life and death."

They looked at each other, puzzled by the sight of a man and a woman outside their door on a Saturday morning, declaring a life-and-death emergency. Without speaking, the man opened the door and nodded with his head.

"If it's about my grandmother's badge and pin, I already told the other man I am not interested in selling them," the woman said, as Diane and I sat down together on their sofa. Mrs. Tremblay sat on a wooden rocker near the window, and her husband put on a robe and sat in a recliner by the television. The room was small, and the furnishings were sparse and mismatched. There were no decorations on any of the walls.

"Do you know how Deirdre Mulholland came to possess the Crown Jewels of Ireland?" I asked.

Mr. Tremblay's jaw dropped. "Crown Jewels of Ireland?"

"There's no such thing as Crown Jewels of Ireland, Maxime. They have the same king we do," she said to him. Turning to me, she asked, "And how do you know my grandmother's maiden name? Who are you?"

"I told you; my name is Clay Howard."

"And I'm Diane Hayward," said Diane.

"I've heard that name," she said. "Where?"

Her husband sat up straight in his lounge chair. "You're the guy who killed the movie star. We were watching it on the news. The Sûreté said you are hiding in Quebec!"

"He didn't kill anybody," said Diane. "Olivia Hunt is my daughter. She's alive. At least we hope so. She was kidnapped by hoodlums, and the police blamed him because they were too stupid or too lazy to go after the real criminals."

It took the Tremblays several minutes to take this in, then Emilie asked, "So, what does this have to do with us? Why are you asking about my grandmother's jewelry?"

"Because the kidnappers want those jewels. It's the only ransom they will accept," I answered.

"There has to be some mistake, monsieur," said Emilie. "My grandmother's badge and pin are just rhinestones and colored glass. They're precious to me because they are my only connection to my past, but they certainly aren't anybody's crown jewels."

"And who ever heard of Ireland having crown jewels? My wife is right. Ireland doesn't have a king," said Maxime.

"They weren't to be worn by a king, they were given by the King of England, William IV, to the Lord Lieutenant of Ireland, and they weren't called the Crown Jewels of Ireland until much later. Their real name is the Order of Saint Patrick."

At the name Saint Patrick, Emilie gasped. Her eyes widened and her face lost its color. "Grandma used to say that her mother told her the badge and pin belonged to Saint Patrick."

"The regalia of the Order of Saint Patrick were crafted in the early nineteenth century," I said. "They didn't belong to Saint Patrick; they were just named for him."

"I still can't believe my grandmother's trinkets are part of some famous collection of jewels. How in the world did she get them?"

Diane reached into her bag and pulled out a parcel about the size of a book, wrapped in brown paper. She unrolled the paper to reveal a small wooden box, richly stained, with broken hinges in the back. She pulled the top apart from the bottom to reveal a cobalt blue velvet interior with two impressions, a star-shape, four inches in diameter, and an oval, about three inches wide and six inches long. "This is the box made for the jewels, Mrs. Tremblay. Does it look about right to you?"

"What do you want from me?" she asked, suddenly defensive. "Why are you here?"

"We need your grandmother's jewels to rescue my daughter," Diane answered. "Please, you have to help us. You're our only hope."

"I know we're asking a lot," I said. "If there were any other way, we wouldn't have come."

"You have no idea what you're asking!" she shouted. "Those jewels are the only thing I have from my childhood. You have no idea what price we nearly paid for them."

Maxime shifted in his chair and said, "You don't need to go there, mon chéri."

"Please, tell us," I said.

"You must know about the fire in Lac-Megantic," she replied.

"Yes, of course. Such a tragedy. I was profoundly saddened when I read about it."

"Our home was on Rue Milette, between the train tracks and the lake. The night of the fire, we were awakened by explosions. We watched in horror as our neighbor's home started steaming and then suddenly burst into flames, like a guimauve."

"Like a what?" Diane asked.

"Marshmallow," I told her.

Emilie continued, "As I was looking out the window, my hand touched the glass, and it burned me. That's when I knew we needed to run. We woke up our son, Olivier, and started out the door. Then I remembered my grandmother's jewels."

"She was more afraid of losing the jewels than she was of burning in the fire, monsieur," said Maxime. "I knew I had to go back for them."

"He was so brave, and so stupid," she said with a tear and a smile. "He went back into our house, but by the time he came out, poof, another... marshmallow."

"Oh dear," said Diane. "I can see that you made it out, but what about your dear boy?"

"Olivier was outside with me, and yes, Maxime made it out. He was badly burned, but he's alive. Thank God."

"Indeed," I said, nodding and unsure how to proceed.

"So, you see," continued Emilie, "these jewels mean the world to me. I don't care if they are real or not; I don't care if they came from the King of England or from a factory in China."

"But my Olivia, Mrs. Tremblay!" pleaded Diane. "If your Olivier were inside the burning house, you wouldn't go back for the jewels. You would save him first. Now, it's my Olivia inside the burning home and only your jewels can get her out."

"I'm truly sorry about your daughter, madame, but I am not responsible for her kidnapping. I simply will not part with my grandmother's jewels. I hope you can save her, but you must find another way. These heirlooms are my only connection to my past."

"Interesting that you should say that!" I exclaimed, suddenly inspired. "I never answered your question when you asked how I knew your grandmother's name. Aren't you curious how I knew she was in possession of these jewels?"

"Precisely," said Maxime. "I was wondering that very thing."

"If you would indulge me one moment, I think I have found a win-win solution to this impasse."

CONNECTION TO THE PAST

I excused myself from their living room and ran toward Nigel's waiting car. Nigel saw me and jumped out of the car, ready to spring into action. "Where's Diane?" he shouted at me.

"They're inside. Everything's fine. I just need my briefcase."

"You almost gave me a heart attack, kid. What's taking so long in there? We don't have much time."

"Patience, kid," I said to him, grabbing my bag from the back seat. "Isn't that what you always tell me?"

He looked like he was about to say something, then stopped. He nodded his head in agreement, and said, "Go, but hurry it up," as I returned to the house.

"Thank you for waiting," I said as I took my seat on the couch. The Tremblay's eyes were on me as I began to tell the story of a Belgian woman named Louisa Peeters, whose father died preventing the Irish Crown Jewels from falling into the hands of German spies in World War One.

"As her father lay dying from injuries he sustained in a car crash in Brest, France, he gave Louisa the jewels and told her to bring them back to England, to be returned to their rightful owner," I began. "But the Germans followed her to England, so she sailed for the New World, landing in Quebec City. Aboard ship, she met an Irish immigrant named Michael, who brought her to Burlington, Vermont to become his bride, Mrs. Michael Mulholland."

"Mon arrière-grand-mère!" Emilie marveled.

"Yes, Louisa Peeters Mulholland was your great-grandmother."

"Burlington Vermont is where they said the actress was killed!" Maxime pointed out.

"The Mulhollands lived on what was then Grafton Street in Burlington.

166

In that very home were born to them two children, Deirdre…." I paused for effect, then added, "…and Edward."

"Edward? I think you're mistaken. My grandmother was an only child; she always said so."

"Your grandmother had a brother named Edward. Louisa had to flee Burlington because of those jewels, but she couldn't bring both children with her. She had to make an impossible choice. In order to save her family, she had to divide them. She took Deirdre and the jewels, leaving Edward with his father in Burlington."

Emilie looked out the window into the trees and said, "I can't believe it. Can it be true?"

"Edward Mulholland never left their home in Burlington. He never married, never had children. He lived until the ripe old age of ninety-something and was murdered in his bedroom—the same room in which he and your grandmother were born—probably by people tearing the house apart looking for these jewels," I said, pointing to the box Diane was still holding.

Emilie stood up and paced about the room, waving her arms up and down. "How can you know so much about my family, Mr. Howard? Why should I believe you? How can any of this be true?"

I pulled Louisa's book from my briefcase, stood up, and presented it to Emilie. "This is the true connection to your past, Emilie. This book was written by your great-grandmother, in her own hand." I opened to the pages where she described the painful decision she was forced to make. "Look at these blotches in the ink made by her own teardrops."

Emilie swayed as if she would faint, and I helped her back into her rocking chair. Maxime, with some difficulty, stood up from his lounge chair and stood behind her chair to see it for himself. She opened the book slowly and wiped her own tears with her sleeve as she turned the pages. With her other hand, she ran her fingers over the text, feeling the imprint of Louisa's sharp-tipped pen.

"And look," I continued, not missing a beat. "These are letters written by your great grandmother to your grandmother's brother, your grand-oncle."

Emilie took the letters in her hands and gaped at the trove of family history that had fallen into her lap. "I'm utterly speechless, monsieur," she said, finally.

"I will give all of this to you, along with my translation into contemporary English, in exchange for your grandmother's badge and pendant," I said.

She looked over her shoulder at Maxime, and he shrugged his shoulders, uncertain how to counsel her.

"Furthermore," I said, "although I know you are not interested in exchanging the jewels for money, if you are willing to exchange the jewels for my book and my letters, I will add a financial benefit as well."

Maxime jumped on my question, and asked, "How much of a benefit?"

"May I ask, Maxime, why you have not yet rebuilt your home on Rue Milette?"

He staggered back to his lounge chair and said, "That's a difficult question to answer."

"Surely, you were given a cash settlement after the train accident, no?"

"We were, yes. We hired a contractor to clear out what was left of our home and to rebuild it. He promised to add all kinds of modern upgrades. The deal was too good to be true," he replied. Then, he pointed to his wife and said, "Emilie warned me, but several of our neighbors had signed on with the same contractor—guys who knew a lot more about this sort of thing than I did. I told her she was being overly suspicious, and I signed on the dotted line. I pre-paid all of what we had been given by the insurance company."

"Oh my," said Diane. "What happened?"

Emilie looked up from Louisa's manuscript as if jolted awake from a daydream. "After the demolition was complete, the contractor came to us for more money. There was fine print in the contract, stipulating the money we paid only covered demolition expenses. If we wanted a new home built, we had to pay more—far more than we could afford."

"I've been on disability since the fire," Maxime added, his eyes searching the ground before his chair.

"How many of your friends were victimized by this scoundrel?" I asked.

"Four," he said. "The guy scammed more people, but there were five of us on my block. I'm not sure they would count me as their friend anymore, seeing as how they blame me for introducing them to this pirate."

"Then here is my offer: in addition to the manuscript, the letters, and the translation, I will pay to rebuild your home and the home of your four soon-to-be-reconciled friends," I said.

Maxime burst into tears and stumbled backwards. Bawling profusely, he cried out in groans that shook me to the core. Emilie placed the book and the letters on her rocking chair and walked into another room. Diane looked around and found some tissues, which she gave to Maxime, whose face was covered with mucus and tears. Diane and I needed the tissues, as well.

Emilie returned carrying a brown canvas pouch, tied at its mouth with a black string. She opened the pouch and removed an eight-pointed silver star encrusted with hundreds of tiny diamonds, with a cross of rubies and a crown of emeralds in the center. She handed the star to me, and it was my turn to swoon. Next, she handed Diane a pendant suspended from a silver harp and decorated in diamonds, rubies, and emeralds.

"The box," I croaked to Diane. "Let's reunite them with the box."

After many tears were shed by all four of us in that living room, Emilie went to the kitchen and brought each of us a glass of wine. "I know it's early," she said, "but this moment requires a toast."

I let them know that due my situation at that time, with criminal charges having been filed against me, I was unable to say when I could transfer the funds. I promised, however, that once cleared, I would see to it that a reputable builder would carry out construction of all five of the demolished homes.

With Diane clinging to the box that contained the keys to rescuing Olivia, I told the Tremblays that we needed to be going. As I was walking to the door, Emilie asked, "One thing I don't understand is, how did that man find us? How did he know I had the jewels?"

I had been hoping to avoid that question. "Uh," was all I could think to say.

"Out with it, Clay," said Diane. "They deserve to know."

"He didn't find you. I did."

"But you said you didn't send him."

"I didn't. I wanted to come here yesterday, but the guy waiting in my car persuaded me to send Mr. Rendelman, instead."

"So, how did you find me?" she asked.

"It's embarrassing, Madame Tremblay, because it involves an invasion of your privacy."

"What kind of invasion of privacy?" interjected Maxime.

To Emilie, I said, "Do you remember sampling some coffee at Food Lion?"

She thought for a moment, then said. "Yes, I do. In the parking lot. I told the woman I don't really care for coffee. I only did it for the ten-dollar coupon. What has that to do with this?"

"We tested the cup for a specific snip of DNA that showed a relationship to Louisa Peeters Mulholland."

"You what?" she asked.

"We were able to extract DNA samples from the envelopes that contained the letters I just gave you."

Emilie just continued staring at me.

"Louisa licked the envelopes to seal them, and we were able to get some good samples of DNA from them. Then, we searched DNA databases for people alive today who share common unique sequences of DNA, called snips. It took a while, but we found an anonymous match."

"If it was anonymous, how did it lead you to me?"

"All we knew was that the sample was sent to an ancestry site from someone who claimed to live in Lac-Megantic, Quebec. We had to narrow it down, so that's when we came up with the plan to check samples from a coffee taste-test at the grocery store."

"Did the Food Lion manager know what you were doing?" Maxime asked, glowering at me with furrowed brow. The friendly atmosphere had dissipated.

"All the manager knew was that we were giving his customers samples of our coffee and a ten-dollar coupon for his store."

Emilie looked at me askance. "I never gave a DNA sample to an ancestry site," she said.

At this, Maxime said, "Uh-oh."

"Did you give a sample?" she asked.

"Couldn't have been him," I said, "he doesn't share any of your DNA. But there is someone who does."

"Olivier? Olivier sent DNA to an ancestry website?" she said to Maxime.

"He asked me if he could do it. It didn't cost much, so I let him pay with my credit card. I thought it was just a little gimmick, like a horoscope or a Chinese fortune cookie."

"How could you do that without telling me?" she asked him.

"You know Olivier inherited your curiosity about the past. I thought, with all his stuff burning in the fire, it was the least we could do for him."

"We can talk about this later," she said to her husband. Then she turned to me and was about to speak when Diane cut her off.

"As a mother, Emilie," she said, "I think you of all people can understand why we did this. What would you do if your son had been abducted. I make no apology for this harmless ruse. This is what we needed to do to save my baby girl, and I would do it again in a heartbeat."

Emilie smiled and put her hand on Diane's shoulder. "So would I, madame. So would I. When you find your daughter, please give her our love."

They embraced and Emilie kissed Diane on both cheeks. The tender moment was interrupted by an urgent rapping on the door.

It was Nigel. "Something's happened at the shop," he shouted through the storm door. "We need to leave, now!"

CRAWLING HOME

My head was spinning as I tried to take in all of Nigel's instructions. When we left the Tremblay's home with the Crown Jewels of Ireland in Diane's possession, Nigel told us the FBI had searched the café, looking for me. He told me I needed to leave the area, and quickly. Recognizing that at any time, the kidnappers might be calling to arrange the handover, it was imperative that I cross the border into the United States.

And so it was that I found myself standing in my underwear, swatting mosquitos, at the remote trailhead of an overgrown hiking path near the Maine border.

"These are quick-dry hiking pants. Put them on," Nigel said. "When this is all over, you might want to go to the gym and beef up those chicken legs of yours."

"For sure," I replied. "First thing."

"This is a backpack," he continued.

"I know what a backpack is."

"Have you ever worn one?"

"You mean, personally?"

"Thought so."

"I've seen people wearing them. This one seems heavier than those," I said.

"You've got enough water in there to keep you alive. There are a couple protein bars, but that's it for food."

"All those days in front of Food Lion and you didn't have time to buy groceries?" I asked.

"We had enough time to get all this used gear for you, didn't we? If you are caught, you're to say you're on a day-hike and you got lost. They'll have no trouble believing the part about you being lost. But if you were carrying a lot food, your story wouldn't check out."

"What's in this can?" I asked, pointing to what looked like a fire extinguisher hooked onto the outside of my pack.

"Bear spray," Nigel said, in a matter-of-fact tone that concerned me. "Lots of bears out here. More bears than mosquitos, but that's a good thing."

"And why is that a good thing?" I asked, shivering a little.

"The Customs and Border Patrol have motion sensors all along the border between Maine and Quebec to deter people from doing what you are about to do. But the bears are constantly creating false alarms, so the CBP doesn't follow up on most of them."

"Uh-huh. And given a choice between a CBP officer and a bear, I'm to prefer the latter?"

"CBP won't run if you shout at them and start banging sticks together."

"What if I spray a CBP officer with this stuff?" I asked, holding the can.

"That's not recommended," he said. "We're trying to get you out of trouble, not make it worse."

He handed me a cell phone and said, "This is a satellite smart phone. You'll start out following this trail, but at the top of the hill, you need to go due east. You can check the map on the phone from time to time to make sure you are on course, or you can call me in an emergency. Otherwise, keep it out of sight."

"You're sure this is a good idea?" I asked.

He pointed to the compass he gave me earlier and asked if I remember how to use it. I lied and said yes, but he showed me again anyway. "Get to the top of the hill, then follow this heading for seven miles," he said using his hand to indicate the direction I was to walk. "If you don't dawdle, you should make it before dark."

"Make it where, again, I forget the name of the town."

"Jackman. When you walk into town, you'll see a Citgo station and convenience store across from a motel. Diane and I will drive up to the border crossing at Sandy Bay, and then down to Jackman on the other side of the border. We'll be waiting for you at Citgo."

"You sure I can't just ride in the trunk of your car?"

"They X-ray all vehicles now. This is our best play. You'd better get going. You need to make it to Jackman before dark."

After confirming I was decent again, Diane stepped out of the car and hugged me. She thanked me for all I was doing to rescue Olivia, but I reminded her that it was my fault Olivia was in this predicament. She kissed me on the cheek and thanked me again.

Then I watched the car drive away.

I walked to the trailhead and began following the path up the hill. Never in my life had I heard such quiet. There were no people, no cars, no airplanes. The dense pine forest around me was eerily quiet, so quiet, I could hear my heart beating. The pine needles made such a thick cushion beneath my feet, that even my footsteps produced no sound, except the snap of the occasional twig. The silence was only pierced by the whine of mosquitos searching for any patch of my skin that wasn't slathered in DEET.

I walked for what felt like more than seven miles before stopping to eat a protein bar and drink some water. I was happy to see neither man nor beast along my path to that point. I took off the boots Nigel's staff had bought me because they felt little too tight for my right foot. Removing my sock revealed a dark red spot along the side of my toes and the back of my heel. I decided to check the satellite phone to see how much farther I had to walk, and I was shocked to discover it must have been malfunctioning. According to that device, I had only walked about one mile with almost six more ahead of me.

I was heartened to hear the sound of rushing water in the distance. On my right side, some distance away, I could hear what sounded like a stream. I checked the satellite map, hoping to see a small river near Jackman that would confirm I was near my destination. On the contrary, it established my position was in fact only about a mile from where Nigel dropped me off. The stream that lay to my righthand side, about a half mile away, formed the American border. "Six miles to go," I said aloud and resumed my trek.

I saw my first bear as I approached the border of Maine. It was drinking at the edge of the stream, which was much wider than I had envisioned. Nigel's only instructions for overcoming this obstacle were, "Find a way across, but don't get wet. Hypothermia is a killer." When I got close enough, I threw a rock into the stream—nowhere close to the bear—but it was enough to startle him or her into running away. Unfortunately, it seemed to me that the bear was running straight in the direction of Jackman, Maine.

I scouted for a place to cross the small river and enter United States territory. There was a spot where large boulders were almost close enough to jump across from rock to rock, but I wasn't confident of my ability to leap safely with a backpack, and Nigel's admonition to stay dry at all costs played in my head like a public service announcement on repeat. The satellite image of my location indicated that the river widened considerably several hundred yards to the south, so I started in that direction, hoping that a wider river meant a shallower river, and that I might be able to put my waterproof boots to the test and ford the stream.

Before I reached that spot, however, I came across what looked like a better option. A dead tree with roots in Canada had fallen over and invaded America. The tree trunk was plenty wide on the Canadian side, while dubiously thin across the border. Undaunted, I ventured atop my serendipitous tree bridge crossing.

On the Canadian side, the tree was almost two feet wide, which posed no difficulty for me, as it was resting on the safety of terra firma. However, once I started over the water and realized I was walking several feet above a river of unknown depth, it seemed not nearly wide enough for comfort. To make matters worse, the tree tapered toward the other side, and the thinner it got, the more it sagged and rose beneath my feet. By the time I was half-way across, the width had narrowed considerably, and the wobble had become treacherous. I looked at the running water below me, and my legs started to shake, rustling the leaves at the far end of the bridge.

I told myself to stay calm, and even tried taking deep breaths to ease the tremors in my legs. "Peace," I said to myself. "If this tree were on the grass in Central Park, I'd could walk across it with no hesitation whatsoever." My self-talk must have worked because the sound of rustling leaves ahead of me stopped. Another sound rose from upstream to the north, however. At first, I thought it was a new breed of flying insect, but as it got closer, it sounded less natural and more technological. Seconds later, I realized it was a drone, and it was getting closer at incredible speed.

"Idiot!" I said. "Bears don't cross streams on tree bridges." I reasoned that I had set off the border patrol's motion sensors in an un-bear-like manner. The drone would be on top of me in seconds, and it wouldn't be long before the border patrol followed in person. I looked at the path ahead of me and realized I had no choice but to try sprinting across.

I started to run and was encouraged by the ease with which I took my first steps, but the tree trunk bounced more and more with each stride, and my stability abandoned me. I was only one or two strides from the riverbank on the American side when my right food landed on the curved edge of the tree. My ankle turned and my foot slid off the tree. I slipped forward and struck the tree with my crotch, sending a wave of pain throughout my body. The next thing I remember seeing was the tree trunk pass the corner of my right eye as I fell backward, face-up, and splashed into the frigid water below. As the water covered my face, I could see the drone hovering above me. Then all I could see was darkness.

The underwater current was incredibly strong, and I was being dragged across the bottom of the rocky river, anchored by the weight of my backpack. With all my strength, I freed myself from its dead weight and looked about me for the lighted surface. Initially, I saw no sign of it because the current had flipped me upside down without my realizing it. When I looked in the direction I thought was down, I could see bubbles rising up to daylight and to the surface.

As I swam to the surface, the current carried me along, and I was scratched and scraped by rocks, but none of that mattered to me. My lungs were aching, longing to breathe again. I only cared about getting my head above water. I finally hit a rock that pinned me against its bulk, and I was able to use its surface to claw my way to the top. With the icy cold water flowing around my neck and shoulders, I opened my mouth for several gulps of sweet, wonderful air.

Looking downstream to the left of my rock, I could see only a slow-flowing eddy, so I slid sideways as best I could. I was still being pushed against the rock by the strong current, but with effort, I was able to slide into the eddy and onto US soil.

I rested for only a moment because I could still hear the drone flying above the river upstream. Before they could spot me with their camera, I decided to make a dash for the cover of the forest, crawling on all fours, as bear-like as possible, to avoid detection. I ambled over sticks, mud and rocks, not looking up, until the din of the river and the whine of the drone were muffled by the welcomed stillness of the pines.

LOST AND BOUND

I flexed my arm, shoved my face into the pocket of my elbow and screamed every expletive in every language I had ever learned.

Everything Nigel gave me was gone. I had no water, no food, no compass, no bear spray, and no satellite phone. Furthermore, Nigel's cautionary advice, "Don't get wet," was no longer an option. I was wet, and I was cold, very cold. I knew I had roughly six miles to go before I reached Jackman.

I decided to move as quickly as possible to make time and stay warm, keeping the sun behind me in roughly the five o'clock-position, as it had been on the other side of the river. I knew it wasn't a very accurate way to navigate, but I estimated that even if I strayed off course, I would eventually hit Route 201 that ran north-to-south through the town. Once on the road, it would just be a matter of figuring out in which direction I would find the Citgo station where Nigel and Diane would be waiting.

Hours passed; I don't know how many. I've no idea know how long I walked, or how far I walked. There were times when I thought a particular tree or pinecone looked familiar, but then I convinced myself that all trees bear a certain resemblance to one another and kept marching with the sun behind my right shoulder.

At one point, I stumbled into a small clearing where three young black bears were tumbling and wrestling each other. When they saw me, they were as startled as I. For a moment, I thought they were going to invite me to tumble with them, but the largest one let out a bark that sounded like bear-speak for 'stranger danger!' I didn't wait around for mama bear to come and investigate. I gave the frightened cubs the widest possible berth, but in so doing, I wandered far from my path.

As the day wore on, I stopped occasionally to listen for drones or search parties or the sound of cars on Highway 201, but I heard nothing. The sun was much lower by that point, and it was getting increasingly more difficult to follow my guiding star. As it sunk lower, I was also losing my solar heating, and I realized I was shivering.

I was not only cold; I was also exceptionally thirsty. Hiking for hours in the autumn air had dehydrated me, and all I could think of was water. My longing for a drink was made more excruciating by the sloshing of water in my waterproof boots. In the river, my boots had filled with water and the lining designed to keep rain out, was keeping the river in. It was as if my feet were playing in swimming pools as the rest of me died of thirst. Desperate, I sat down on a rock surrounded by pine needles and untied my shoes. I carefully pulled one foot at a time out from the shoe and removed the sock from my wrinkled toes. Holding the sock over my open mouth, I wrung it with all my might and sucked out as much water as possible. Then I put the boot to my lips like a goblet of fine crystal and poured into my mouth the liquid that had pooled inside my foul-smelling shoe.

Shivering in the woods, penniless, lost, and bereft of my identity, drinking river water wrung from my dirty socks and shoes, I recalled the party at Philip's new apartment in Manhattan where I first met Olivia. I remember asking Philip for a glass of water, and I remember grumbling about my life, which I felt had been cursed by abundant wealth. Purpose, challenge, and meaning had been taken away from me, I believed, and I was bitter about having too many material resources. "If I get out of this alive," I vowed, "I will never complain about my life again."

I put my socks and shoes back on and started out as best I could in the direction I was pretty sure I needed to go. The sky got darker, but I pressed on for more hours, hoping beyond hope to find the town or the road before I succumbed to hypothermia or dehydration, or both.

My memory of the remainder of the hike is hazy at best. I remember becoming inexplicably hot and removing my shirt, and even my long pants, as I journeyed on. I remember the sound of what I thought was thunder and wishing for rain. When no rain came, I remember lying down on a flat sandy surface with sharp stones cutting into the side of my head. And then I remember seeing a bright light coming closer and closer. "So, the stories are true," I said, and closed my eyes, yielding to death.

The next thing I remember is waking up with a sharp pain in my left arm. The morning sun was streaming in a window beside my bed. A woman in dark blue surgical scrubs was struggling to insert a large needle. When she saw my eyes open, she said, "I thought that might wake you up. Sorry, but your veins are a bit floppy."

"Where am I?" I croaked.

A man stood up from a chair on the right side of my bed. He was wearing a dark brown uniform shirt with light brown pockets. A star-shaped gold badge was pinned above his left pocket, and a name plate that read 'York' hung on the right. "Welcome to the United States of America, Mr. Howard," he said. "And, oh, by the way, you're under arrest for the murder of Olivia Hunt."

The nurse jabbed my arm with the needle again, a bit harder, I thought.

"Olivia is alive," I said.

Officer York continued, "And you'll be charged with improper entry into the United States."

"I'm a citizen."

"And of course, the Canadians have some questions about the manner of your arrival in their fine country, as well."

"I want to call my lawyer," I said.

"All in good time, Mr. Howard. Mind if I call you Clayton? We're informal folk up here in the woods."

"Where am I?" I asked again.

"You are in Jackman, Maine, miles from where they found you. Where did you think you were going?"

I ignored his question. "Who found me?"

"You collapsed along a logging road, about ten miles from here. A very alert truck driver spotted you and stopped his truck a few feet before his front tire squashed your skull like a watermelon."

"You suffered severe hypothermia," said the nurse. "Your body temperature was eighty-three degrees when they brought you in. Another hour or so, and you'd have had irreversible organ damage."

"Or your brains would have been squirted all over the logging road," added the officer.

"When can I call my lawyer?" I asked.

"My job is to make sure you don't go anywhere," he replied, picking up my right arm and pointing to the handcuff on my wrist. "You're a VIP: a very important prisoner," he chortled, apparently pleased with his joke. "FBI is sending agents all the way from Boston to book you."

"They're wasting their time. I am going to speak with my lawyer before I cooperate in any way."

The officer puffed out his chest and pursed his lips. "I couldn't care less about your cooperation. You are under arrest, and you'll go where we tell you, when we tell you."

"No problem, but I will speak to my lawyer, or the first judge I meet will release me from your custody forthwith."

"When will he be released from the hospital?" the officer asked my nurse.

"The doctor will check him again this afternoon. If he's stable, then he'll be released today."

"I hope so," he said. "I want him in my jail before those federal agents show up."

Officer York did not get his wish. The doctor was delayed in checking on me because of an emergency that required his attention. By the time he got around to clearing me, it was late in the afternoon, and the FBI's arrival was imminent.

I had never been hospitalized before, so I had no idea how to check out. Was I to drop off my wrist tag with the concierge on my way out the door? A small older woman, with graying hair and a red sweater that hung over her hunched shoulders approached the side of my bed after all the tubes and telemetry had been removed. I learned later that she was the hospital bookkeeper. She had a clipboard and many papers, which she read through the half-glasses perched on the end of her long nose. "How will you be paying your bill?" she asked.

"I have no money," I replied. It felt incredibly strange to admit that to another human.

"Any credit cards?" she asked.

"Nothing."

"How about your phone? We take everything: PayPal, ApplePay, Venmo, et cetera."

"I've no phone, no wallet, nothing but the shirt on my back."

"You don't even have that," said a familiar voice, entering the room. It was the FBI agent who had traveled to Burlington from Boston, what seemed ages before, Agent McClurg. "They told me they found you in your skivvies. Hypothermia does that to people. Makes them think they're hot, just before they die."

"I've seen you before," I said. I knew who he was, but I couldn't remember his name.

"McClurg, FBI," he said and flashed a badge quicker than I could blink. "You, sir, are my prisoner now."

"I need to call my lawyer," I repeated. "If for no other reason than to arrange for him to pay my hospital bill."

"Uncle Sam will cover it," he told the bookkeeper. "At least, until he starts earning a salary in prison. Then we'll garnish his wages until he pays it all back, with interest. And let's buy him a set of those blue scrubs. His hospital gown is a little drafty in the back."

While I changed into hospital scrubs behind a privacy screen, the Jackman police officer was trying to persuade Agent McClurg to keep me in the local lockup overnight. No doubt, he had some mischief planned for me. I was thankful that McClurg held his ground and insisted on taking me to Boston immediately. He cuffed me with his own handcuffs and led me by the arm past the frowning Officer York to his car, parked outside the door behind the ambulance.

McClurg placed me in the back seat, and we turned onto Highway 201 from the hospital lot. A few minutes later, I saw the Citgo that had been the destination of my hike. I was craning my neck to spot Nigel's car, so I didn't notice we were slowing down. When I turned around, I could see McClurg was making a lefthand turn into the motel across from the gas station.

"I thought we were going to Boston tonight," I said as he reached behind my back and unlocked my cuffs.

"I'm not sure where we're going," he said. "We're not calling the shots. King is." Then, he picked up his brief case and he led me to a room on the second floor of the motel and knocked on the door. "McClurg!" he bellowed.

When he opened the door, I was face-to-face with Nigel.

RANSOM

"I thought I told you to not get wet, kid," Nigel said, patting me on the back. "When are you going to learn to follow my advice?"

"That was no stream you had me cross," I said. "It was a proper river."

"That's because you didn't cross it where I told you to, but none of that matters now. You're here, so let's get to work."

Nigel picked up the hotel phone and dialed a number. After a brief pause, he said, "Yeah, he's here."

Seconds later, Diane burst into the room and threw her arms around me. "Clayton!" she cried.

Agent McClurg tapped me on the shoulder and said, "King's man called the burner phone last night. They weren't happy to hear you went missing. They will call again tonight, and they made it clear that you need to answer this time."

"Right," I said. "This part should be easy compared to what we've been through so far."

"Nothing's easy when these guys are involved," said McClurg. "They're killers and scum."

"Do you think Clayton will be in any danger?" Diane asked.

Nigel didn't give him a chance to answer. "The first thing you need to do, kid, is get proof of life. You need to hear her voice before you give them anything. We have the jewels; we can call the shots."

"Bad move," said McClurg. "We don't even know if she is alive."

Diane gasped and placed both hands over her mouth.

"That's the whole point of demanding proof of life," Nigel insisted.

Ignoring him, McClurg said to me, "You need to demand to see King. You will hand the jewels to King himself, and no one else."

"What I need to do," I answered both of them, "is whatever the hell these guys tell me to do. They have Olivia. *They're* holding all the cards, as far as I'm concerned."

Diane nodded in agreement. "I know she's alive. I can feel it. Let's just do what needs to be done to get her back."

McClurg took a small bag out of his briefcase and pulled out a set of jewels like the ones given to us by the Tremblays.

"How did you get that?" I asked him.

He smiled and said, "Not bad, huh? Show him, Nigel."

Nigel opened the oak jewelry box and revealed the original Order of Saint Patrick. I looked back and forth between the original and the replica, and I could not tell the difference.

"The likeness is striking," I said. "I guess you went through a lot of trouble for nothing, getting the replicas from the Brits, seeing as how we have the real jewels now."

"What are you talking about?" McClurg said. "No way in the world can I allow you to hand over the original jewels to those thieves."

"What?" Diane and I said, almost simultaneously.

Nigel put the box down on the bed and said to McClurg, "Let me see those things. How do we know they're good enough to be passed off as original?"

McClurg handed the bag to Nigel, who proceeded to examine the forged jewels under a light on the wall. "They look good enough to me," McClurg said. "You are the only people alive today who know what the originals look like. How would King be able to spot the fake?"

"It's too risky," said Nigel. "The first thing King is going to do is have some expert look at what we hand him. If we give him a fake, he'll kill Clay without a second thought."

"Nigel's right," I said. "King will know they're fake, and who knows what he'll do to Olivia if we try to make a fool of him. I'd rather not give King the satisfaction of possessing the Crown Jewels of Ireland, but Olivia is the only one who matters to me in this transaction."

"It's not up for discussion," said McClurg.

"You're right, it's not. I'm giving King the real jewels. End of discussion." I answered.

"You are in no position, Mr. Howard, to insist on anything," said McClurg. "You are wanted for two murders. Yes, two. They still haven't found the antique dealer. You are in my custody. You'll do what I say, or you will find yourself buried so deep in the bureaucracy of the federal prison system that even Tobias Rendelman won't be able to find you."

"I'm afraid he's right, kid," said Nigel, shaking his head in resignation. "It's his way or none. But, I checked out the replicas, and they look really good. I doubt King will spot the fake."

McClurg grabbed the bag from Nigel's hand. "Wise man," he said. "You should listen to him. Remember what happened the last time you ignored his advice. Splash!"

"McClurg," Nigel said, "I think we should use the original box. Switch yours with the ones in here, so they will look even more authentic."

"Good idea," he said, and he took the jewels out of the box and placed them in his briefcase. Then he took the ones from his bag and placed them in the box. "There's one more thing we need to go over before the killers call," he continued.

"Now what?" I asked.

"Tracking devices. We need to know where you are at all times."

"Forget about tracking devices," I said. "You don't need to worry about me. I don't want to do anything that will jeopardize being reunited with Olivia."

"Very noble of you, Mr. Howard, but remember what Nigel said. It's my way or none. The tracking devices I give you will enable me to know your location very precisely, but King's goons will have no way of finding them on you. Government-issued. Latest technology."

"I really don't see the need for this kind of risk," I said. "Do you think I should do it, Nigel?"

"Nigel has nothing to say about it," answered McClurg. "Consider this your way of paying your debt to society. Instead of going to jail yourself, you will help us locate a real killer. And let's not forget, this is the madman who kidnapped the love of your life. Don't you want to nail him?"

"I just want Olivia back."

"And you don't care if the kidnappers get away Scot-Free?"

"We just want to get my daughter back," Diane insisted.

McClurg cackled, "And what makes you think they won't do it again? Huh? These scumbags know an easy mark when they find one. Your daughter will live the rest of her life looking over her shoulder because they know they can grab her, and then her billionaire lover boy will go to the ends of the earth to give them anything they want."

"I hadn't thought of that," Diane replied. She looked as if she had been punched in the gut.

"Fine," I said. "I'll wear your AirTags, or whatever they are."

"They are several generations more advanced than AirTags, Mr. Howard. You won't even know they are there. I will affix them to your clothes."

Nigel handed me my overnight bag, and we found the clothes I had been wearing in Quebec before I changed into my hiking outfit. McClurg went to work placing several tiny chips, about the size of a dime, inside my shirt, pants, and even my underwear.

"Why so many?" Diane asked.

"In case they find some," said Nigel, quietly.

"I thought they would never be able to find them," she said.

Nigel rolled his eyes and didn't respond.

When McClurg was done, I went into the bathroom and changed into my own clothes again. "Anyone hungry?" McClurg said, when I rejoined them.

As he was talking, the burner phone began to ring for the second time.

AN AUDIENCE

"Is this the boyfriend?" squawked a man's voice.

"This is Clayton Howard. Who's this?"

"Shut up and listen," he said. "Do you have it?"

"Yes," I said. "I want to talk to Olivia."

"Don't make me tell you to shut up again. Your girlfriend's alive, barely. If you do exactly what I tell you, you'll see her again."

"What do you want me to do?"

"Meet me in Boston. Forty-seven Boylston Street. Parking garage. I will be waiting on Level B3."

"Olivia will be there?"

"They told me you were stupid, but I had no idea just how dumb you could be. Come alone to the Boylston Street parking garage and bring the thing we want. Wrap it in aluminum foil, lots of foil. You'd better write this down; you're such an idiot. If you get lost again, the girl dies."

I wrote his instructions with a small pencil and pad of paper on the motel nightstand. "I'll be there. When?"

"Whenever it's convenient for you, Mr. Howard. Moron! Now! Drive to Logan Airport and rent a car, then drive alone to the parking garage. Get one of those little clown cars, so I can see if anyone else is inside."

"It's going to take me a few hours to get there," I said.

"Then you'd better hurry. I don't know how much longer your girlfriend can hold on."

"I'm on my way," I said as he hung up on me, and I told the others what he said.

"Parking garage on Boylston, huh?" McClurg said. "That's downtown, near Chinatown."

"They're going to put you in a vehicle and take you somewhere else," Nigel said to me.

"Agreed," the FBI agent said. "That's when you tell them you will only hand the jewels to King himself."

"I don't think the guy knows what I'm carrying," I said. "He kept saying 'it' and 'the thing we want.' He didn't say 'jewels,' and he never spoke of the ransom in the plural."

"We can use that in our favor," said McClurg. "It makes sense. King wouldn't trust these guys to know what's inside the package. That's probably why he wants you to wrap it up in foil."

"I need to get going now," I said. "I've got to pick up some foil and drive to Logan Airport. Can I take your car, Nigel?"

"You're not really going alone, are you Clay?" asked Diane.

"The man was quite emphatic."

"Of course he's not going alone," said Nigel.

"I'll drive you to the airport," said McClurg. "Nigel can go directly to the garage and scout it out."

"Good," Nigel said. "I'll wait near the exit, so we can follow whatever vehicle they put him in."

"You do that. I'll go to my office and track him from there," he answered as we left the hotel room.

In the parking lot, McClurg handed me the wooden jewelry box and led me to the back seat of his car again, no handcuffs this time. "Take good care of the package," he said, laughing. "Remember, you're responsible to the British government for what's inside."

"I'm about to hand fake jewels to an organized crime boss," I said. "I don't think there's much chance the Brits will ever see them again."

"No chance in Hell," he replied. Then he added, "There's one more thing I need you to do, Mr. Howard." He produced a wristwatch from a box on the front seat of the car. "I need you to wear this watch. When they bring you in to see King, press the button on its side."

"What does it do?" I asked.

"It's a signal. You're wearing tracking devices, so I'll know where you are the whole time, but I won't know when King is with you until you use the watch to signal me."

"Sounds like you're not expecting me to make it back alive, Agent McClurg."

"You're a brave man, but I'm not taking any chances," he replied, and he sped south on Highway 201.

I fell asleep shortly after leaving Jackman. I don't know how long it took us to get to the airport; the watch McClurg gave me didn't actually tell time, its face and hands were just for show. We must have stopped somewhere along the way, because when I woke up in the airport parking lot, there was a roll of aluminum foil on the seat next to me.

"I'll go in and rent you a car," he said. "You stay here and wrap up that box."

He came back about thirty minutes later, driving a car that looked like it was more suited for the narrow streets of Milan than the American highways. "Is that a Smart Car?" I asked. "I've seen them in Europe but never driven one."

"King's man said he wanted you in a small car," McClurg replied.

"They didn't have a Mini Cooper?"

"Sorry, but Uncle Sam is on a tight budget. They practically paid me to take this car."

"Does it have GPS? I've no idea how to find the place."

McClurg shook his head and said, "Don't need it. I'll call you on the flip phone and give you directions. I can see your location on my computer." Then he handed me a twenty-dollar bill for the parking fee and told me to leave the airport, following signs for Highway 1A.

Several minutes after leaving the airport, the reality of what was about to happen began to sink in. I was alone and headed for a rendezvous with another killer who worked for King. The previous time I met up with these guys didn't end very well, and the realization that I was potentially walking into a death trap brought flashbacks of that awful night. My gut tightened, remembering the thrust of Joey Kilbane's boot in my gut and the bite of his stun gun on my back. Then I remembered the softness of Olivia's skin and the warmth of her kiss just before the nightmare began.

"I got you into this mess, Olivia," I vowed, "I will get you out."

"That's the spirit, Mr. Howard," McClurg said into the telephone. I had forgotten he could hear what I said aloud. "Be brave and remember that the only way Olivia will ever be really free from these guys is if King is locked up where he can't hurt her again. You need to get in front of him in person, and when you're there, signal me with that watch."

"You could have given me a watch that tells time," I said as I turned onto I-93, a central artery that passes in tunnels beneath Downtown Boston. "What time is it, anyway?"

"Just watch the road," he said. "The tunnels you're driving through can be very confusing, and your exit is coming up."

I turned off the highway onto Berkley Street and made a right turn onto Boylston Street, a one-way thoroughfare that took me past Boston Common, a large park on the south side of town. It was late, and there wasn't much traffic, but the road was well-lit. "I see the parking garage," I said to McClurg. "I'm signing off."

Before I hung up, he reminded me for the last time, "Get face-to-face with King and signal me when you get there."

Winding deep into the nearly empty garage, I found a sign for level B3. The jewelry box, wrapped in layers of aluminum foil, was on the seat next to me. I drove past the sign slowly, looking for any indication of the kidnappers' presence. I didn't have to wait long. A dark blue van pulled out of a parking space behind me and flashed his lights in my mirror.

When I stopped my car, a man got out of the passenger seat of the van. He wore a ponytail and a thick beard. He was well over six feet tall and almost as wide. He reminded me of the bouncer who once threw me out of a rowdy nightclub in college. He was holding something in his hand, which I initially took to be a gun. In fact, it was a bright flashlight, and he used it to look inside the back of my car. When the beam landed on the aluminum foil that covered the jewelry box, it lit up the whole interior.

"Is that it?" he asked, while standing behind my open window.

"Yes," I said, being careful to keep my hands on the wheel and visible.

"Park your Matchbox Car and get in the van; bring it with you."

I did exactly as he said, and as soon as I entered the van through the sliding door, he slammed it shut and the driver took off. The van had no windows in the back, and those in the front were tinted.

"Where are we going?" I asked. "I want to see King."

The bouncer just sneered and said, "Strip."

"Excuse me?" I replied.

He handed me a bag and said, "Your clothes," he said, flashing a smile that revealed two gold front teeth. "Put them in here. Everything."

I stripped down to my underwear and handed him the bag.

"I said everything," he snapped at me and shoved the bag in my chest.

Sitting naked in the back of van, I was thankful for the lack of side windows, although I tried my best to look out the windshield to see where they were taking me. We made several turns on city streets before entering the tunnels of I-93 under Downtown Boston. With my clothes stuffed in a bag under the back seat I wasn't sure that McClurg was still able to track me, but I was hopeful that Nigel and Diane were following at a safe distance from behind.

Inside a tunnel, the van screeched to a sudden halt, and I slid off the seat onto the console between the front seats. The foil-covered box fell on the floor. Horns were blaring from behind as cars tried to make their way around us. The side door opened, and the gold-toothed bouncer grabbed me by the elbow and pulled me from the van. Debris on the side of the road dug into my bare feet.

"Where's the package?" he asked me, looking at my empty hands. I pointed to the box on the floor of the van. "Pick it up!" he shouted, then slammed the door shut and pounded twice on the side of the vehicle.

To my horror, our van sped away into traffic, leaving me standing stark-naked and shoeless in the right lane of I-93 beneath the city of Boston. Cars horns honked, and passengers leaned their head out the window to whistle, gawk, and shout unflattering epithets. I was mortified to think that Diane was in one of those cars whose headlights illuminated my pale bare skin. The large man grabbed my arm and hauled me up onto a raised platform along the side of the road. We took a few steps and came to a silver door, marked, 'No Exit,' which he proceeded to open with a key. The door led to another tunnel, parallel, with traffic running in the opposite direction. To my surprise, I saw another van—this one white—surrounded by cones and parked along the side of the road. The van door slid open, and I was thrown inside, leaving the gold-toothed bouncer behind.

There were two men in the vehicle, besides the driver. Another bouncer-looking figure sat in the front seat, and a smaller man was in the very back. As soon as the side door was slammed shut, the van lurched forward, and the man behind me, whose heavy accent told me he was born and raised in London, leaned forward and said, "I'll take the parcel, if you please."

I reluctantly handed him the jewelry box, and he said, "I hope you aren't daft enough to listen to McClurg."

"Who?" I replied, unconvincingly.

He just nodded and laughed. "Aye, you are that daft. There are pants, trousers, and a jumper in the laundry sack, unless you enjoy going full Monty." I tore open the bag to find a pair of boxer shorts and some jeans, along with a sweater, socks and a pair of loafers inside. Happy to be clothed again, I tried looking out the front window to see where we were headed.

"No need to look," he said. "Nothing to see here." Then he placed a cloth hood on my head and tied the drawstring around my neck. Once I was blind, he grabbed my hands and bound my wrists with plastic zip ties.

I teetered back and forth like a metronome as the van made several quick turns through city streets before accelerating onto the highway. Time is hard to measure when one is wearing a black hood, being led to certain slaughter, but I estimated we drove for over an hour when the van came to a stop and the side door opened.

From the fragrance in the air and the sound of water splashing, I knew we were at the ocean, but I had no idea where. "Mind the step," said the Brit, who took me by the arm and led me out of the vehicle. The bouncer wrapped his hand around my other arm with a grip like a tourniquet. Together, the two of them led me across a gravel driveway and pulled me up onto a ramp. The sound of our footsteps sounded like we were crossing a metal bridge, and I realized I was being led along a small pier. At the end of the pier, the bouncer lifted me by one arm and dropped me like a sack of potatoes into a boat that had been tied there. I crashed into a bench and fell to the floor. My face, still covered by the cloth hood, landed in a puddle of seawater.

"Mind the step," he mocked, then he and the Brit also climbed into the boat just before it started to move.

"Where am I?" I asked, "and where are we going?"

My questions garnered no response from either man. After a few moments, the boat's outboard motor, which had been running at a low hum, became louder and higher pitched. I reasoned that we had left a harbor area and were heading out into open sea. The furious sound of wind rushing past my hood grew more and more intense as our speed increased. With each passing moment, I became increasingly convinced they meant to take me out to sea and throw me overboard.

Did they know the jewels were fake? I asked myself. *Or were they all along planning to kill me anyway?* Then my stomach tightened. *Maybe McClurg was right; maybe Olivia is already dead,* I thought. I began to weep inside my hood.

The boat was plowing relentlessly through the water, continually rising to the crest of a wave, then slapping the surface of a trough, shaking me to my core and dousing me with sea spray. Although we were clearly traveling at high speed, time seemed to move in slow motion as I replayed the events that brought me to this day. Light had started to permeate the fabric of my head covering. I wiped my tears with its inner surface, and I smiled at the memories of Olivia—every fight, every tender moment together.

I had launched our quest to find the jewels not because I was hunting for hidden treasure. I already had more treasure than I wanted. That which was hidden from my life was meaning. I was searching for a purpose, searching to find a reason to live. I thought the journey would make me feel alive, but I was wrong. What brought meaning into my life wasn't the hunt for treasure, but the treasure who was Olivia Hunt.

I had been in so many toxic relationships—women who I wanted to exploit or women who wanted to exploit me—that I didn't think love was worth the pain it created. However, my short time with Olivia taught me something different. Olivia accepted me for who I was, and her acceptance fortified me to become someone better. Her love for me began closing a chasm in my heart that had been growing ever wider since my childhood in boarding school. And as my heart grew more sound, my capacity to love others began to surge. My love for her gave me the meaning I had been craving for all those dark years, and I knew it was worth any sacrifice that I would make and any pain I would bear. I thought it ironic that I finally found meaning in my life just as it was coming to an end.

I regretted all the days I wasted lamenting over the vanity of my meaningless life, foolishly ignorant of the proximity of purpose. Instead of hiding from love, and the pain it engendered, I should have pulled back the curtain and embraced the affection of the people who were within reach all along. Loving my friends, even my severely dysfunctional family members, would have given me more than enough reason to live.

My thoughts went to my father. I marveled at how I had misunderstood him. He had hurt me, and I knew it. Sadly, I never stopped to ask why. I never tried to understand the man who sent me away and told me to never return. I wish I had been less offended and more curious. I wish I had to tried to understand what would cause a man to do something so preposterous. Now, with no more opportunities to reconcile, my heart went out to a widower who would soon be burying one son in the ground and losing his only other child to the open sea.

Will he even know that I'm dead? I wondered as I heard the boat motor slow to a stop.

Rough hands pulled at the drawstring around my neck and pulled the hood off my head, and my eyes began to adjust to the sunlight, which had become quite bright by that time. I was facing the stern of the boat, and looking behind us into the distance, I could not see any sign of land. *There's no way anyone will find my bloated body,* I thought. Then I turned around and was shocked to see that our boat was drifting close to a much larger vessel. Directly ahead was a yacht, whose white hull blocked all else from view in that direction. The large man who accompanied me in the second vehicle stood before me, struggling to keep his balance in the choppy waters, and used a pair of scissors to cut the plastic ties that were binding my wrists.

I massaged my forearms and hands that were aching terribly and said, "Thank you," to my captor. I wondered if those would be my last words. He picked me up out of my seat and I closed my eyes, expecting to be thrown overboard into the sea. To my surprise, he shoved me into a bosun's chair that had been lowered from the deck of the yacht. The canvas seat was held aloft by a long climbing rope, and I was strapped into the chair by large Velcro fasteners and hoisted upward. Next to me and above me, was a second chair, already near the deck. In that chair was the British man, holding a life jacket to which was taped my foil-covered box.

The ship's crew swung me over the railing, and once on deck, I looked around, quickly realizing this yacht was the most luxurious I had ever stepped foot upon. I stood beside a harp-shaped swimming pool, trimmed with gold. Astern, was a massive hot tub, surrounded by posh couches situated on an opulent stone surface, textured and perfectly round. To my left, between me and the hot tub, was an enormous island that served as a wet bar made of white marble with veins of green stone. To my right, amidships, was a glass wall that led to inner chambers hidden from my sight. Above the wall was perched a dual prop, jet helicopter.

I didn't see what became of the British man and my box because a deckhand brought me behind the glass wall to a spiral stairway that led directly into a luxurious office suite, several levels below. The room was lit only by small portholes just above the surface of the water. It was filled with dark leather couches and darkly stained mahogany furniture with gold fixtures. An enormous desk, empty except for a green banker's lamp and my foil-covered box, stood before a floor-to-ceiling bookcase. A life-size marble bust of Julius Caesar was on a pedestal in the middle of the room.

I walked toward the bookcase to try and get the measure of the man, for it was most certainly a man's office, who worked in that room. Before I could get to the bookcase, however, two men entered from a door that blended into a cabinet near a grandfather clock. The smell of cigarette smoke accompanied them. One of the men was the Brit. The other man, I had never seen before.

He was an important-looking man, virile and strong. He was wearing a tailored suit of fine wool and strutted across the room like someone who was accustomed to getting his own way. His face was hardened, as if he bore many concerns, but his eyes were penetrating, and he gave me the impression he could see right through me.

"You must be Mr. King," I said as he approached.

WHO CAN SEPARATE?

"I'm Danny King," he said, in a rasping Boston accent. "And if you did what I think you did, you're my new best friend, Clayton Howard."

I didn't like the sound of my name on his lips, and I didn't want to be his friend, but for that moment, I was willing to play along because I was alive and I had renewed hope that Olivia might still be alive, too.

"Speaking of best friends," I said. "I think you know where I can find a friend I haven't seen for a couple weeks now. I would like to see her now, please."

He nodded in the affirmative but said, "No idea what you're talking about. Let's see what you brought me." He walked to the desk and picked up the jewelry box in his thick, manicured hands. "Did you scan this?" he asked the man before opening the foil wrapper.

The Brit nodded and said, "Clean."

King opened the foil wrapper and marveled at the oak box. His eyes widened, and he looked at me. "Is this the original box?"

"It is," I said. "The hinges were damaged when I found it. I don't know when that happened."

"You've done very well, Mr. Howard. This is beyond my expectations."

We shall see, I thought to myself, hoping beyond hope he would not detect McClurg's deception.

He then opened the box and let out a low, almost effeminate gasp, then quickly looked at us, as if he was wondering if we had heard him. He pulled the eight-pointed star out of the box and held it up to the lamp on his desk. He ran his fingers across the Brazilian diamonds and caressed the emerald clover and ruby cross in the center. Then he handed it to the Brit, who had a magnifier in one eye and was stretching out his neck to see what King was seeing. Next, he picked up the badge and examined the words, *'Quis Separabit,'* Latin for 'Who shall separate?' and Roman numerals MDCCLXXXIII formed by the rose-colored diamonds, commemorating the formation of the Order of Saint Patrick in the year 1783, surrounded by a wreath of clover made of emeralds. He handed the British man that piece, too, and sat behind the desk, facing me.

The British man had placed the jewels on King's desk and examined them with the magnifying eyepiece loupe and his flashlight. I could feel beads of sweat forming on my forehead, and I began to feel like I might faint. He took the loupe out of his eye and started by saying, "There is no doubt." I expected to hear him pronounce the jewels a fake, but to my surprise, he continued and said, "these are the original jewels presented to the Grand Master of the Order of Saint Patrick by William IV in 1831."

Is he mistaken? I wondered, *or is he just telling the boss what he wants to hear?* Whatever the reason for pronouncing them authentic, a tremendous sense of relief flooded over me, and my hope of seeing Olivia surged. As I was reflecting on my good fortune, however, I did not notice the effect his pronouncement had on King. When he heard the jewels were real, King sank back into his colossal leather desk chair and began to weep. The dreaded crime boss, likely responsible for untold bribery, corruption, maiming, and murder, wailed and wept in our presence. I was reminded of the line from Milton's poem, *Il Penseroso*, where he penned that Orpheus' music was so powerful, it 'drew iron tears down Pluto's cheek and made Hell grant what love did seek.'

"Mr. King," I said, emboldened by Milton's words and the hope of seeing my Eurydice, "I have given you that which your heart has sought to possess, would you now grant that I could recover the one I love?"

He wiped his tears with the silk handkerchief from the front pocket of his suit jacket. "Do you know why I have sought these jewels, Clayton Howard?"

"It's none of my business, Mr. King, I am only concerned with seeing Olivia Hunt again and bringing her to freedom."

If he heard my response, he didn't show it. "You've probably been told that I am living out some kind of delusional fantasy about being the King of Ireland, or some such nonsense, and that I want these jewels as a symbol of my power. Is that what you think?"

"I don't know what I think," I said. "I am in love with Olivia, and your men took her. They told me you wanted the jewels, and you'd return Olivia to me and her mother if I found the jewels and gave them to you. That's all I need to know."

He looked intently at me, examining me. "Have you ever heard of Francis Shackleton?"

His question caught me off-guard. "I've done some reading about the history of the jewels. I know Shackleton was the brother of the famous Irish explorer to Antarctica, Ernest Shackleton, and was a suspect in the theft of the jewels in 1907."

"That ends now," King said.

"What ends now?"

"Very few people know this, but my mother's mother was Cecily Shackleton, daughter of Ernest and Emily Shackleton. All her life, my mother lived with the shame of being associated with the man who 'was a suspect in the theft of the jewels,'" he said with air quotes at the end of the sentence.

"But your great grandfather was a celebrated explorer. He made several important expeditions and was considered a hero for saving the lives of his crew when disaster struck. Why should suspicions concerning his brother taint that legacy?"

"You tell me, Clayton Howard. They shouldn't, but they do. After they moved to Boston, my mother's family was attacked brutally by people trying to get ahead of them in social circles. I saw it with my own eyes. They ruined her life."

"I'm sorry to hear that; I truly am," I replied.

"So, I made two promises to my mother. I told her I was going to get back at those people who snubbed her and made her feel less important because of our family history. That's why I built the business I run today, and I'm proud to say I've avenged my mother's embarrassment seven times over."

"What was the second promise?" I asked, not wanting to think about the first.

"That I would clear the name of Francis Shackleton from having anything to do with the theft of these jewels."

I debated whether or not to offer more information, then I said, "It was Goldney who stole them, not Shackleton."

He paused again, staring at me, then nodded, "I've heard that theory, too, but even if we could prove it, people would say Shackleton and Goldney were in it together. No, the only way to clear Shackleton's name from the theft is to prove there was no theft at all."

I jumped back in surprise at this, and it made King laugh. "How can you do that? Do you have a time machine?"

"Don't need one. Now I have these," he responded and placed the jewels back in the box. "Not only do I have the original jewels, but you also gave me the original box. I like it when people go above and beyond for me."

I didn't do it for you, I thought to myself. "I don't really understand what you're saying."

"You don't need to," the Brit said. "Just be thankful you didn't follow McClurg's plan and bring us the fake jewels."

"Who? What are you talking about?" I replied, trying to act surprised.

"Who? What?" the British man mocked. "You know precisely who and what."

King said, "How well do you think you know Agent McClurg?"

Realizing there was no point in denying it anymore, I said, "I only met him a few times. He's not my favorite person."

"Nor mine," King laughed. "Did you know that being a federal agent is only his day job? He's on the take."

"He works for you?" I asked.

Shaking his head, he said, "He is in the employ of my competitor. His current assignment is to rid the earth of Danny King, and he will stop at nothing to achieve that end."

The Brit continued, "Didn't you think it odd that McClurg came by himself to take you from police custody in Maine? He's a renegade. The poor chaps who were sent by the FBI to take you into custody are at sixes and sevens wondering where you got to."

"And why was he so keen on getting you to carry tracking devices?" King asked. "Did you wonder that? How many were you carrying on your clothes? We found about twenty."

"I have no idea," I replied. "He put them in my clothes and told me to wear them."

"Well, it's a good thing you took them off," King said. "McClurg knows I'm living on my yacht; he just doesn't know where it is. He has torpedoes on a gunboat ready to fire. All he needs is my location. That's why he gave you fake jewels. He knows we would spot the fakes, but he doesn't care, because he intended to sink my yacht with you, me, and the jewels inside."

"Professionally," said the British man, "I find it insulting that anyone might think I couldn't spot the fakes. After all, I made them."

This surprised me. "*You* made them?"

"I was a guest of Scotland Yard, doing time for bad behavior, when they offered me a deal. If I made a replica set jewels for their little museum, they would take two years off my sentence."

"Kudos are in order," I admitted. "When I saw them, I couldn't tell them apart from the originals."

"To the uninitiated, they look the same," said the forger. "But I knew right away that the jewels you brought me today were not the fakes. William IV commissioned the Rundell, Bridge, and Company of London to use Queen Charlotte's gems when making the originals. Her emeralds and rubies are richer in color than any I could find today. But the real proof is on the back. I made the copies based on drawings of the front of each piece. There were no existing images of the back. These pieces have markings on the back that I didn't know existed."

But I saw McClurg himself take the originals out of the box and replace them with the ones in his pouch, I said to myself. Then I remembered that Nigel was briefly in possession of both sets, examining them in the light. He must have put the originals in McClurg's pouch and put the copies in the box, gambling he could persuade McClurg to switch them back.

King stood and said, "It's time for you to leave us, Clayton Howard. But we can't have you repeating anything you heard in this room."

A man entered from behind me. He was large and bald with sunglasses and a dark goatee, wearing a gray track suit. Without a sound, the man approached me, fastened my wrists with a zip-tie, and fastened heavy chains around my ankles. "Goodbye, Clayton Howard," said King.

"Please, just tell me if Olivia is still alive. I don't care what you do to me. Let her go home."

King sat back in his chair, closed the oak box containing the jewels, and fingered the edges of the wood. He looked at the man in the track suit and said, "Go."

Taking awkward, short steps, I was led out the door from which the man had entered. My chains rattled with each step, and my gait sounded like that of a Dickensian ghost. He took me to an elevator that brought us all the way to the upper deck of the yacht, where the helicopter stood ready.

The deck was flat, and he pushed me closer and closer to the edge, where no railing stood between us and the sea, far below. The man with sunglasses seemed to be almost as reticent as I was about getting any closer to the edge, but the bouncer with a ponytail who had been in the van was standing at the edge, waving at us to come over to him. Once we got there, the man in the tracksuit held me, while the other man strapped more weights to my legs and arms. I felt like I was being prepared as a piece of bait for bottom-feeding fish.

They spun me around to face the water. I could see an island with a lighthouse in the distance. *Too far to reach by swimming,* I thought, *even if I could survive the fall, and if I wasn't loaded down with lead weights.*

I took a deep, satisfied breath, knowing it might be my last. I was about to die, but I had found meaning and my purpose for living. I knew there were many people who couldn't say as much. "I love you, Olivia," I said as the men put their hands on my back to push me overboard.

They began to push, and I began to resist, even though I knew it was a losing battle, when suddenly a voice called out from the elevator. "Stop," the voice said.

It was King. "Change of plans," he said to my great relief. "It was the box," he continued. "I couldn't stop thinking about the box. You didn't have to bring the box, but you did. Having the original box is going to make my plan much more likely to succeed, and I always reward the people who help me succeed." I could tell the last part was said more for the two thugs than for me.

Then, he said to them, "Cut him loose, bring him in the skiff to the island, and leave him there."

"Thank you," I said to him, with a renewed understanding of the Stockholm Syndrome.

"But mark my words, Clayton Howard. If you breathe a word to anyone about what you heard in my office, I will make it my life's new purpose to kill you and everyone you love."

TREASURE ISLAND

I was back in the motorboat for the second time that day, but unlike the previous trip, I was able to see where I was going this time. I was alone with the pilot. My hands and feet were free, my face was open to the sun, and the wind was caressing my face and tousling my hair. A million thoughts were going through my mind. All of them were about Olivia.

King had never acknowledged he knew anything about her, so I had no idea if she was still alive. Although I was alive, I was no closer to finding Olivia than I had been a week earlier. In fact, I was even less hopeful because I had found the jewels and provided the kidnappers with their designated ransom, but I still had no word on her condition or whereabouts.

The island was growing closer more quickly than I expected. Either the boat was traveling faster than it felt, or the island was smaller than it looked. My next step, so I thought, would be to find a way of contacting Nigel before anyone ashore recognized me as a man wanted for murder. I had no money, no phone, no identification, but at least I no longer naked, so I had a leg up on Odysseus at Scheria.

When the motorboat arrived at the island, I discovered it was, in fact, quite small. It looked to be no more than two hundred yards long, with a gray weathered lighthouse on an outcropping of rock unattached to the island. There was only one structure on the island that was visible from our boat, a small Cape-Cod-style cottage with a steeply pitched roof. As the pilot tied up to the dock, I noticed there were no other vessels tied there. "This is your stop," the man said with a smile when he saw that I wasn't moving.

"How do I get back?" I asked.

"You want to go back there?" he laughed.

"Well, not really, but I want to get the mainland."

The man indicated with his thumb that it was time for me to get off his boat, so I climbed onto the wooden dock, and he immediately untied and sped towards the yacht.

"Now what?" I said aloud as I stepped off the dock onto dry land. The cottage was to my right, and it was nestled in a crop of trees. Directly in front of me, about fifty yards away, was the opposite shore and open ocean. To my left were some rock formations that lifted the island to about twenty-five feet above the undulating sea level. There was no sign of mainland in any direction.

I decided to approach the cottage carefully. If there were any people inside, they probably wouldn't be expecting company, so I wasn't sure what kind of reception I would receive. I was afraid of being shot or harpooned. I walked along a well-tended path from the dock to the cottage made of small, white pebbles that crunched under my feet.

As I approached, I noticed that behind a screen door, the cottage door was open, and I could see into the home. Coming closer, I saw a figure standing in a doorway on the opposite side of the cottage, silhouetted, looking out at the sea in the other direction. It was a woman, barefoot, wearing jeans and a sweater, with long blonde hair, standing in the doorway. Her left arm was leaning on the side of the door frame and a coffee mug was in her right hand.

It was Olivia.

"Did you bring the books?" she asked without turning around.

"I don't have any books," I said.

"Then why did you…" she stopped mid-sentence, then spun around and dropped her mug. "Clay!" she shouted in disbelief. "You're alive!"

"So are you!" I shouted back, nearly walking into the screen door.

Olivia raced across the room and flung the door open, narrowly missing my face. "Clay!" she said again, hugging me and kissing me repeatedly. Then she stopped to touch my head and chest. "Wait. I want to make sure I'm not hallucinating."

"Pinch me," I said and kissed her again.

"That only works for the one who thinks she is having the hallucination, but because it was such a bad joke, now I know it's really you."

"I can't believe I finally found you. I must be the one hallucinating. All along I was picturing you, bound and gagged in a storage locker—in New Jersey. Here you are on a private island, sipping coffee!"

"How did you get here? How did you find me? I thought they killed you— how are you even alive?"

"Those questions will take a long time to answer," I said, caressing her face as tears streamed down mine.

"Can we leave? Do you have a boat?" she asked, looking over my shoulder at the dock behind me. "Do you know where we are?"

"The guy who dropped me off took the boat back to that yacht over there. When I asked about getting to the mainland, he just laughed at me."

"Do you know where we are?" she asked again, not at all surprised to hear that I, too, was trapped there. "I think there must be a city to the south and west of us. On a cloudy night, I saw a faint glow in the sky over the horizon in that direction. Also, there seems to be boat traffic to and from that spot, but I don't know where I am."

"That must be Boston," I said. "I was there yesterday. It's where they told me to bring the jewels."

Her eyes widened and her mouth opened wide. "You found them?"

"Yup," I said, with a satisfied smile. "Louisa's great-granddaughter lives in Quebec, and she still had the jewels."

"She sold them to you?"

"No. She wouldn't sell them. She said they were priceless to her—the only thing that connected her with her past. But I showed her the book Louisa had written and convinced her an autobiographical manuscript was a much better connection. Also, your mother did a great job telling her how priceless and precious *you* are."

"My mother? My mother traveled to Canada?" Olivia wept and smiled and began to quiver, thinking of her mother.

I held her in my arms and asked, "Is there any place to sit on this island? We have a lot to talk about."

Inside the cottage, we sat together on the love seat, looking out the window facing west. We talked for hours as we watched the sun traverse the sky and hover low on the horizon before us. We didn't know what time it was, and we didn't care. We were alive, and we were together.

She told me that the final time they attacked me with the stun gun, she assumed I was dead. The larger man dragged her out to their car, which was parked next to hers, while the other man did something inside the house. In the back seat of their car, they injected her in the neck with something that knocked her out. When she awoke, it was morning, and she was in the cottage, lying on top of the bed. She never saw the kidnappers again. The only person she has seen since that day is the pilot of the motorboat who came a few times to bring her food and clothing.

"Have you seen any other boats?" I asked.

"Just the yacht out there," she replied. "It was here the day they dropped me off, and then it left. I didn't see it again until yesterday. None of the other marine traffic comes anywhere near this place."

"What about the lighthouse?" I asked.

"It works," she replied. "Made it hard to sleep the first couple nights with the strobe going all night, but I've grown used to it."

"If it's a functioning lighthouse, then the Coast Guard must come around to check on it from time to time," I said.

"Now that you're here, I'd be fine staying here forever if I could only get word to my mother."

I kissed her again. "Sounds good to me. But I'd also want to notify my friends, and Nigel, and my father."

"Your father?" she said, jumping back a bit to look at me. "That's a surprise, coming from you."

"I have so much to tell you," I said with her head in my lap, "but right now I just want to be here with you."

We watched silently as the last bit of the sun's orb set below the horizon, and sometime after sunset, we fell asleep in each other's arms.

I awoke alone on the love seat. The beam of a bright flashlight tracked across the room. "Olivia!" I called out in a hoarse whisper. "Olivia!"

Olivia turned on her nightstand and laughed. "Are you afraid of the big bad lighthouse?" She had changed into her pajamas and gone to bed.

"Was Odysseus afraid of Cyclops?" I shot back.

"His crew probably wished he was," she said with a yawn.

"Good point," I replied, admiring her pajamas. "The motorboat guy has good taste in clothing. You look great."

She looked at me and smiled. "There's only one bed in this cottage. We can sleep together, but I'm not ready for anything more than sleeping."

I wonder if a motorboat pilot can perform a wedding ceremony, I thought to myself as I climbed into bed beside her.

EURYDICE

It was several hours later before I finally fell asleep. The sound of the surf outside and Olivia's rhythmic breathing alongside me was hypnotic, yet every time I drifted off, the lighthouse beam slapped me in the face as it swept the room. At some point, exhaustion took over and I finally slept.

When I awoke, Olivia was standing at the kitchenette, still in her pajamas, brewing coffee and cooking eggs. The sun was visible as a white disk, low on the eastern horizon, through the cloud cover. The sea breeze was salty and strong.

"Our friends are gone," she said with a nod toward the western side of the island. I looked and saw the yacht was no longer at anchor beside us. There was nothing in any direction except gray skies and choppy seas.

"I wouldn't want to be here in a bad storm," I said.

"It rained a little the day before yesterday, but this is the most wind I've seen so far," she said, handing me a mug of coffee. It tasted heavenly.

After breakfast, she took me on a tour of the island. About the size and shape of two football fields placed end-to-end, the island tour did not take long. It was shaped like a cigar, with the long axis running north to south for about a two hundred yards. Once she had shown me everything, we sat on the highest rock with our backs to a large boulder that offered some protection against the wind. We were looking south and east, trying to determine how far away were the ships on the horizon.

"We could make a signal by lighting one of those trees on fire," I said, pointing to the grove at to the south of our cottage.

"Why not just start with the house and cut out the middleman?" she scoffed.

"I'm just saying, if the Coast Guard sees a fire next to one of their lighthouses, they'll send a crew to check it out."

"You're right, but I don't want to risk burning down the cottage. In this wind, a fire would burn out of control."

"How about up here?" I asked. "It's nice and high, and these rocks are far enough away from anything flammable."

"Good idea. In the afternoon, we can gather dead wood from among the trees and light a bonfire up here after dark. Right now, however, you need to tell me everything that happened to you since the time they took me away."

We walked back to our love seat in the cottage, and I told her all that had transpired since I woke up on the floor of the bed and breakfast, beginning with the moment I crawled over to Mrs. Kennealey's table and scared the daylights out of her. Olivia laughed when I told her the Burlington police didn't believe my story about the kidnapping and were planning to arrest me for her murder.

"*You?* Murder *me?*" she laughed. "I'd like to see you try."

She cried, however, when I told her about Grayson, his shooting, and about the disease he inherited from my mother, and the meaningful conversations I had with my father.

"I wish you had more time with your brother, but I'm so thankful your father finally stepped up and came through for you, Clay. That's really special."

"Nigel was amazing, and so were Robert and Roberta, Philip and Stephanie, and even Brian played a key role," I continued. "And, of course, I wouldn't have been able to get the jewels if it weren't for your mother's passionate plea for her daughter's life."

"How in the world did you find the jewels?" she asked.

"You're not going to believe it, but I got the idea from your TV show."

She turned her head to look at me from the corner of her eye, and said, "Are you making fun of me again?"

"We collected DNA samples from the envelopes that were in the box with Louisa's diary. Those were letters she wrote to Edward, and he kept. When she licked them shut, she left us enough genetic markers to connect her with one of a few thousand residents of a small town in Canada."

"You're serious?" she asked, then said, "Wait. If you narrowed it down to a few thousand residents of a small town in Canada, how did you find the one you were looking for?"

I told her about our scheme to set up a coffee-tasting station and the tent where we secretly screened for snips that matched Louisa's DNA profile.

"You're crazy! I can't believe you did that," she shouted.

"I'm madly in love with you. I couldn't stand the thought of life without you, nor could your mother."

"You leave her out of this. I don't know how I feel about you invading people's privacy to rescue me."

"I would invade Hades itself to find you, my Eurydice," I replied.

"Now you're my Orpheus?" she laughed. "That doesn't bode well for my chances to get off this island alive."

"Ah, but you must know that in the earliest Renaissance operas, Orpheus succeeded in bringing her back, and they lived happily ever after till the end of their days."

"Is that what will happen to us?" she pondered. "We're still trapped on this island, and I get a deep sense of foreboding whenever that yacht silently appears. I don't know whose it is, but I think this must be their island, and I am still their prisoner."

So, I told her the rest of my story. I told her how they took me from the parking garage in Boston to the yacht alongside the island, although I left out the part about standing naked in the middle of I-93. Then I told her about my audience with Danny King and his family history concerning the theft of the jewels.

"They were going to kill me," I said, at last. "They had me up on the roof of the yacht, tied hand and foot, with weights on my arms and ankles. They were going to push me in, but Mr. King stopped them. Want to know why?"

Her eyes were wide, and her brow furrowed. "Yes, why?"

"It was the jewelry box," I chuckled. "He was so touched by the fact that I also gave him the original jewelry box that he couldn't bring himself to kill me."

"What?" she asked.

"My life was saved by an antique jewelry box. Is that ironic or what?"

"So, no more complaining when I take you antique-hunting?"

"No more complaining about doing anything with you," I replied. "Do you want to know what I was thinking about as they were trying to push me off that boat?"

"Yes, tell me," she said, placing her hands on mine.

"I thought my search for you had cost me my life, but I knew it was worth it because my love for you brought the meaning I had been craving for so many dark and desperate years. Two of King's men had their hands on my back, pushing me toward the precipice, and if he hadn't intervened, my last words would have been, 'I love you, Olivia.'"

We cried together and held each other for who knows how long. Then she wiped her tears, blew her nose, and said, "I love you, too, Clayton Howard, my Renaissance Orpheus, and I want us to live happily ever after until the end of our days. But not on this island."

"Time to build our fire?"

"Time for inferno."

SIGNAL

We spent the afternoon gathering logs, sticks, and leaves and carrying them to the highest rocks on the island, which were on its northern end, close to the lighthouse. By evening, we had collected enough kindling to create an impressive blaze. The weather was continuing to deteriorate, which improved our chances of rescue. In rough seas, the Coast Guard would be on high alert, scanning the horizon for any trouble.

At dusk, we took buckets of sea water and splashed the north side of the cottage to protect the wood siding in case our 'inferno' got out of hand. As darkness fell, we lit a flame, beginning with some sticks on which we had poured cooking oil. Before long, we had a decent fire going, with flames licking up well over our heads. We quickly realized, however, that large fires are hungry fires, and we needed a lot more wood to feed it.

Rushing back and forth between the trees and the rocks, we watched the southern horizon continually to see if any of the Boston maritime traffic was coming to investigate the fire. We could see plenty of ships in the distance, but none that were headed our way. Hours past, and we were exhausted after running scores of two-hundred-yard dashes carrying wood. When I could run no more, I stood on a rock searching the horizon but only saw vessels running in and out of Boston Harbor. None were venturing toward us.

"Clay," Olivia called out from the other side of the fire, "I think I see something."

I ran to her and scanned the sea to the north and west. After my eyes adjusted to the darkness, I pointed in the direction of her gaze and said, "That boat there?"

"Yes. I think it's coming toward us."

"No," I said, "It's going away. You can tell by the running lights. The one

206

on the left is green, which means it's going away from us. Green for go."

She frowned and looked at me with one raised eyebrow. "If we are going to live happily ever after, you need to learn something about mansplaining. It's bad enough to be condescended to by a person who's short one X chromosome, but it's even worse when the guy doesn't know what he's talking about."

"Is it the other way around?" I muttered.

"The green light is on the starboard side of the boat, and the red light is on the port side. Green is a longer word than red, and starboard is a longer word than port," she instructed. "So with the green light on the left, the boat is going away from port."

"So, I was right; green is for go."

"If you need to believe that, it's fine with me. But there is another way I can tell the boat is headed in our direction."

"How's that?" I asked.

"Because every time I look at it, it's a little bit closer."

Suddenly energized, I sprang up and started jumping in front of the fire. "If they have binoculars, I want them to see us signaling for help," I said to Olivia.

We jumped and shouted for several minutes, and it soon became clear the boat was headed directly for our island. When it was several hundred yards away, and quickly moving closer, Olivia grabbed my arm and said, "What if it's them?"

"Who?" I asked.

"The guys who put us here. What if they saw the fire and it made them angry?"

"I hadn't thought of that," I said. "Let's hide in the woods. If it's King's people, when they get out of the boat and start putting out the fire, we can run into the boat to get away."

She looked at me like I was a different person. She said, "I think that's the plot of a television show. Are you feeling OK?"

"TV screenwriters must get it right once in a while," I replied. "Hurry up, or they'll see us."

We ran into the woods and we each hid behind a large tree in the shadow of the house, being careful to avoid the beam of the lighthouse that had begun searching the darkness. The boat circled the island and approached the dock cautiously, eventually tying up on the far side. Because the cottage was obstructing my view, I couldn't see who was disembarking. Olivia's tree was closer to the west side of the island, giving her a better look.

"Who is it?" I whispered, but she didn't hear me.

Suddenly I heard her scream, and I felt my heart sink into my gut. Not again, I thought. But when I looked over at her, I saw she was running toward the dock.

"Mom!" she shouted, "Mom, I'm here!"

Standing on the dock, looking confused, were Nigel and Diane.

By the time I got there, Diane and Olivia were already hugging each other on the white-stone path near the cottage. Nigel was behind them, surveying the surroundings.

"It's great to see you, kid!" he grinned and shook my hand heartily. "Are you two alone?"

"It's just us," I said, nodding. "King's yacht left some time last night. How did you find us?"

"He called Rendleman. The infamous Danny King, himself, called Tobias Rendelman and gave him this message," Nigel said. He handed me a piece of paper, which read, *Drive to Nahant Dory. Rent a boat to The Graves. Alone. No FBI. No McClurg!*

"The graves?" I said. "Are we supposed to be buried here?"

"Not at all. That's the man's name."

"Who's name?"

"Admiral Thomas Graves," he replied. "British navy. Killed in action in while this was still a colony." Then, looking around, he added, "Although I wouldn't be at all surprised if King has some enemies buried around here. He would enjoy the irony."

"He was about to bury me right over there," I said, pointing in the direction of the yacht's mooring pin, west of the island. "Speaking of which, that was a smooth move you made, switching the jewels before giving them back to McClurg."

"I didn't think I'd get away with it, but I had to try," he said with a smile. "So, King decided to let you go, even after spying out his location?"

"He told me lots of things that should have gotten me killed, but he was so moved by the gift of the original jewelry box that he relented."

Diane overheard me say this, and after hugging me and kissing me, she said, "Olivia told me about that. It was an inspiration from above. I don't know why I brought it with me from home. I just thought the jewels belonged in that box."

"Well, it saved my life," I said.

"I'm so thankful to see you again," Diane said. "I thought I wouldn't see you again after that night in the tun—" she stopped short before finishing the sentence.

"You saw me in the tunnel?" I cried.

Nigel said, "Saw you? I almost ran into you. Your pearly white skin reflected my headlights and nearly blinded us."

"What are you talking about?" Olivia asked.

"Didn't he tell you they took all his clothes and made him stand on an interstate highway buck naked?"

"I didn't see a thing," Diane said, with a wink and an OK sign to Olivia.

"He must have forgotten that part," she said, laughing.

"Believe me," I said, "That's not something a guy forgets."

REUNION UNION

The reunion was held the following February at the newly opened Café Belgique du Louisa in Lac-Megantic, Quebec. In the months prior to the reunion, Robert and Roberta sold their Burlington bed and breakfast and became residents of Canada. Philip and Stephanie were married and went on a long honeymoon in Thailand and throughout Southeast Asia. Brian's newest video game hit the market and was doing well, or so I was told by others; Brian, being not in the least concerned about such things, knew nothing of the sales he generated. Nigel quit his job at Starr-Troutman and went back to school for a master's degree in psychology.

Agent McClurg met a fate less fortunate than the rest of us. Becoming the target of an investigation into his relationship with a known Boston crime boss, he fled the country. He was later arrested in France, attempting to sell a bag full of Brazilian diamonds, rose-colored diamonds, emeralds, and rubies to an undercover police officer. He died mysteriously in the custody of Interpol while awaiting extradition. The last person to see him alive was a man who claimed to be his lawyer and bore a striking resemblance to Big Bill Donahue.

Tobias Rendelman brokered our return from The Graves. After taking us from the island to Nahant Dory Yacht Club in the rented boat through rough surf, Nigel drove us non-stop to Rendelman's home in Westchester County, New York. In the morning, Rendelman arranged for a judge to summon representatives from the FBI and the Burlington Police Department to Federal Court in New York City. No doubt, they were expecting to find the murderer, Clayton Howard, in the courtroom ready to turn himself in. The look on their faces when they entered and saw the alleged perpetrator holding hands with the very-much-alive victim, was worth more than the Crown

Jewels of any country. Charges were dropped forthwith, and lawsuits were avoided in lieu of mea culpas in every form of public media known to man.

My father was the first person to greet us when we exited the courthouse. He was unrecognizable: smiling, crying, singing—I had never heard him sing a note in my life—he was positively ebullient. Olivia did not believe it was him. Diane ran to us while we were jumping for joy, and the four of us skipped all the way to my place on Forty-Sixth Street. Then, we spent the better part of the day straightening up the mess made by the FBI when they ransacked my home. Later, we celebrated with dinner at *Per Se*, a trendy French restaurant overlooking Columbus Circle and Central Park. It was my father's favorite, in part because of the nine-course tasting menu and the award-winning wine list, but I suspected even more so because it was located in the Deutsche Bank building, which I was pretty sure he owned.

Olivia went home to live with her mother and begin the long process of post-trauma recovery. Her days in captivity on the island were not as horrific as they could have been, yet being subjected to such violence and powerlessness, held against her will not knowing if she would ever be returned to her loved ones, added considerable emotional damage to an already fragile psyche. Nigel recommended she reach out to a non-profit organization that specialized in helping kidnapping victims and their families recover emotionally from the trauma of captivity. They connected her with a mental health practitioner in Summit, New Jersey, which was about half-way between her mother's place and Manhattan.

We saw each other often as autumn turned to winter and she suffered flashbacks, nightmares, bouts of depression, anxiety, guilt, anger, and most of all, a sense of helplessness. Her therapist recommended she empower herself to make her own choices whenever possible and establish some kind of routine for her everyday life based on her own preferences.

So, I met her twice a week after each therapy session, and she drove me wherever she wanted to go in her Chevy Biscayne, which she restored from the damage done by the Burlington Police Department as they searched for clues in the 'car dash.' In fact, I was thankful she decided to add air conditioning, power steering, and seat belts, but keep the bench seats, so I could slide over next to her while she was driving. One day after Christmas, she drove us to the Delaware Water Gap, where the Appalachian Trail crosses into New Jersey. Looking out over the river, she told me, "My counselor suggested I choose a therapeutic pet to accompany me on my walks in the wilderness."

"Are you thinking of getting a dog?"

She patted the top of my head, shook me by the ears, and used a baby voice to say, "Who wants to hike the Appalachian Trail?"

I yelped playfully and asked, "Yikes. Two thousand miles?"

"Two thousand one hundred ninety, give or take."

"Give or take what?"

"Give me your agreement, or take your leave," she replied.

"Looks like I'm going to need a sleeping bag. When do we start? I have some unfinished business up north."

"April first," she said. "No joke."

That gave me plenty of time to fulfill my promise to Emilie and Maxime Tremblay to begin rebuilding their home and the homes of the four friends who were also cheated by Maxime's contractor.

I spent the month of January commuting back and forth between New York and Quebec, meeting with the Tremblays and their friends in Lac-Megantic and taking walks with Olivia after her therapy sessions.

It was around that time I read an interesting news item out of Ireland in the *New York Times*. It read:

Workers restoring the Wardrobe Tower in the Dublin Castle, which served for centuries as the headquarters of the British administration of Ireland, discovered a small wooden box in a chest of early twentieth-century clothing believed to have belonged to Sir Arthur Vicars, the Ulster King of Arms from 1893 to 1908. Inside the box was a star and a badge composed of rubies, emeralds, and Brazilian diamonds, mounted in silver, which were determined to be the Order of Saint Patrick, commonly called The Crown Jewels of Ireland. Since 1907, the jewels were the object of one of the most mysterious crimes in Irish history. Many prominent families had been implicated in their disappearance, including that of Ernest Shackleton, the famous Antarctic explorer. Their discovery amongst Vicars' clothing sheds new light on the mystery and suggests they were, in fact, never stolen. It seems that Sir Arthur, known for being absentminded, placed the box inside a chest of clothes and had it moved from his apartments in the Bedford Tower to the Wardrobe Tower, where it was forgotten for nearly one hundred twenty years.

I smiled when I read the article. Danny King had managed to turn back time, and now his mother could rest in peace. Ironically, Louisa Peeters' father was also granted his dying wish. The jewels had finally been returned to their rightful owners.

On February first, we all came together to celebrate the opening of Louisa's Belgian Café. Olivia was by my side, along with her mother. My father was there, having flown in from Switzerland, and he was joined by Nigel and Mr. Rendelman. Philip and Stephanie flew in directly from Thailand, arriving at the café darkly tanned and thoroughly frozen. Brian had planned to attend, but something distracted him, and I was pretty sure he simply forgot. The Tremblays were there as well. Emilie had proudly scanned several key pages of Louisa's diary, enlarged them, had them framed, and presented them to Roberta as decorations for the café. The effect was stunning.

Emilie was particularly taken by Olivia. "I'm ashamed to think," she said to Diane in English, "that I thought for a single moment of holding onto those pins instead of saving your daughter's life."

Ever gracious, Olivia replied, "You made a tremendous sacrifice for someone you had never met. I will be forever grateful to you and your husband."

"You must come visit us in our new home," her husband replied, "once it's finished."

"It won't ever be finished if you don't stop changing the design, Maxime," Emilie said.

"That's my fault," I said. "I told him I want him to have the home of his dreams, but every night, he has a new dream."

Then, I gathered everyone together for a toast to the proprietors of the new café and said I would like to say something in front of my closest friends. With Olivia standing next to me, I took from my pocket a small wooden box, custom-made and deeply stained. I opened it to reveal its cobalt blue interior that held a gold ring, on which was set a three carat Brazilian diamond. I got down on one knee and asked Olivia to marry me.

She said yes, and we were married seven weeks later, on the first day of spring in a small ceremony in her mother's backyard.

We hiked the Appalachian Trail—all two thousand one hundred ninety miles of it. When the other thru hikers recognized us, they gave me the trail name, 'Killer.' I lobbied hard for Orpheus, but Killer was the name that stuck. Olivia, they called 'Revenant.'

After we completed the trail, Olivia moved into my home on Forty-Sixth Street and resumed her acting career—on and off Broadway.

She auditioned for a part in *Hadestown*, but she didn't get it, which was fine with me. I didn't care for the ending. In my story, Orpheus and Eurydice live happily ever after.

The End.

ACKNOWLEDGMENTS

I want to thank my editor and friend, Rebecca Franks, for her excellent work editing this book. I also want to thank my wife, Cheryl deMena for her encouragement and input during the writing and review process. Each one made a significant contribution to make this story better. All my readers will benefit from your input. I also want to thank my son, David, for giving me the inspiration to write narrative fiction and my daughter, Maria, for her beautiful cover design. And I want to acknowledge my two other amazing kids, Bethany and Luke for their encouragement along the way to keep writing. My wife and I are blessed to have four talented children, all of whom have contributed in one way or another to the story you just read.

IF YOU ENJOYED READING THIS BOOK...

If you enjoyed my book, would you please leave a review on my Amazon page? Tell me and my other readers what you liked about the book. Leaving a review does three important things. First, it helps others decide whether or not this book is for them. If you liked it, they might like it, too. It also helps me learn what's good about my writing, so I can do more of it in the future. Furthermore, when you leave a nice review, it brings a smile to my face... and I like to smile, don't you?

To leave a review, or look for other books I've written, you can go to my author page at Amazon.com/author/demena

ABOUT THE AUTHOR

Paul deMena never expected he would write a book. Even though he has always harbored an active imagination, he thought writing was the bailiwick of people with a different personality and skill set.

Then, in early 2019, he injured his knee during a weekend warrior workout. Forced to stay still for long periods of time, he found himself looking for a creative outlet that didn't involve movement. He was inspired to write by his son, David, who is pursuing a career in writing, but it didn't seem feasible because of the time it would take to complete a project. One day, he heard a friend say we can achieve a major goal if we break it into small, micro-goals. We only need to make a tiny step today, and every day, until it is complete. That was the day Paul started to write. He wrote a little bit that day, and the next day, until he finished his first book, *True Masterpiece*, in just a few months. It was so much fun to write and share with others that he decided to keep on writing.

Paul and his family have been living in Wuhan, China for over twenty years. During that time he launched a consulting company and co-founded an international school, where he currently serves as Secondary Principal.

ALSO BY PAUL DEMENA

True Masterpiece: a novella
Peter Huber learns that his grandfather was in possession of a painting that was stolen by Nazis in World War II.

A Bit of Healing: a novella
John Pablo Casals discovers his late wife's computer contains several million dollars in cryptocurrency, but all he has is a cryptic message to figure out the password.

The Cost of Payback: a novella
A woman has been murdered in the Grand Canyon, and rookie ranger Alexandria Daws needs to solve the crime before the killer strikes again.

Race for Mercy: a non-partisan novella
Chris Bradley is a young idealistic pastor with a heart for the needy who decides to fight city hall by running for office during the COVID-19 pandemic.

Hypatia Lost: a novella
Dr. Zoe Karagiannis discovered papyrus scrolls in Egypt that had been lost for two thousand years; then she and the scrolls went missing.

Song of the Innocent: a novel
Music pastor Billy Joel Mitchell was wrongly convicted of murder based on evidence from artificial intelligence. As he pursues justice, he learns that being released from prison is not the same as being truly set free. Inspired by a true story